"Where do you hurt?"

"Everywhere. My leg, mostly."

Remo tilted his head down. A dark splotch stood out on one of her thighs. It nearly blended in with her rain-drenched jeans, but staring at it made him sure it wasn't just water.

Blood. Damn it again.

"The ambulance will be here soon," he said, careful to keep the growing concern from his voice. "Hold my hand as hard as you want. Sometimes that helps."

She gave him a weak squeeze. "Promise me."

"I can't do that." It pained him a bit to say it.

"Xavier, Remo."

He glanced toward the car. The engine was crumpled so badly that it was barely recognizable, the hood disintegrated. No doors. No steering wheel. An empty back seat. Except...

What was that?

Remo pulled off his glasses, gave them another wipe, then looked again.

A stuffed bear.

His gut churned. She didn't just mean there was another person in the car with her. She meant there was a kid in the car. A kid named Xavier.

* * *

**If you're on Twitter, tell us what you
think of Harlequin Romantic Suspense!
#harlequinromsuspense**

P9-DMJ-390

Dear Reader,

Like many of my books, the idea for *First Responder on Call* came to me in the form of a single vision. This time, it was that of a young mother lying on the road as a shadowy figure stood over her. From there, I built up Celia—a woman who can't remember anything except that she absolutely must keep her son safe.

I've got to admit, I had a bit of fun researching the effects of trauma-induced memory loss. (Not in a macabre way! The science and psychology is very interesting!) I even got to interview someone who experienced it. And of course, I'm also excited to bring you the very dreamy first responder himself— Remo. I write a lot of police heroes, but it was great to step outside that box and bring to life this lovely EMT. I hope you enjoy their journey as much as I did!

Happy reading,

Melinda

FIRST RESPONDER ON CALL

Melinda Di Lorenzo

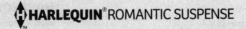

HARLEQUIN® ROMANTIC SUSPENSE

Recycling programs
for this product may
not exist in your area.

ISBN-13: 978-1-335-66212-5

First Responder on Call

Printed in U.S.A.

Amazon bestselling author **Melinda Di Lorenzo** writes in her spare time—at soccer practices, when she should be doing laundry and in place of sleep. She lives on the beautiful west coast of British Columbia, Canada, with her handsome husband and her noisy kids. When she's not writing, she can be found curled up with (someone else's) good book.

Books by Melinda Di Lorenzo

Harlequin Romantic Suspense

Undercover Justice

Captivating Witness
Undercover Protector
Undercover Passion
Undercover Justice

Worth the Risk
Last Chance Hero
Silent Rescue
First Responder on Call

Harlequin Intrigue

Trusting a Stranger

Harlequin Intrigue Noir

Deceptions and Desires
Pinups and Possibilities

To all the real-life first responders
fighting the good fight.

Chapter 1

The buzz came first. A hundred—no, a thousand—bees, circling her head and making it vibrate with an indescribable pain. Next came the stinging. Over and over, the sharp points hitting her face, each one worse than the last.

If she could've made a noise, it would've been a whimper.

She tried to turn her head, to steer it away from the angry swarm. But she was clamped down. Something viselike held her in place, stopping her from even the slightest movement. All she could do was blink, and even that yielded little more than a blurred picture overhead. She wasn't even sure what it was she could see above her. The night sky, maybe? A dark swirl of clouds, blocking out every star and barely letting through the moonlight?

Typical Vancouver.

The thought temporarily overrode the pain, probably because it was something concrete. Something that

grounded her. Yes, the muted gray tone definitely embod-
ied the city's weather. Even in mid-July, a rainstorm like
this one could be expected. It was usually a small sacrifice to make in exchange for being wedged between the
Pacific Ocean and a half a dozen mountain ranges. But
right now, it gave her a chill.

The rain...

It's what beat down on her face, the source of the sting.
She blinked again. A string of wires—power lines, she
thought—came into focus.

The buzz...

The vicious drops were hitting the wires as well, and
the zap of water on live electricity filled the air.

The accident...

A flood of memory came rushing to the forefront of
her mind. It was disjointed, like the pieces of a puzzle
that had been scattered across a table. But it was memory nonetheless.

The storm, rushing in from nowhere.

The road, slick beneath her tires.

The slam of...something.

Then the horrible sound of metal on metal.

And blackness.

The buzz and the sting were muted now, taking a back
seat to the struggle to remember anything else. What kind
of car had she been driving? What was the source of the
anxious pressure in her chest? And most important...what
was her *name*?

Oh, God.

She didn't know. She couldn't recall it, even though
when she dropped her lids closed, she could picture her
own face. She could see the swirl of her ash-blond hair
and the overwhelming number of freckles that dotted her

complexion. Her gray eyes and fair lashes were there, too, well above the surface of whatever blocked the rest.

Please let me remember. And please....someone help me.

As though her silent plea willed it into existence, a new noise caught her attention. Boots on pavement, approaching slowly, like their wearer was trying to disguise his steps. But whoever he was, his feet were too heavy for subtlety. And the gait had an odd, shuffling cadence, too. One that struck a familiar cord. She squeezed her eyes shut even tighter.

Not good.

The two-word thought was hardly strong enough to match the abrupt increase in her heartbeat, which thrummed so hard against her rib cage that she was surprised it didn't drown out the rain, the buzz *and* the footsteps. But maybe the man attached to the boots—she wasn't sure why she was so certain about what he wore, but she was—*did* hear her heart. Because his movement stopped. And a gruff question, spoken from a few feet away, carried to her ears.

"Where is he?"

Both the query and the voice itself sent a thick slap of fear across her whole body. She couldn't answer. She didn't *want* to answer.

The man repeated himself, a little louder, biting off the words. "Where. Is. He?"

She tried to shake her head, but of course met with the same resistance she had before. The boots hit the ground once again. She still refused to look. She knew he was close enough to be leaning over her, because his body blocked out some of the rain. It should've been a relief. It wasn't. Nor was the rush of air that came as he reached down and lifted off whatever it was that held her down.

Because she still couldn't move. And now she was exposed.

"I know you're awake," he said. "You might think I don't remember what you look like when you're sleeping, but you're wrong. I remember everything."

It struck her as unfair that he could claim perfect recall, while she had nothing but bits and pieces.

But maybe listening to him will help you. Maybe it will give you a clue. Maybe he'll even say your name.

She forced her attention to his chilling ramble.

"The way you smell," he was saying. "The way you always thought you could hide. How you believed you could get away with it. With *him*."

Finally, she did move, albeit without conscious effort. She shivered. And he saw it. She knew because he laughed, a low, dark chuckle that was harsher than the weather. He followed the eerie sound with touch. Just a small one—fingers to shoulder. But it was enough to send her mind reeling. She could feel the man's hands on her everywhere. Sometimes balled into fists, sometimes stroking her with a tenderness that made her skin crawl.

Why would the accident leave me with those *memories, but take away my identity?* Her stomach swirled into a tight ball of nausea.

"If you don't tell me where he is, baby, things are going to be much worse for both of you," the man warned.

Baby. It was the endearment that brought another name—not her own, and not the man's, either—to the surface. *Xavier.*

She clamped her lips tightly to keep from crying it aloud. Somehow, she was sure that even if she could say nothing else, the name would come out.

"You're awake," said the man above her. "And now

you're thinking about him. Tell me. You want to. You hate lying and you hate secrets."

The cajoling tone was just as frightening as the threatening one. It made her want to cry. She suspected that once upon a time, she might've given in to the tactic. And she hated the thought that she could be manipulated so easily. Especially by the man who had his hand on her now.

As if he could sense her internal suffering and wanted to make the outside match, he began to squeeze. Or maybe he just wanted to hurt her, plain and simple. His fingers tightened, and his thumb drove into her collarbone. If she could've gasped, she would've. Instead, silent, unshed tears built up behind her sealed eyelids, then stayed there, burning with an inability to fall freely.

If I tell him what he wants to know, he's going to kill me, she thought. *And maybe even if I don't.*

But then it stopped. Just like that. His hand was gone. He cursed under his breath, and his footfalls hit the ground hard and fast—fading away at not *quite* a run. It took only a moment to figure out why. Tires squealed on pavement. A door slammed. And a second set of feet hit the ground.

Thank you.

She didn't care who they belonged to. All that mattered was that whoever it was had driven away the angry man with the rough hands.

"Holy hell."

In spite of the fact that the voice was gruff, and the two words a curse, relief washed over her. Something in her gut told her *this* man harbored her no ill will. The feeling increased as he dropped to the ground and placed a hand directly on the spot that the first man had squeezed so relentlessly. His touch was warm and gentle and imbued with concern.

"Miss, are you with me? Blink if you can hear me."

She fluttered her lids. A set of dark-lashed, bright blue eyes stared down at her from behind a pair of tortoiseshell glasses. His gaze filled with relief.

"Thank God." He ran a hand over his damp jaw and breathed out.

From under her lashes, she watched as he leaned back on his heels and yanked a phone from his pocket. He dialed without looking, then spoke in a low voice. Was he doing it for her benefit? Maybe to keep her from worrying? She thought maybe he was.

After a few moments, he dropped the phone from his mouth and said to her, "Sit tight for one second, okay? I'm not going anywhere."

He stood up and strode away. Panic threatened, but she fought it. She could still hear his feet sloshing over the wet ground, and only a heartbeat passed before he came back into view, dangling a white, mostly shredded purse from his fingers. He spoke into the phone again, this time loudly enough for her to hear.

"She's got a bag here. Just gonna make sure she knows I'm opening it." He held out the purse, and she blinked her assent.

"Okay," he said. "No medical card and no driver's license. But I've got a Port Moody Public Library card. Name on the card is Celia Poller. That'll have to do." There was a pause. "Okay. Yeah. I have to. See you as soon as you can get here."

He hung up, then crouched down beside her again, his dark hair plastered to his forehead. "Miss Poller? Celia?"

She turned the name over in her head. Was it familiar? She honestly wasn't sure, but she had a feeling she should lay claim to it. She blinked again.

"Okay, Celia. If you had to get into a car accident right here, right now, then I'd call you about as lucky as can be under the circumstance. My name is Remo DeLuca, and I'm a paramedic with BC Ambulance Services." He paused and met her eyes before he went on. "What I'd *like* to do is keep you very still. Unfortunately, I can't do that right now. There's a downed power line just over there, and with the way the puddles are growing, we're right in range for a solid electrocution. So, Celia…I need your consent to go outside of normal protocol."

As if to punctuate his statement, a flash of lightning and an accompanying boom ruptured the air.

And she blinked as hard as she could.

Ten minutes earlier, Remo would've said the storm overhead suited his mood perfectly. A twelve-hour shift on a Friday night was pretty much his least favorite thing. He didn't know if he'd ever been so thoroughly glad to have a workday over with. A recent new article in the *Vancity Gazette* claimed that EMT service wasn't what it should be. As a result, rowdy drunk calls and calls about broken washing machines and calls about heart attacks all got an equal amount of attention. The former two both got in the way of the latter—the ones for people who actually needed his help.

Now, though, his sour thoughts had pushed themselves to the far corners of his mind. The immobile woman on the side of the road commanded his full attention. He could tell she was near shock. Unaware of her surroundings and oblivious to the danger that skirted the edge of her body. Adding to the problem was the part he hadn't told her about. The other local EMTs were tied up at a house fire, and he was going to have to wait at least fifteen minutes for the backups to arrive. Her slate-gray eyes were fixed on him and him alone, full of both hope and fear. He didn't want to let her down.

"Another quick second, all right?"

He gave her shoulder a quick squeeze, then pushed to his feet. His eyes flew over the scene, filtering out the things he already knew were there—the devastated car with its crushed front end, the cracked pole and the downed wires—in search of something he could use as a stretcher. As easy as it would be to scoop up the pretty blonde and carry her out of harm's way, he knew better. He couldn't see any external afflictions, and he suspected—based on instinct, mostly—that distress was what kept her from moving rather than an injury, but experience and training had taught him not to rely on gut alone. Some of the most heinous injuries were invisible to the naked eye. So what he needed to do was keep her as still and straight as possible.

Then he spotted it. The car's windshield, sitting on a patch of grass a few feet away. It was miraculously intact, and he suspected that somehow, the impact had dislodged it and sent it flying. It might even have been the thing that saved the woman's life. With the windshield missing, she'd had a clear path out the vehicle. He could almost picture the sequence of events.

Incredible.

Remo glanced down at her. Did she have any clue just how lucky she'd been? He doubted it. Not at the moment, anyway.

With a disbelieving head shake, he slipped off his glasses, wiped them with his T-shirt, then stuck them back on his face and headed up the road. There, he positioned himself in front of the glass. He bent down, closed his hands on the slippery edges and lifted. It came up with surprising ease, and it took him only a second to get it stable enough to cart it back over to Celia. Careful to keep it from hitting the ground with any kind of force, he eased it down beside her. Then he took a breath, pushed his knees as flat as they would go, stiffened his arms and positioned the windshield against her body.

"Okay, Celia. Here we go."

Moving as slowly as he could and being extra cautious in keeping her head and neck stable, he inched the glass underneath her. In spite of the rain, he could feel sweat beading along his forehead and his upper lip. He ignored it. By the time he got her into position, he couldn't see a damned thing. He was dripping, his glasses were completely fogged up, and the sky had darkened even more. Breathing heavily, he dragged the windshield and its passenger out of range of the sizzling power lines, then knelt down beside the makeshift gurney.

"You still with me, Celia?"

She blinked, then inclined her head. He was relieved to see that she was no longer frozen, but he still didn't want to take any chances.

"Try not to move around," he cautioned with a smile. "Hard to say if anything's broken, and I'd like to retain the role of hero for a little longer."

One corner of her mouth tipped up and she breathed out. His relief was short-lived. As quickly as her little show of amusement came, it left. Her whole face drooped and her eyes dropped shut.

Damn, damn, damn.

Remo dragged his hands up and clasped Celia's face. She was cold.

Because it is *cold out here*, he told himself.

He clasped her wrist and pressed his head to her chest. Her pulse was strong and steady, and her breathing was slow and even, and that was something.

"Did you faint on me, Celia?" he murmured, brushing her hair back from her face.

He leaned back and studied her for a second. Her skin had a hint of a tan, but mostly it was a connect-the-dots palate of freckles.

More than pretty.

She had that clean-faced, granola-girl feel that made it easy to picture her hiking up the side of the Grouse Grind. Remo liked it. Which made him sigh and question his sanity.

"Obviously even more tired than I thought," he said.

Checking out a girl—a patient…sort of—was very low on his list of priorities. Right below the washing machine emergencies. Remo gritted his teeth and told himself to stop before he even got started. Except as soon as the self-directed order made its way into his mind, her hand lifted and found *its* way into his palm, and a shot of heat cut through the chill.

He looked down in surprise. "Celia?"

Her eyes opened wide. "Xavier."

For a second, he thought she'd mistaken him for someone else. "Sorry, honey, I—"

She cut him off. "Please, Remo."

"What do you need?"

"Xavier."

"Where is he?"

"The back."

"The back?"

Her eyes flicked toward the shattered car. She couldn't possibly be saying there'd been someone else inside. Could she? He looked down at her, hoping he'd see a hint of delirium in her gaze. Instead, he just saw faith. She didn't know him at all, and she still believed in him.

"I'm not even wearing the uniform," he muttered.

"Help him." Her fingers tightened around his.

Remo inhaled. "I don't think Xavier's here, Celia."

"He *is*. In the back." Her eyes closed for a second. "I hurt."

"Where do you hurt?"

"Everywhere. My leg, mostly."

Remo tilted his head down. A dark splotch stood out on one of her thighs. It nearly blended in with her rain-drenched jeans, but staring at it made him sure it wasn't just water.

Blood. Damn again.

"The ambulance will be here soon," he said, careful to keep the growing concern from his voice. "Hold my hand as hard as you want. Sometimes that helps."

She gave him a weak squeeze. "Promise me."

"I can't do that." It pained him a bit to say it.

"Xavier, Remo."

He glanced toward the car. The engine was crumpled so badly that it was barely recognizable, the hood disintegrated. No doors. No steering wheel. An empty back seat. Except…

What's that?

Remo pulled off his glasses, gave them another wipe, then looked again.

A stuffed bear.

His gut churned. She didn't just mean there was another *person* in the car with her. She meant there was a *kid* in the car. A kid named Xavier.

She had to be mistaken. She had to be confused. There was no car seat. No other sign that a child had been there. Yet there was that horrible instinct again, telling him he'd read the situation correctly.

"Celia?"

But her eyes were still closed, her breathing even and slow once again. She had a small crease between her brows, like her worry carried over into her lack of consciousness. Remo freed his hand from hers and smoothed his fingers across the wrinkle. It faded for a second, then reappeared. He sighed.

"All right, honey," he said. "I promise. If there's a kid around here named Xavier, I'll do my best to find him."

He stood and stepped woodenly toward what was left of the car. The rear seat was shredded, its leather split and its foam exposed. Rain thumped down on the remainder of the roof, then poured down onto the remainder of the floor.

"Xavier?" he called softly.

There was no answer.

"You there, kid?"

He took another step and called out a little louder.

"Xavier? I've got a lady here who's pretty worried about you."

Still nothing.

He swiped the rain off his chin and squinted through his glasses, considering whether both Celia *and* his gut feeling were off. He tossed another quick look her way. From a few feet back, she looked smaller and more vulnerable.

Shouldn't have left her lying there.

He moved to go back to her, but sirens cut through the air then, startling him so badly that he jumped. He stumbled a little, trying to catch his footing. He wasn't quite successful. Cursing his own overreaction, he put out a hand to stop himself from doing a face-plant. The new position—one knee on the ground, body bent over—gave a different perspective.

Between the split cushions of the car seat was a gap that led to the trunk. And inside that gap was an unmistakable object. A small, limp hand.

Chapter 2

The sirens he'd been counting on and the flashing lights that accompanied them became secondary. Remo raced over the puddle-drenched ground, desperate to free the child from inside the trunk.

The trunk. What in God's name was he doing in there?

He brushed off the question as secondary, too. Something he could deal with later. He reached the rear end of the car just as the first emergency vehicle arrived. Vaguely, he noted that it was an ambulance. A good thing, because he would likely know whoever rode in it.

He stared at the tiny hand for a tenth of a second before deciding two things. One, he shouldn't wait for anyone else, and two, he shouldn't try to go in through the trunk itself. He dropped to his knees, stuck his own hands into the crack and pulled. At first, he met with resistance. Then the seat groaned. It creaked. And finally, it cracked and sprung forward. Soaking wet pieces of fabric and shards of plastic flew out, and a chunk of foam smacked Remo directly in the forehead, then stuck there. He brushed it away, straightened his glasses, then bent down. His breath burned at what he saw.

The little boy was splayed out on his back, his legs spread wide, the one arm flung near Remo, the other tucked up on his chest. He had his thumb jammed in his mouth, which hung slightly ajar, and his eyes were wide-open.

For a moment, Remo feared the worst. Then the boy—*Xavier*, he reminded himself—blinked slowly. He pulled his thumb from between his lips and reached out his arms. The needy gesture tugged at Remo's heart, and without thinking it through, he bypassed protocol. He leaned deep into the trunk, slipped his hand under the kid, then scooped the boy to his chest.

"You're okay, Xavier," he said gently. "I've got you, kiddo."

He pushed to his feet, spun, and just about smacked straight into one of the first responders. He recognized him immediately—a senior EMT known for his by-the-book standards. Of all colleagues, this man was his least favorite. The one he'd least want to run into, even under normal circumstance.

He forced himself to back up and nodded an acknowledgment. "Isaac."

The older man blinked. "Remo?"

"Yeah."

"What are you doing here?"

"Lucky coincidence."

Isaac glanced down at Xavier. "What are you doing *now*?"

"Saving this kid's life." His voice was embarrassingly thick with emotion.

"You moved him?"

"Had to."

Isaac's eyes went from the boy's small body to a spot over Remo's shoulder to the shattered vehicle. He opened his mouth. Before he could speak, though, a thunderous rattle came from all around. Something popped. And from the corner of his eye, Remo spotted the source.

The electrical pole.

A crack as wide as his arm split the damned thing down the middle. Its two pieces shuddered, then tilted. One went backward, but the other came forward, and as they watched, it fell fast and hard. Straight into the car.

Remo wished he could feel smug. Instead, he just felt relieved. Maybe a bit stunned. He swung back to Isaac, but the other man didn't acknowledge the fortuitous result of his rule breaking.

"Guess you moved the woman, too?" he asked.

"She would've been electrocuted otherwise."

"Fine. What's done is done. I'll get a gurney over here so you can put the kid down."

Xavier buried himself in Remo's chest, his small hands gripping his shirt tightly.

"I don't need a gurney. I'll hold him in the back."

Isaac blinked. "What?"

Remo shook his head, not buying the ignorant act for a second. "You heard me."

The older man narrowed his eyes. "You want to keep ignoring protocol?"

"Done it twice in the last twenty minutes. Saved a woman and a kid. Think I'll stick to my own rules for just a little while longer."

"I'll have to put it in the report."

"Go for it."

Isaac's expression didn't change, but the tightness in

his jaw told Remo he was annoyed. The irritation rolled off him, and the seconds ticked by with neither of them backing down. Finally, the second EMT—a younger, part-time kid named Tyler—called out, breaking the tension that radiated through the air.

"Isaac! Need a hand over here, please!"

The older man twitched, then spun to offer his assistance. Remo didn't bother to gloat. All he cared about was keeping his promise to Celia and making the kid feel safe. He stepped over to the ambulance, murmuring that Xavier's mom would be fine, and explaining that he'd made sure himself that she'd be safe.

"It might be a little scary in the ambulance," he said, "but it's just science, and there's nothing *really* scary about that, right?"

For the first time, Xavier pulled back and looked up into Remo's face. His eyes were the same unusual shade of gray as Celia's, and he had a smattering of freckles that matched hers, too. There was no doubt that the kid was her son.

"Science?" he repeated in a small, curious voice.

"Science," Remo confirmed. "Do you like science?"

"Yes."

"Me, too. Do you want me to take you inside so you can see?"

"Yes, please."

"Okay. Let's get in before they bring your mom around, okay?"

Xavier nodded, and Remo used his height—six foot four, and sometimes an inconvenience but right that second an advantage—to propel them up together.

"One," he grunted. "Two."

"Three!" added the little boy, quiet, but almost gleeful, too.

"Wow." Remo put some extra awe into the exclamation.

"What?"

"You can count."

"Yeah."

"I dunno. Are you *old* enough to count?"

"I'm five!"

Remo suppressed a chuckle and let out a whistle instead. "Holy cow."

"How old are *you*?" the boy asked.

"Old."

"That's not a number."

"Maybe I'm so old that I don't remember."

"A hundred?"

"Hey, now. Do I look like I'm a hundred?"

Xavier leaned back and studied Remo's face like he really had to think about it. "I dunno."

Remo suppressed a grin. "Is my hair gray? Or falling out?"

"No."

"Is my face wrinkly?"

The kid lifted a hand and pressed a finger to Remo's forehead. "A little right here. The same kind of wrinkly my mom gets when she worries about me."

"Yeah, I'm a bit of a worrier myself."

"Do you have a boy like me at home, too?"

"'Fraid not."

"How come?"

"Well. For starters, I don't have a wife."

"My mom doesn't have a husband."

Remo couldn't quite block out a trickle of interest at the statement. "No?"

Xavier shook his head. "My dad isn't in the picture."

It had the ring of something oft-repeated, and this time,

Remo couldn't stop a smile. "Well. I guess that makes you the man of the house, hmm?"

"That's what my mom says, too."

"Glad she and I agree."

The little boy's gaze flicked toward the open doors at the back of the ambulance. "Is she okay?"

Remo considered the question and how to answer it. Over the course of his career, he'd learned more than a bit about how to read people. Some wanted a gloss-over. Others wanted the worst case scenario presented in black-and-white. A kid, though, was a bit of a curveball. Protectiveness was a reflex, spurred on by the solemn, needy gaze zeroed in on him. No dad in the picture. Celia could be all the boy had. But Remo's own history made it hard to tell a lie. The kid didn't deserve it. Especially not if things took a bad turn.

So he chose his words carefully. "She could be hurt, buddy. Car accidents are tricky. But those guys out there are experts. Do you know what that means?"

"Kinda."

"Well, just in case, I'll tell you, all right? It means they have lots of training for emergencies just like this one. They're going to check her over really well before they load her up in here. Then they're going to take her to the hospital, where they'll check her over even more."

"Can I watch?"

"At the hospital?"

"Yeah."

"Probably not, kiddo. The doctors like to keep things pretty private while they're doing their job. And the hospital's like school—it's full of rules and bossy grown-ups."

Xavier's face fell. "Oh."

Remo gave his shoulder a squeeze. "But hey. There's always pudding to sneak. And when they're done, I'll make sure you're the first one to see your mom."

"You'll stay with me?"

"Sure I will. Unless you'd rather call someone else. Grandma, or a babysitter or something?"

The kid shook his head. "I'd rather be with you."

"Then it's settled. You and I will steal pudding, eat it until we feel sick, then check in on your mom."

"My mom says stealing is wrong."

A chuckle escaped. "All right then. We'll *ask* the nurses if we can have some, and if they say yes then we'll eat it."

A smile cracked Xavier's face. "I like chocolate best."

"Me, too."

"I think they're bringing my mom in now."

Remo turned his eyes to the door. Sure enough, Isaac and Tyler had the blonde woman on the stretcher, which they were wheeling closer.

"You good in there, Remo?" called the younger EMT.

"Yep. We're ready for you."

"All right. Up we come."

With another reassuring squeeze, he tucked the kid in a little closer and gave his colleagues room to climb in.

Because of the ring, Celia was sure she was in a dream. It sat on her index finger, catching the light and sparkling in an unnatural way, especially considering all the darkness around her. But it wasn't the unusual contrast that made her so sure. It was the fact that the ring was her own personal trick. Something she'd learned in therapy. A lucid-dream tool. She could see it. Feel it. And use it to protect herself from the onslaught of seemingly endless nightmares.

When the counselor had first introduced the idea—a subtle implant in the back of her mind—Celia hadn't bought the idea that it would work. In fact, she'd assumed it wouldn't. But on the third night after the initial subliminal suggestion had been given, she'd been tossed into the throes of the familiar, terrifying dream.

It was the same as always. The pause before she realized she had to run. Then her feet hitting the floor of the long, pitch-black corridor. Dread not just pooling in her gut, but overwhelming it and making her heart thunder so hard against her rib cage that it felt bruised. And of course, the fear was warranted. Because next came the furious growl from behind her. The bellowing of her name and the warning that she wouldn't make it out alive. She didn't have a name for who chased her—half man, half monster maybe. All she had was the belief that she would never break free. So she ran harder. But the effort lasted only a few seconds before she had no choice but to slow down. Under her aching ribs was something that forced her legs to cease their pumping. Something huge and cumbersome—an undeniably pregnant belly. Which startled her into stumbling and brought the man-monster so close that his self-satisfied laugh cast a breath over the back of her neck.

But on that day…she'd known it wasn't real. And while she couldn't force herself into consciousness, the knowledge made the experience just palatable enough. It would end. She would wake. Life would go on.

Just like it would at that moment.

So in her present-day dream, Celia lifted her hand for a second to stare down at the shimmering stone and glittering gold. She acknowledged it with a resigned nod, then moved on. And it happened. The run. The never-ending hallway. The man, the baby, and the laugh. But strangely, it didn't end in the same way it always had. Instead of the sheer terror and the awareness that her time was up Celia normally experienced, a light appeared. And the light became a door.

Startled, Celia blinked at the newly added element. Then the chill-inducing laugh came again, and she realized that she might—for the first time ever—be able to escape it. As a contraction clutched at her abdomen, she stepped forward. The movement somehow brought the door closer to her, rather than the other way around. But she didn't stop to question the phenomenon. She simply took advantage. She reached out her fingers, grasped the handle, turned it, and flung the door open.

On the other side was a man. He had dark hair and kind eyes. And he was beckoning to her, his palm turned up and his fingers crooked.

Celia didn't even hesitate. Squeezing her eyes shut, she dived forward, swollen stomach and all, and let the strange man enfold her in a protective embrace. Behind her, the door slammed. She inhaled. His scent filled her nose. Clean and fresh, with no hint of cologne or aftershave. The smell was so real—so distinct—that Celia felt compelled to check again for the ring. And it was there.

But when she opened her eyes, her senses were assaulted by something else entirely.

Voices, churning all around her. Frantic, mechanical blinking. Over all that, the wail of a siren. And under it, a pervading disorientation and feeling of separation from reality.

"What…" The word came out as a cracked whisper, and she knew it couldn't possibly be heard. She swallowed and tried again, willing her voice to be stronger. "What's happening?"

A hand found hers. It wasn't a grip she was acquainted with, but it was warm and strong and reassuring, and Celia clutched at it, glad for its solidity. For a blissful second she felt safe. And though she couldn't pinpoint why, she was sure it was actually *the* safest she'd felt in a long time. Then an odd thing happened. There was a shift— like the person was adjusting to a better position—and a face came into view.

It's him.

And it *was* him. The man from her dream. Only real. Celia was certain, because their clasped hands would've driven the ring into her palm.

She stared up at him, held transfixed by the incredible blueness of his eyes. They were azure. Stunning. And though Celia didn't think she knew the man, there was still something familiar about his stare. She was so enraptured by his look that Celia nearly missed the fact that his mouth was moving.

She tried to focus on what he was saying, but it seemed to be a mumble of medical jargon. It distracted her.

Was the man a doctor? Was he *her* doctor? Was she hurt or sick?

Of course you're hurt or sick, said a voice in her head. *If you weren't hurt or sick, you wouldn't be in this ambulance.*

The thought jerked her attention away from the man's blue, blue eyes, and her gaze swept back and forth. It was true. There was a narrow strip of light on the metal roof, bright red medical bags and a variety of equipment hanging from the sides. She could feel a thin mattress under her back. An IV line ran directly into the hand not held by the stranger. And when she tipped her head back a little, she also saw a blue-clad leg that she was sure belonged to a paramedic.

But...why?

She swallowed. She had no idea how she'd gotten into the back of the ambulance. And now that she was thinking about it, she realized she couldn't remember much of anything at all. Not what she was doing before she got to the spot where she was now. Not where she lived, or what she did for a living. She closed her eyes, trying to grasp at something from her past. Anything, really. But it seemed just out of reach.

It was so frustrating. So frightening. And Celia felt a need to *do* something about it.

She opened her eyes and tried to sit up. Her head spun. Badly. And the blue-eyed man's palm slid from her hand to her shoulder, and his voice filled her ear.

"You have to lie back down," he said gently.

For no good reason she could think of, Celia fought against the soft suggestion.

"Let me go," she said. "I have to…"

Have to what? Oh, God. Why can't I remember?

Her heart thudded even faster, and one of the machines in the ambulance chimed an alarm. Celia squeezed her eyes shut again and willed her pulse to slow. She had questions, and if she wanted answers, she needed to be calm. She needed calmness *around* her so that the blue-eyed man—another paramedic, maybe?—would answer them. She breathed out, counted to ten, then opened her eyes and found herself face-to-face with that azure gaze again.

"Celia."

He knows my name.

And it was good. It brought a very small, very recent memory to the surface. Him, holding her library card—with its distinct logo—in his hands. Her, not even knowing who she was until that moment. The wave of gratitude tempered her panic, but only momentarily. Because it no sooner washed over her than a tiny, worried voice cut through all of it, and it was the most familiar thing she'd heard, seen, or felt in what seemed like a decade.

"Mommy?"

Xavier.

She knew little else, but she knew her son. Five years old. Freckled face. Too much intense seriousness for such a little person. She loved to make him laugh. Loved it when he let go of that little frown of his and giggled so hard that he said his tummy hurt.

Celia dragged her eyes open and sought him out. There he was, his small frame tucked against the big one that belonged to the blue-eyed man. How she hadn't noticed him first—or even sensed his presence—was beyond her. He looked scared. But undeniably safe.

And I have to keep him that way. I have to keep protecting him.

She didn't know where the thoughts came from, but they were accompanied by another, dizzying rush of blood. It thumped through her body, up through her chest, and straight to her head. It wasn't just fear; it was absolute terror.

The world swam. Celia desperately wanted to say something to her son. To reassure him that everything would be fine. But her mouth didn't seem to be in a co-operative mood. And worse than that, her mind was slipping again, headed straight back toward the oblivion it'd just barely crawled out of before.

She blinked, trying to clear away the impinging blackness. It was impossible. But as she faded even further, she made a last-ditch effort to communicate by sending the blue-eyed man a look. A plea. And for a moment, she thought she failed. The man said something else—more indecipherable medical stuff. But then turned his attention to her son. And even though she couldn't hear his words, Celia was sure that they were the right ones. Xavier's eyes cleared. His tense little body relaxed. And then there was nothing.

Chapter 3

As Celia's eyes fluttered shut and her pulse evened out, Remo wanted to holler at the driver to go faster. He actually had to grit his teeth to keep from doing it. He knew better. Tyler—the kid at the wheel—had the sirens going, the lights flashing, and he was negotiating the streets of Vancouver at a pace that was both quick and safe. Isaac had done everything right, because that was how the older paramedic rolled. Carefully, perfectly set IV. Heart rate monitor secure. Pain meds, blankets, gurney…all as they should be. Remo was sure of it. Yet he still wished he'd done it all himself.

For no good reason.

He stared down at Celia, wondering where the unusual desire came from. The blonde woman was beautiful. No doubt about it. He'd already acknowledged that. Her physical vulnerability was a given. And Remo had been told on more than one occasion that he had a bit of a hero complex. Except neither of those things—alone *or* together—usually affected him. He ran into beauty and vulnerability in his job just as often as he saw the ugly side of things, and he always took it in stride. Patients were just that—patients. They needed him, and he got paid to meet those needs.

So not that, then.

Remo ran his eyes over his "patient" once more. The rush of protectiveness didn't ease in the slightest. If anything, it grew. He watched the rise and fall of her chest—consistent but weaker than he would've liked—and reminded himself that she wasn't as frail as she seemed in that moment. Underneath it, she was strong. The proof was evidenced in her determination to save her son's life. In the pleading look she'd sent his way before she faded out. Pure selflessness. She'd sacrifice herself for her kid, and that was a hell of a thing.

And speaking of the kid...

He dragged his attention down to Xavier. The little guy was tucked right against Remo's side, his forehead creased, his eyes closed, and one of his little hands clutching at his shirt. The sight of the small, nails-chewed-down fingers reminded Remo of something else—the kid had been locked in a trunk. Undoubtedly because Celia had put him there. And if she'd done it, then it had to be because it was the best way to keep the kid from harm.

What could be so dangerous that Celia felt the safest place for her son was hidden in a trunk?

Not what, he thought immediately. *Who.*

Remo's eyes flicked from Xavier's hand to Celia's face, a suspicion creeping in. The kid claimed that his father wasn't in the picture. Could be that it was by design. Remo's heart twisted a little as he considered it. The idea that being locked in a trunk might be the better alternative to putting the kid in contact with his dad was a dark one. Darkness didn't mean it wasn't true. His own life was enough proof of that.

He blinked, genuinely surprised to find even a hint of his past creeping up on him. Sure, it was only in his own head. It was still an unusual occurrence. Something he deliberately avoided.

"Remo, did you hear me?"

He blinked again, this time to focus on Isaac, who was eyeing him with concern.

"Sorry, man," he replied. "Missed it."

The older man opened his mouth, closed it, then opened it again. "Just letting you know that we're T-minus thirty seconds away from the hospital."

On cue, Tyler cut the sirens and the lights, and slowed down as they rounded the bend that led to the hospital entryway. They coasted to a stop, and Isaac prepped the gurney for transport.

Xavier lifted his head. "Are we there?"

Remo gave the kid a light squeeze. "Yep."

"Are they taking her away?"

"Only for a short bit, buddy. Doctors have to look her over, remember? Make sure everything's working right."

"But you said these guys were ess-berts."

"Experts," Remo corrected with a smile. "And they are. But their job is to get people to the hospital."

"Because of science?"

"That's right."

"Oh." Xavier's little face sank. "I wish we could go."

"I know it's hard," Remo said gently. "But you're a brave kid. I can tell."

The little boy nodded solemnly, but a moment later, his face brightened. "And you're staying with me."

"You got it, buddy."

Tyler and Isaac finished pulling Celia out of the ambulance then, and Remo gestured to the open doors.

"You wanna go first so you can see them take your mom in?" he asked. "Or you want me to go so I can lift you down?"

Xavier didn't hesitate. "You."

"All right. Here I go." Remo shot a conspiratorial wink in the kid's direction, then hopped up and out.

Before he could turn and grab the kid, though, a hand landed on his shoulder. Startled, he turned. Isaac stood just behind him, a dour look on his face.

"Shouldn't you be with Celia and Tyler?" Remo said in a low voice.

The other man shook his head. "Handed off the first patient. Now I'm back for the second."

At the statement, Remo's gut flipped uncomfortably. And when Xavier's worried voice carried out from the ambulance, his stomach downright churned.

"Are you catching me?" the boy asked.

"I sure am," Remo told him. "Just sit tight and give me a minute with Mr. Isaac, okay?"

"Okay." The kid slipped back into the ambulance.

Remo turned back to his coworker. "I'll take him in."

Isaac shook his head. "Not necessary."

"I want to."

"Riding along with us was one thing. But you're going to have to wait in the waiting area like everyone else. Tyler and I will see that the patient is taken care of, and the child care worker will—"

"No."

"Pardon me?"

Remo dropped his voice and gestured toward the ambulance. "That kid's scared. His mom is unconscious. He has no one else here, and he seems to like me."

"You're not on duty," the other man reminded him.

"And?"

"It'd violate the rules, DeLuca. Once we get behind those sliding doors, though, you're a lawsuit waiting to happen."

"And?" Remo repeated.

Isaac gave him a puzzled frown. "What's with you?"

"What's with *me*? Have you ever *been* that kid?"

"What?"

"Have you ever sat there and waited while your mother—" He stopped himself abruptly and shook his head as he realized his coworker had a damned good reason for looking confused; Remo was far from heartless, but he had no problem checking his emotions at the door. Usually. What *was* with him? He had no idea.

But I'm not backing down. The kid needs more than a pat on the head and a bandage.

"I'm going in with him," he stated firmly, his words a little calmer.

Isaac wasn't done being his stubborn, by-the-book self. "I'm running this shift, DeLuca."

"And that means what? You're going to *fight* me, to stop me from taking the kid in? Block my way into the hospital?"

"Don't be ridiculous."

"I'm not. But one of us sure is." Ignoring his coworker's irritated expression, Remo turned toward the ambulance. "C'mon, kid. I'm ready for you."

There was a shuffle, and then Xavier appeared at the doors. He looked uncertainly from Isaac to Remo, and Remo could've given the other man a knock straight upside the head for making the kid worry even more.

"S'alright, Xavier," he said. "I've got you."

"Do you promise?" the little guy asked.

The plaintive question dug straight into Remo's heart. "I promise."

Xavier nodded, then reached out his arms, and Remo scooped him up. When he turned toward the hospital, though, he found Isaac standing there with his arms crossed over his chest. Was the other man actually going to block him out, ridiculous or not? If so, would Remo genuinely push his way through?

Only a heartbeat went by before he was saved from having to find out. One of the hospital's administrators— one who favored Remo, thank God, but knew him well— stepped into view.

She shook her head of tightly curled gray hair and frowned at the three of them. "Are you going to stand out here all night with that kid, DeLuca, or are you going to bring him in?"

"He's not on duty, Dr. Hennessey," Isaac said immediately.

The woman pursed her well-wrinkled lips, moved closer, and fixed a kindly smile toward Xavier. "What do you think, son? Should we bend the rules so Remo can bring you in?"

"Yes, please," the kid replied with barely contained enthusiasm.

Dr. Hennessey chucked his chin, then lifted her head. "You have a good rest of your night, Isaac. I think your colleague and I have it from here."

With entirely more relief than was reasonable, Remo exhaled and followed the wizened doctor—a woman he'd known most of his life—into the building. Sensing something was up, he let her take the lead. She said nothing as she guided him through the halls and up a flight of stairs to a relatively unused part of the hospital. She continued to keep silent until they finally reached one of the small, unoccupied family rooms. There, she gave Xavier a speedy but thorough once-over, and everything she said was related to that. It wasn't until she'd issued a clean bill of health and set the kid up with a juice box and a colorful book that she finally asked Remo to join her outside for a moment. After making sure it was all right with the kid, Remo complied. The moment they crossed the threshold from the room into the hall, the older woman's demeanor changed. She put her hands on her hips and issued a stern look.

"All right," she said. "What's going on?"

Remo blinked. "I kind of thought *you* were about to tell *me*."

"Any idea why someone might be looking for that kid and his mother?" she asked.

His earlier thoughts about an angry ex sprang to mind, but he shook his head. "What do you mean?"

"Five minutes ago, I was in Emergency getting a signature from triage. A very well-dressed man pushed his way through the ten people waiting and demanded to know if a mother and son had come in, and when the nurse explained they couldn't give out information like that unless he could prove he was a family member, he left." She paused. "It rubbed me the wrong way. And a minute later, I overheard another nurse mention that *you* were outside arguing with another paramedic about a mom and her son."

With the term "walking lawsuit" leaping to mind, Remo quickly decided in favor of telling her his fear—that Celia was on the run from an ex-husband. As he spoke, the senior administrator studied him with unveiled concern, and he knew what was coming before she even spoke.

"Remo…" she said. "You know I love you like a wayward nephew."

"Thanks, Auntie Tanya," he replied dryly.

"Uh-huh. And you know how close I am with your mother," she added.

Remo feigned a look up and down the empty hall. "Shh. Nepotism."

"Monthly coffee with a fellow hospital employee hardly counts as nepotism." She smiled a sharp I-know-everything-anyway smile. "Stop deflecting. You can guess what I'm wondering."

"Am I letting my past cloud my view?"

"Exactly."

For the briefest second, Remo closed his eyes. In the last hour, his mind had strayed to his childhood at least twice. That was double the number of times he let himself think about it at all in an average year. So he had to admit—at least to himself—that it was there, under the surface. Was it affecting his objectivity? Maybe. Was it affecting his reaction to the kid and the kid's mom? Definitely. But it didn't change the bits and pieces of evidence that led him to the conclusion.

He opened his eyes and shook his head. "I might not be unbiased, but I'm also sure my opinion is sound."

The older woman sighed like she was hoping to hear something else. "Okay. I believe you."

"So what do you think? You want to call the police?" For no good reason, the idea bothered Remo, and he was thankful when she shook her head a little.

"I don't know," she told him. "Nothing illegal happened. Not yet, anyway. And domestic violence…" She let out another soft breath. "It's a fine balance here, Remo. If what you think is true, then exposing their location and identities could put the two of them at more risk, and patient well-being is my number one priority. Particularly when there's such a large element of vulnerability involved." Her eyes strayed toward Xavier. "But protecting the hospital's needs is a part of my job, too. Not doing anything and them getting hurt because of it could put us in a bad spot."

"I'll take responsibility," Remo said immediately. "I'll watch the kid. I'll see what I can find out from his mom. And if there's the slightest hint of danger, you know I'll do the right thing."

"Do you think the child's in danger *right now*?" she asked.

"Did you see any signs of abuse?" he countered.

She shook her head. "Considering that fact that he was just in a car accident, he's in damned near perfect shape."

"So…"

Her gaze hung on him, her expression thoughtful. She was clearly weighing it all, and he had to fight an urge to make an uncharacteristic plea. Instead, he waited with as much patience as he could muster.

"All right," she said at last. "But you're going to stick like glue to that boy in there. As long as his mom's a patient and you're here in the hospital, I don't see a need to involve social services."

Relief washed over Remo. "You're the boss."

Tanya issued a nod. "I'm trusting you both personally and professionally here. You're the best paramedic I know, and you're a good man, too. So at the slightest hint of anything that could put *anyone* at risk… I expect to be informed. And I'm sure I don't have to tell you that as far as the kid is concerned, it's a legal obligation."

"Got it."

"I'll give you a call on your personal phone as soon as I hear anything about the kid's mom."

"Thanks, Tanya."

"And, Remo…" She trailed off, then cleared her throat. "One more thing."

His heart thumped an unusually nervous beat. "What?"

"It hasn't escaped my notice that the little boy is about the same age as your niece would've been now."

Her words hit him hard, and square in the chest, and he was thankful that once she'd said them, she simply nodded, then spun and walked away.

This time, consciousness slammed into Celia like a cold wave. It smacked her in the face, forcing her to open her eyes and gasp in a breath at the same time. For a moment, she was too stunned to move. Then a thought jumped to the front of her mind and forced her to act.

Xavier.

Her son's name took the wave to the next level. Her rib cage squeezed a protest, while her vision fought to adjust. Trying to stay calm was an impossible endeavor, and Celia gave in to the panic. She whipped her head back and forth in a frantic search. On the periphery of her mind, she noted her surroundings. She was tucked firmly into bed. The room was dark. And quiet, too, except for a light, mechanical hum. And it was all a concern. But it was also secondary to the fact that Xavier was nowhere to be seen.

"Where is he?" The words came out in a raspy whisper, and they were met with silence. "Where am *I*?"

She tried to sit up, and met with resistance. Her fear doubled. She tried harder, and a new noise overrode the relative silence—the beep of some kind of alarm. And it was followed by the rapid thump of feet hitting the floor.

No.

She had to get away. She had to find Xavier and keep him away from the man who threatened the life they'd built together.

Celia drew in another sharp, burning breath. She could

see his face. See the craggy outlines of his cheeks and feel the heat of his breath.

Then there was a zap, and the relative darkness became a soft, artificial glow.

Nowhere to hide.

"God, God, God." It was a prayer and a plea and a curse.

Ignoring the indistinct voices that suddenly filled the air, she fought against the hands that were on her now, holding her in place. Her flails got herself free. Partly. Something else gripped the back of her hand and made it sting.

The IV.

A rush of recall swept through her. The ambulance. The accident.

"Remo," she whispered as a pair of blue, blue eyes filled her memory.

The thought of them—of *him*, dark-haired, rough-spoken, and protective—brought the panic down to a reasonable level. Her heart rate eased, and the decrease of blood roaring through her let the sound of a patient female voice reach her ears.

"It's all right," the voice was saying. "Just breathe in and out."

Celia complied. It would be easier to communicate and locate her son if she was calm.

Slow suck of oxygen in.

Steady release out.

And again.

"Just like that," the voice encouraged.

In. Out.

"You're safe and sound now," the voice added.

In. Out.

Celia at last blinked away the last of the fog and cast

a careful look around, trying to get a handle on her surroundings. The nearly drawn blinds drew her attention first. They revealed that night reigned, and that a rainstorm raged.

Still raged, she thought, as she remembered it hitting the windshield of her car before she was blindsided.

But that wasn't what she wanted to be thinking about now.

She swiveled her head, noting that the room was pale blue and lit with soft light. Her gaze finally landed on a plump, olive-skinned, sixtyish woman—the source of the voice, obviously—who was smiling at her from a safe couple feet away. She was dressed in scrubs, wore a stethoscope around her neck, and had on a name tag that read Jane. As Celia took in the woman's appearance, she connected the dots. The soothing ambience, the tube hanging from her hand, and the nurse added up to one thing.

I'm in a hospital.

That realization provided her with some relief. But where was Xavier? In the hospital somewhere, too? Could the nurse be trusted?

And why do I have to wonder if a nurse *can be trusted?*

Her head ached, and Celia briefly closed her eyes to minimize the pain. From behind her dropped lids, a vision of her son filled her mind. In it, he was tucked under the blue-eyed man's arm during the ambulance ride. *Remo.* She knew it was his name, even if she didn't recall why. Was Xavier still with him? For no tangible reason, she kind of hoped so. Deciding she had no choice but to ask— trust or no trust—she opened her eyes and her mouth at the same time. But the nurse—Jane—spoke first.

"Hello, Mrs. Poller," the other woman said, stepping closer. "Welcome back to the land of the living."

"It's Miss," Celia croaked automatically.

"I'm sorry?"

"Miss. I'm not married."

"Well. That's one more thing we know about you, isn't it? Your name and your marital status. It's a start."

Celia eyed her and tried to keep her heart from fluttering. Something in the back of her mind told her she didn't *want* to be known. And not knowing why it was true was frustrating. Especially since she wasn't sure how it affected her son. Regardless, she needed to know he was okay. She started to clear her throat, and the action brought a cough-inducing dryness to the surface. Jane moved nearer again, grabbed a cup and a straw from the bedside table, then held them up to Celia's lips.

"Don't drink too much, too fast," she cautioned. "You don't want to make yourself sick."

Celia nodded and took a miniscule sip. The icy water slid down her throat and cooled the burning sensation.

"Better?" asked Jane.

"Much," Celia replied. "Thank you." She took one more taste, then met the nurse's eyes and chose the direct route. "Was my son brought in, too?"

"Your son?" The blankness in the woman's tone spiked Celia's pulse again.

She forced herself to answer as calmly as possible. "He's five, but on the small side for his age. Brown hair, gray eyes, and freckles. He was wearing a red T-shirt with a fire truck on it."

Jane set down the cup, then moved to the foot of the bed and pulled a chart from a clip fastened there. She flipped through a couple pages and shook her head.

"I'm sorry, Miss Poller," she said. "I don't see any notes on here about your son. I can call down to Pediatrics and—"

"No."

"What?"

Celia exhaled. Whatever it was she feared, the thought of further exposing her son made it that much worse. She *had* to keep the attention off him. It was a compulsion.

"What about Remo?" she asked.

"Remo DeLuca? The paramedic with the dreamy eyes?" Jane smiled.

Even though she wasn't sure of the last name, Celia nodded. The description fit. And besides that…how many Remos could there be hanging around the hospital?

"He's the one who brought me in," she added.

Jane took another look at the chart, and her brow furrowed. "He's not listed here."

Doubt crept in. Was there a reason he'd left his own name off her admission documents? Was it significant? And did she even have time to think about it when her instincts told her she needed to get to Xavier as quickly as possible? Then, from somewhere in Celia's mind, a full-body image of the man popped up, and in it, Remo wasn't wearing a uniform.

He was off-duty.

Celia exhaled and made herself smile. "That's because Remo wasn't acting in an official capacity. He's…a friend. Which is why I think my son might be with him."

Jane thoughtfully tapped the chart for a second, then sighed. "Okay. Let me do a quick check of your vitals, and then I can send out a general page through the hospital. If Mr. Blue Eyes is here, I'm sure he'll come running."

Celia nodded, sat back, and pressed her lips together to keep from impatiently demanding that the nurse do her job as fast as humanly possible.

Chapter 4

Remo smiled as Xavier put the last piece of the jigsaw puzzle in place, then let loose with a triumphant fist pump.

"Did you *see* that, Remo?" the kid asked excitedly. "There were fifty pieces, and I got them *all*."

"I did see it," he agreed. "And I'm pretty impressed. Should we put this one away and start another? Or do you want to go back to coloring?"

"Another puzzle." But the kid no sooner started to pull apart the pieces than he stopped again and lifted a hesitant look in Remo's direction. "Do we have time?"

"You mean how long until we see your mom?"

The kid didn't answer immediately. He just flicked his thumb over the bumps of the completed puzzle. Remo waited. For the last thirty or so minutes, the little boy had been painstakingly pressing the bits together. Though he had to be tired and scared, he'd managed to elevate keeping a stiff upper lip to a whole new level. He'd chatted about cartoons and YouTube and his friend Kevin from school. The one thing he *hadn't* brought up was his mom, and Remo was sure it was on purpose.

Even though the door to the subject had been opened now, Xavier's next sentence came out in a small voice. "She says patience is a virtual reality."

Remo fought a chuckle. "A virtue?"

Xavier nodded without looking up. "Yeah."

"And she's right, buddy," Remo told him. "But I know you're worried, and it's okay to talk about it."

The little guy sighed a deep, far too adult sigh before lifting his face and asking, "They're going to fix her, right?"

"That's their job."

"Does that mean yes?"

For the first time in his life, Remo wished he was better at making grand promises he couldn't personally guarantee. Reassurance was one thing, but sugar-coating wasn't his forte. Even when it came to children, he believed it was better to be honest. Kind but forthcoming. Something he'd always appreciated as a kid himself, but not received often enough.

Everything will be fine was the last thing someone had said to him before his seven-year-old world imploded, and he wouldn't lay that on someone else.

So instead he said, "It means they'll do everything they can to make sure she's fine, buddy. They have science and medicine on their side, and from everything I could see myself, she looked good."

Xavier's face screwed up like he was thinking about the lacking-of-promise answer, but when he spoke, it was to ask a seemingly random question. "Why are they saying your name?"

Remo frowned. "What?"

The kid aimed a thumb toward the hall. "Over the speaker thing. Like the one they have at kindergarten."

Remo cocked an ear. Sure enough, a second later, a crackling page came to life.

"Remo DeLuca, if you're in the hospital, please report to room 414. That's Remo DeLuca to 414. Thank you."

Xavier's face lit up with hope. "Do you think room 414 is my mom?"

Remo ruffled the kid's hair. "I sure do. And that's good news, because 414 is the perfect room."

"It is?"

"You bet. Should we put away the puzzle and go?"

Xavier quickly swept the pieces into the box, then jumped up, visibly excited and truly childlike for the first time since Remo had met him. Smiling, he let the kid grab his hand and tug him into the hall. Room 414 truly *was* good news. It was in recovery, but not intensive care. If the medical staff had found any issues with Celia Poller's well-being, they would've moved her to one of the wards that offered a better chance for one-on-one care. Knowing that lightened Remo's own steps as he led the kid to the nearest staff-only elevator. He was gladder than would be expected of a stranger, and he was eager to speak to Celia.

What would the woman have to say about her situation? He couldn't help but wonder just how much she'd be willing to disclose. Maybe nothing. Maybe she'd see him as no more than the stranger he was. Or maybe— hopefully—he'd get lucky, and she'd choose him as a confidant. If she and her son *were* on the run, then there would be few people who understood it better than Remo did. The peculiar need to continue to help her and her son only strengthened as he acknowledged that his past had to be one of the main reasons behind it.

But there's a difference between admitting it to myself and saying it aloud to a stranger.

He cast a glance down at the kid. The sandy-brown curls were pressed to the outside of Remo's thigh, and the easy trust made his chest compress. What kind of man would he be if he didn't make that trust worthwhile? Not the kind of man he wanted to be, that much was for sure.

The elevator dinged then, and he started to move forward before realizing that he'd acquired a human ankle weight—the kid was standing up, but was also sound asleep. With a chuckle, he reached down and scooped the boy up. As Remo cradled him to his chest and stepped out of the elevator, Xavier barely did more than sigh. Even when someone tapped Remo's shoulder and made him do a startled spin, the little guy didn't stir.

"Hey, DeLuca," greeted the nurse attached to the hand that had made him jump. "I didn't mean to scare y—whoa! Is that Celia Poller's kid?"

Remo looked down, then smiled and feigned surprise. "Well, I'll be damned, Jane. Where did *he* come from?"

The nurse rolled her eyes. "Pipe down, DeLuca. I'm just surprised to see that the patient's claim about you having her kid was true. I wasn't aware that you *had* any friends."

"I have *you*, don't I?"

"I'm friends with your mother. You're just the leech along for the ride."

Remo's smile became a grin. "Your bedside manner must be impeccable."

Jane's eyes crinkled, but she put her hands sternly on her hips. "No complaints yet."

"Today or…"

"I did say pipe down, didn't I?"

"Not sure. I've been told my listening skills aren't great." He paused, then turned serious. "How is she?"

Jane studied him curiously. "She really *is* a friend?"

Remo forced a casual-sounding evasion because it seemed odd to admit that not only was she not a friend, but that he didn't know her at all. "Not on duty, so she can't be a patient."

"Right. Well. Your friend is doing just fine. Worried about her kid and a little groggy and understandably confused, but aside from that, she's all right. CT scan came back normal, so…" She shrugged. "You know the drill. And I won't tell anyone if you wanna sneak a look at her chart."

"Thanks, Jane. Room 414?"

"You got it."

He started to turn away, but the nurse's voice stopped him. "Remo…"

He braced himself for a comment similar to the one made by the hospital administrator. Something about the kid's age or size. Instead, Jane met his eyes, bit her lip, and shook her head.

"Nothing," she said. "Just glad to see you're not as friendless as I thought."

Remo swallowed. He tried to muster up a joke about Jane getting soft in her old age, but he couldn't quite manage it. So he just nodded, then finished his turn, and made his way toward room 414.

If Celia hadn't been stuck in her bed and attached to an IV, she would've paced the room a hundred times over. Maybe a thousand. It felt like a millennium since the page for Remo DeLuca had come through the speakers. Where was he? Did he have Xavier with him?

Please, God, let him have Xavier. Because if he doesn't…

The thought trailed off. She closed her eyes. She refused to let her thoughts go to any kind of dark place. The blue-eyed paramedic would have her son. He'd bring him in. And then she'd take him far away from the hospital and whatever unknown danger it was that lurked on the frustratingly dim periphery of her mind.

"Hurry up, Remo," she murmured.

"Don't want to go too much faster or I might drop him."

The unexpected reply—spoken in a slightly dry, slightly familiar masculine tone—made Celia's eyes fly open. And even though she was expecting him to be standing there, seeing the dark-haired, blue-eyed man in the doorway made her tongue stick to the roof of her mouth. When she'd seen him before, she'd been out of it, and he'd been either crouched down or sitting. Now that she was a little more lucid, and he was on his feet, she couldn't help but note a few things. One, he was tall. Six-five, probably. Two, he was intimidatingly broad-shouldered. And three, he was breathtakingly handsome. The kind of man who would draw the attention of every woman within a three-mile radius. And his looks were so distracting that it actually took Celia a few heartbeats to clue in that what he'd said actually meant something—the "him" he'd mentioned was her son. Held tightly against his wide chest, his sandy-colored lashes fluttering against his freckled cheeks.

"Xavier," she murmured, her voice breaking with the one word.

The big man stepped into the room, then to the edge of the bed. "You want to wake him?"

Celia exhaled, then shook her head. She had no idea what time it was, but it was definitely well into the wee hours of the night. Xavier needed his rest. Especially since they were going to have to be on the move again. Soon.

Swallowing against the ache in her throat, Celia met Remo's eyes. "Could you maybe put him on the bed?"

"Sure can," replied the blue-eyed man.

With more care than his big frame ought to have allowed, he leaned down and gently settled Xavier into the small space between Celia and the guardrail. She tried to offer him her gratitude, but she was too overwhelmed to speak. Her son's body was warm and soft, and he gave off just a hint of baby powder scent that she recognized as the fabric softener she used in his laundry. The relief at knowing he was okay made her want to weep. But she knew there was no time for indulging. She gave Xavier a brush of a kiss, then peeled off her blankets and eased sideways.

A strong hand abruptly took hold of her elbow, stilling her movement. With the contact, a zap of heat slid along her arm. She looked up, startled. The big man was staring down at her with his eyes fixed on her face. She stared back for a moment before her gaze slid to the spot where his palm met her skin. Seeing his large fingers wrapped around her elbow did nothing to change the peculiar little zaps she felt. Warmth continued to radiate from his touch—maybe it even heightened—and Celia couldn't pretend that it was unpleasant. Then Remo seemed to notice the extra attention she was giving their position, and he quickly dropped his hand back to his side and stepped a little farther from the bed.

"Hang on there," he said softly, glancing toward Xavier and dropping his voice even lower. "Are you trying to get out of bed?"

"He's a sound sleeper," she replied in a normal voice. "And I'm not trying. I'm doing."

He took a small step forward, his hand coming up again. Celia tensed with the anticipation of another touch, but he stopped just shy of reaching for her, and a strange stab of disappointment pricked at her for a moment.

There's no time for this, she told herself. *Even if I don't really know what "this" is.*

She gave her a head a little shake, then pushed the blankets down even more. She put her hand on the guardrail opposite her son and pulled her body down the bed.

"Okay," said Remo. "That's not happening."

Celia frowned up at him and continued her shimmy. "What's not happening?"

"Are you kidding me? You're not getting out of bed."

"How is it your business?"

"For starters, I'm a medical professional, and I don't think you're well enough to be going anywhere."

"Are you my doctor?" She sat up and swung her legs over the bed, pretending that a rush of dizziness didn't accompany the motion.

His eyes hung on her bare knees for a moment, and Celia fought a creeping heat in her cheeks. Apparently, finding her pants was the first order of business.

Remo cleared his throat, his gaze back on her face. "I'm not *anyone's* doctor. But I was there immediately after you sustained your injuries, and even if you weren't hooked up to an IV, I could tell you from what I personally saw out there that you're not in any shape to be up and moving around."

"You said that already."

"Because it's true."

"But you're not a doctor."

"No."

She took a breath and formulated what she hoped was a believable lie. "Look. I don't like hospitals, I have terrible insurance, and I feel all right."

"Celia."

She was surprised to hear genuine worry as his voice

wrapped softly around her name. And she responded without thinking. "Do I know you?"

His dark brow furrowed, making his already oh-so-blue eyes appear that much more vibrant. "You don't know if you know me?"

Celia fought a wince. "Of course I know." And she *did*. Or she thought she did. Hadn't she been thinking of him as the blue-eyed stranger? She blew out a breath and muttered, "It doesn't matter."

But apparently it *did* matter to Remo. His long legs brought him to the end of the bed in less time than it took to inhale again, and he quickly grabbed her chart and began reading it. Celia watched as his tense expression eased, then hardened, then eased again. What did he see? What would make his face change like that?

Who cares? Why are you just sitting here, staring at him, anyway? You're supposed to be moving!

She tried to shake off whatever it was that held her pinned to the spot, but Remo lifted his gaze, and she was immobilized again. Held by the intense mix of emotion in his eyes.

"You didn't suffer a head injury," he said.

"You're making that sound like a bad thing," she replied.

"I'm concerned that you're experiencing memory loss."

"Did I *say* I was experiencing memory loss?"

"You asked if you knew me."

"That isn't what I meant," she argued.

"So tell me what you did mean," he said.

"Maybe I meant that as a pickup line." Her face warmed, but she ignored it. "As in…haven't we met somewhere before?"

He didn't smile, or even bite on her lame attempt to deflect. "Did you tell your nurse about the confusion?"

She shook her head and lied again. "I didn't tell her because there was nothing to tell."

"Do you know what day it is?"

"Yes."

"Tell me."

"Tuesday."

"Do you know what year it is?"

"Yes! And I'm not going to tell you. The nurse already went over all of that."

"So it's just *me* you don't remember?"

"It doesn't matter if I say yes or if I say no… Either way, you'll take it how you want."

She started to move again, but he stepped closer once more, and this time, he *did* put his hand on her.

"Listen to me," he said, his voice low, urgent, and earnest, all at the same time. "We *don't* know each other. But to reiterate. You were just in a pretty serious accident. You lost a lot of blood. You've had a transfusion, you've been stitched up, and you're on some intravenous antibiotics. All of that—combined with common sense—should be enough to keep you in that bed."

As logical as his words were, Celia couldn't quite concede. "And if I don't agree?"

"Then I'll call the nurse—whose name is Jane, and who I've known for twenty-five of my thirty-one years—and I'll ask her nicely to sedate you."

"You wouldn't."

"I sure would."

"I can't stay here."

"Then you'd better give me a damned good reason for that," he replied. "And it better be more believable than a hospital phobia, too."

"My son…" Celia felt tears well up, and as she dropped her gaze and fought to either hide them or hold them in, whatever further lie she'd been about to issue got lost completely.

Remo spoke again, his voice gentle. "Xavier is only going to be in more danger if his mom's too weak to help him."

She lifted her head in surprise. "How did you know he was in danger?"

The big man's expression shifted subtly, and Celia realized her mistake even before he pointed it out.

"I didn't," he admitted. "But now I do."

She pushed her lips together and looked away. After a second, Remo let out a sigh.

"I want to help you," he told her. "But if you're going to keep lying to me, I can't do it, Celia. I need a little trust here."

She echoed his words back to him. "Then you'd better give me a damned good reason for that."

His jaw ticked. She waited for an argument. But what she got instead was his story.

Chapter 5

Remo wasn't a hundred percent sure what he'd expected to tell her. An offer of a brief glimpse into his past? Or maybe just an I-promise-you-can-trust-me hint? Whatever it was, it certainly wasn't a full—if somewhat syncopated—disclosure of his childhood. It wasn't that he was ashamed of it; time and therapy had helped him fully understand that it wasn't his fault. It was just that he preferred to keep his private life private. So even as the words started tumbling out of his mouth, he was surprised to hear them.

"I spent the first seven years of my life in a house where any wrong step ran the risk of violence. My dad wielded the punches. My mom was the bag. I spent a lot of time being told to hide. I did it, because it was what my mom wanted. She was sad all the time, and anything I could do to make her smile…"

He shrugged and met Celia's eyes. There was understanding in her gaze. Far more than sympathy, and Remo was sure he'd guessed her situation correctly.

"It played out exactly how you think it did," he added.

"You stopped hiding," she filled in softly.

"It was just once," he told her. "I don't even remember what was different, to be honest. Maybe just because I was getting older and realizing our normal wasn't really very normal at all. Either way, the end result was the same. I stepped up, and it earned me a black eye and a broken arm. And it was a wake-up call for my mom. We were out of there the same day."

Celia's face clouded for a moment, then became a mask. Remo wasn't sure what she was trying to cover up or deny, but he wasn't going to let her form a lie.

He spoke before she could try. "You know what else I saw on your charts?"

Her mouth puckered, and then she shook her head like she'd changed her mind about whatever she was about to say, and instead asked, "What did you see?"

"X-rays. They show old injuries, Celia. A broken arm that wasn't set properly. Previously fractured ribs." He said it gently, careful to keep any and all judgment out of his tone. "I've seen it enough times in my job to know what it means."

For several seemingly long heartbeats, Celia said nothing. She stared at him, her expression unreadable. Remo let her take her time. The evidence was all but irrefutable, but that didn't mean she wouldn't try to deny it, anyway. He didn't want to pressure her, but he hoped with an unreasonable amount of gusto that she'd choose trust and honesty. But when her implacable expression finally crumbled, it wasn't to confess to him that he was right. Instead, it was to burst into silent tears.

Automatically, Remo stepped in and sank down beside

her. Careful not to disturb Xavier—who was still oblivious to the world—he slung an arm over Celia's shoulder and folded her into a sideways embrace. She shifted, and for a second Remo thought he might've overstepped. They were strangers. He was a foot taller and eighty pounds heavier than she was, and as natural as it felt to offer her comfort, it wasn't crazy to think maybe the contact was unexpected and unwelcome. But it took him only a moment to realize Celia wasn't pulling away. She was settling in.

Her head pressed to his chest as her body noisily shook. Another few breaths, and one of her hands came up to slide across his abdomen and clutch at his shirt. It was an undeniably intimate pose. Yet it was innocent, too. She needed the outlet, and Remo was more than happy to provide it. He brought his own hand up to run in a soothing circle over her back, and murmured that it would be all right. A good two minutes passed before Celia finally drew in a shaky breath and pulled back just enough that Remo was able to look down at her. Her lower lip was trembling, and when she spoke, her voice was just as wobbly.

"The things is…" she said. "You were right. I *don't* remember. I know I need to keep Xavier safe. I know he's in danger. From what you said, and what you saw on the X-rays, I feel like the conclusion is easy. It fits. And as cloudy as my brain is, it's not arguing against it, which makes me think it's true." Her eyes flicked toward her son's peaceful form, and she whispered, "It's his dad. It *has* to be. But it scared the hell out of me that even though I'm sure of it—logically—I don't actually *know* it."

Remo studied her face. It was still true that he didn't know her, but it was also becoming truer and truer that he *wanted* to.

"Let me help you," he said.

"Help me *how*?" Her voice had a desperate edge. "All

I'm sure of is that if I stick around here for long, I won't be able to protect my son."

Spontaneously, Remo reached out and touched her cheek. She didn't shy away. If anything, she leaned into his hand a little.

"Close your eyes and tell me what you remember leading up to the accident," he said.

"Really?"

"It can't hurt to try."

"Are you going to hypnotize me?"

He had to laugh. "I don't know what you think a paramedic does, but stage shows aren't usually included in the job description."

She wrinkled her nose. "There are perfectly legitimate medical professionals who use hypnosis in their practices."

"Oh, yeah? Like who?"

"Therapists?"

"Is that a question? Because it sounded like a question."

"Therapists," she repeated, without the added inflection at the end.

His grin widened, not because he didn't believe her, but because the lightened conversation felt good. Natural. And Remo liked it.

"I don't know that I'd trust a therapist who wanted to hypnotize me," he told her teasingly. "Who knows what subliminal messages they'd stick in there?" He dropped his best, very bad Sigmund Freud impression. "Definitely something about my mother."

"I can*not* believe you just made that joke," Celia said, but she was smiling, too—a genuine one that made her eyes sparkle—and that alone made it worth it.

"Stand-up might not be my forte, either," he admitted.

"You don't say."

"But I'm pretty damned good at helping. So close your eyes."

She stared at him for a second longer, and then she shifted—regrettably—out of reach, and her eyelids drifted down. As her long, fair lashes hit her cheeks, Remo's amusement wore off, and a stab of remembered worry took its place. He tried to brush it off and couldn't. The two times he'd seen her so still with her eyes closed, it'd been because she was unconscious.

But she's fine now, he reminded himself. *Awake. Under medical supervision. Under* your *supervision.*

So why couldn't he shake the deep concern?

"Are you still there?" she asked softly.

He cleared his throat. "Yeah. Sorry. Just…uh. Tell me the last thing you remember before waking up here."

"Right before, or a long time before?"

"Whatever comes to mind first."

"Being in the ambulance and being confused about why I was there. Then seeing you, and…" She trailed off, a spot of color appearing in each of her cheeks.

"What?"

"I remember thinking your eyes were really blue."

Remo's mood lightened again. "My mom's always said it's the best thing I got from my dad."

Celia opened her own eyes a crack. "But it's not very helpful."

"Compliments are always helpful," he said teasingly. "You can keep them coming. Or you can go back to before the ambulance. Up to you."

Her blush deepened, and she squeezed her eyes shut again quickly. It took her a few moments, though, to say anything else. Remo waited it out. He watched her shoulders rise and fall as her breaths evened out. Then a tiny frown creased her forehead, and her words came out so softly that he almost didn't hear her.

"It's not that there's *nothing* there," she murmured. "But it's all general, jumbled together stuff."

"Why don't you tell me what you *can* remember, then?" Remo suggested. "Some of the general stuff."

"Okay. Well. I know it's just the two of us, and it has been for a long time. I can tell you that my son's teacher is named Ms. Jenny, and I can also tell you that's her last name, not her first name. Xavier thinks that's funny."

"What else?" he prodded.

"Xavier's birthday is September 1, and his favorite food is waffles." Her mouth tipped up. "We had them for breakfast this morning. We were out of syrup, and he was supremely unimpressed."

Remo didn't bother to point out that she'd just recalled something not only very specific, but also within a very recent time frame; he didn't want to derail anything that might come after. "I don't blame him. Not a big fan of waffles without syrup myself. So did you buy him some, or make him suffer through it?"

"I would've bought him more. I'm a sucker for his pouty face. But since we were in a hotel room, I—" Her eyes flew open, and she shot an excited look his way. "A hotel!"

"You remember which one?" he asked.

Her face fell. "No."

"What about a logo? Maybe on a notepad on the nightstand?"

"I think it might be the kind of place that doesn't spring for branded items."

"That's good info."

"Is it?" She sounded completely disheartened. "It feels kind of useless."

Remo reached out and squeezed her hand. "It's a start. It means we can probably rule out anything with a three-star or more rating. When we contact the police—"

"No."

The single word cut him off, but not because it was gasped out or spoken with particularly firm emphasis. Its power was in the fact that Celia had infused it with a genuine fear. And there was a matching terror in her eyes.

Celia had no idea why, but hearing the word *police* was like a switch being flipped. Her heart thundered. Her pulse raced. And her head started to throb. The only thing keeping her grounded was the fact that her hand was clasped in Remo's warm, strong palm. Her body used the contact to keep from bolting. Her mind, on the other hand, refused to stay still.

Was she running from the police? Was she a criminal? Had she broken a law—or more than *one* law—in the name of keeping her son safe? She weighed the question in her head, and quickly decided that if the choice was between protecting Xavier and not committing a crime, she'd definitely choose the former. If she admitted it aloud, would the blue-eyed paramedic feel a need to contact the local PD, just in case?

And if he does *call them...would you blame him?*

But when she exhaled and forced herself to meet Remo's gaze, the concern on his face seemed reserved for her. And his next words confirmed it.

"Hey," he said gently. "If you don't want to contact the cops, I'm not going to force you to do it."

Some of the pressure on Celia's chest eased, but she felt compelled to shake her head and say, "I should probably point out that the cops are the good guys."

"I know."

"So by extension, the people who avoid them…"

"*Aren't* the good guys," he filled in. "I get what you're saying."

"If that makes you uncomfortable, Remo, I understand. Just…give me a head start, okay?"

"A head start?"

Celia nodded. It was strange how badly she wanted him to say that it was fine with him if she was kind of a fugitive. Maybe part of it was just that he was one of the few familiar things in her current world. Maybe some of it was that he'd saved her and—even more importantly—saved her son. But she suspected that underneath that was some other driving factor. An unnamable pull. Whatever it was, it deepened when he released her hand and reached up to touch her cheek. He ran his knuckles over her cheekbone, then turned his palm to cup her face. And the intimate contact didn't feel in the slightest bit wrong or unnatural. Just the opposite. It felt *right*.

Celia tipped into the attention, leaning a little harder against his touch and enjoying the security of the touch.

Her eyes lifted, and she found the same sense of safety in his responding stare. There was an openness in his gaze. An honesty. And as fuzzy as her specific memories were, Celia was sure that was something she lacked in her day-to-day life.

Always hiding. Always running. No one to trust.

The thoughts were disturbing, and the reasons behind them were frustratingly out of reach. But Remo—this man she didn't know at all—offered a hint of hope. And something else. A feeling she hadn't experienced since God knew when.

Attraction.

As soon as Celia acknowledged it, a spark ignited. A current pulsed from his hand to her face. It throbbed in time with the pulse in her throat, and it shortened her breath, too.

A little startled by how strong the zap was—and by the fact that it seemed to mute the world around her—she pulled back. But the moment Remo's palm left her cheek, she realized she didn't want the contact to be cut short. And her body reacted reflexively. One of her own hands shot out to grasp his, pulling it back to the spot it'd just abandoned. Her other hand came up to touch *his* face. Hesitantly, but not without intention. And it was just as pleasant to be on the giving end of the caress as it was to be on the receiving end. Celia took a moment to enjoy it.

Remo's jaw was strong and well-defined. Maybe a little squarer than would be considered perfect, but it only added to his good looks, making him interesting rather than stereotypically model-esque. His chin and cheek were pebbled with the barest hint of stubble. Just the right amount of roughness against her fingers, as far as Celia was concerned. But it wasn't his outward appearance, or the way he felt physically that made her skin tingle. It was the look in his eyes, and what he said next.

"You don't need a head start from me, Celia. I said I'd help you, and I meant it," he told her, his voice low. "And even if that weren't true, I would never do anything that would make you or your son need to run. That's not who I am."

Dizziness hit Celia again, but this time it had nothing to do with her medical state, and instead everything to do with Remo DeLuca and his promise.

And his nearness, she acknowledged.

He *was* close. So close that she could feel the warmth of his lips. And she wanted to be even closer. Instinctively, she tipped her face up to make it happen. He tipped his down in response. For the briefest second, their mouths brushed against one another. It was enough time for delicious heat to fan out through Celia's entire body. Enough time to know that fireworks were waiting under the surface, ready to burst as soon as the kiss deepened. And then her son's sleepy voice forced them apart.

"Is it morning?" he asked, punctuating the question with a yawn. "I'm *so* hungry."

It could've been an awkward moment. Maybe it *should've* been. One where Remo offered her an apologetic look and murmured something about the kiss being inappropriate. Or maybe one where Celia questioned what she was thinking, kissing a man she'd only just met. In a hospital bed. While her son slept two feet away. But the tickle of mingling guilt and embarrassment lasted for only a heartbeat. Just as long as it took for Remo to smile in her direction, then lean around her and offer a wider grin to Xavier.

"You're hungry?" he said. "Well, what's your favorite gross hospital food? Squishy peas, or pudding? If your mom says it's okay, you can pick one of those, my treat."

"Ew," her son replied. "Are squishy peas really a thing?"

"Absolutely."

"Why?" Xavier's genuine bafflement made Celia want to laugh and shush him at the same time.

But Remo just shrugged. "Who knows? People are weird. And I take that to mean you want some pudding?"

"Yes, please!" He turned a pleading eye in Celia's direction. "Please, Mom? Can I?"

Celia nodded. Fighting about middle-of-the-night treats hardly seemed like a priority in light of everything else. Remo shot a conspiratorial wink her way, then stood up. Xavier jumped out of the bed, and Celia's heart banged an anxious beat. The big man clearly picked up on her nervousness. He bent down to Xavier's level and spoke to him in a serious voice.

"Can I ask you a favor, buddy? Because I could really use your help with something," he said.

Her son was quick to solemnly agree. "Yeah. I can help."

"The pudding is just down the hall and around the corner in a little kitchen. It'll only take me a minute to go there and back, but I don't really want to leave your mom alone. Think you can keep an eye on her for me?"

Xavier glanced from Remo to Celia, and Celia's heart squeezed. She knew he'd want to say no. And she couldn't blame him. An adventure to get pudding was undoubtedly more appealing than playing watchdog for his boring, bedridden mom. But she knew, also, that his sense of responsibility was high. *Too* high for a kid his age.

She swallowed against the thick lump in her throat, and spoke quickly. "You know what? I'll be fine here for a minute. You two go."

Remo stood up and lifted an eyebrow. "You sure? Could take us *two* minutes to track down a spoon. Puddings abound, but utensils are notoriously hard to come by. Had to settle for a fork a few times."

She heard the other, unasked question in his words. *Are you sure you're comfortable letting your son leave with a stranger?*

Celia met his eyes. "Don't settle. Take five minutes, if you need to. It'll give me time to regroup."

Remo studied her for a few seconds, as if trying to figure out if she meant it. She offered a nod. She *did* mean it. He'd rescued her son from the wreck. He'd taken care of him while she was unconscious. Those two things alone told her she could trust him. And her instincts heartily agreed.

"All right," Remo said, then tipped his gaze back down to Xavier. "What do you say, my man? That work for you?"

Celia fought a smile as her son practically bounced on the spot with barely bridled excitement.

"Go ahead," she told him. "Freak out. It's pudding."

Xavier's eyes brightened even further, and he jumped up once, then did an enthusiastic fist pump. "Yes!"

Remo chuckled and held out his hand. Celia watched her son's tiny fingers disappear in the paramedic's palm, and her heart squeezed again, this time in a different way. She held her breath until the two of them were gone, then let out a long, shaky exhale and closed her eyes.

She felt lost. The holes in her memory were enough to make her want to cry. And what was worse was that she was starting to suspect that the lack of recall had little to do with her accident, and more to do with not *wanting* to remember. Like her mind was intentionally blacking out the Big Bad Wolf to protect her.

But it's having the opposite effect.

Instead of being insulated, she was just helpless. She *needed* those memories, whether her subconscious wanted to admit it or not. She had to find a way to get them back.

"What am I going to do?" she wondered aloud.

And unexpectedly, a rough, masculine voice answered her. "My suggestion would be to tell me where the boy is."

Chapter 6

Celia didn't even get a look at the man attached to the voice before he clamped a hand over her mouth, blocking anything but a muffled protest.

"Scream," he said in a low voice. "I dare you."

For a second, the challenge made no sense. And Celia was too scared to attempt to force it to. But then the man eased back just enough to give her a view of his *other* hand, and she didn't have to think about it anymore. It wasn't a challenge; it was a threat. His fingers were clasped around a syringe, one thumb poised on the plunger. And the syringe itself was stuck through a rubberized injection port.

Oh, God.

She had no clue what was in the needle, but the possibilities were endless, and not one of them let Celia come out alive on the other end.

"Do you understand?" the man asked.

Celia nodded—the barest incline of her head.

"Good," said her attacker.

He eased back, but only a little. As if he thought the needle wasn't quite enough to buy her silence. It made a silent, hysterical laugh bubble up. But that didn't escape any more than a scream could have done. Sound was an impossibility. It had all evaporated into fear-induced dryness in the back of her throat.

Even when her assailant pulled back more, then settled into the hard-backed chair beside her bed, and stared at her expectantly, all Celia could do was blink back at him. He was dressed in scrubs, but she knew beyond any doubt that he wasn't a doctor or a nurse or a medical professional of any kind. Because the moment her eyes landed on his face—acne-scarred and clean-shaven—a vivid memory sprang to life.

This man, with a gun in his hand.

This man, with a gun pressed to a stranger's head.

This man, pulling the trigger.

"Nothing to say?" His voice cut through the memory, and Celia had to bite back a gasp.

She lifted her eyes and shook her head. Who was he to her? Who was he to Xavier? Looking at him, she was certain he wasn't her son's father.

Ten years too young.

The thought wasn't a vague assumption. It was something she *knew.* Whoever Xavier's father was, he was older than this man. Older than Celia herself.

She breathed out, unsure if it was a relief to know that detail or not.

"Are you listening to me, Celia?"

She jerked her attention back to the man's face—he clearly assumed she knew him—and made herself answer in as sure of a voice as she could manage. "I'm listening."

"Then maybe you're not listening well enough," he replied. "Because if you don't tell me where your son is, I'm going to make sure you don't leave here alive."

His statement made her realize something: he didn't know that Xavier was in the hospital. Celia squared her shoulders and made sure to keep both her face and her voice devoid of the hope that washed through her.

"I'd rather die than let you get your hands on him," she said evenly. "But it doesn't matter. Because even if I *wanted* to tell you where he was, I couldn't. He's with social services."

The man narrowed his eyes. "You want me to believe that? Social services took him, when his mother is alive and well and capable?"

"They didn't take him from *me*," Celia replied. "I was unconscious. He's got no family. Who do you think watches kids in a situation like that?"

He studied her for another moment, then leaned back and said, "He's got family. His dad would be more than happy to 'watch' him."

Her heart tried to plummet toward her stomach. And when she responded, it was like her mouth was on autopilot—saying things she wasn't consciously aware of, but which she knew were true as soon as they left her mouth.

"Xavier doesn't *have* a dad," she stated. "The man you work for has never had that title. And he lost any chance he ever had of earning it the moment he laid a hand on me."

"Self-righteous, aren't you?"

"Completely devoid of morals, aren't *you*?"

He shrugged. "I've got loyalty, and I get paid. And if you can't tell me where the kid is, then I guess I've got no use for—"

He cut himself off and stood abruptly, yanking the syringe with him. And the moment he was on his feet,

Celia saw why he'd made the sudden move. A nurse—not Jane—was stepping into her room.

"Hi, Miss Poller. I'm here to check your vitals," she said, then frowned as she spotted the scrubs-clad man. "Oh. Doctor... Um. Sorry. I don't think we've met?"

"Wrong room," the man muttered, brushing roughly by the nurse to exit out to the hall.

Celia let her body sag. He wouldn't come back. He wouldn't risk being caught and identified. She was sure of it for the same reason she was sure of everything else— her memory told her so, even if it wouldn't tell her why.

The nurse stepped closer, concern playing over her face. "Are you feeling all right, Miss Poller?"

"I'm fine," Celia lied. "Just tired."

"All right. Well you just let me have a quick look-see, and then you can rest."

"Thank you."

Celia closed her eyes and let the nurse do her thing. Where were Remo and Xavier? She prayed that whatever had delayed them had also kept them out of the sights of the unknown man.

Not unknown, she corrected silently. *Not exactly, anyway.*

Whoever he was, he worked for Xavier's father. And not in a pleasant way. God, why couldn't she just remember?

"There you go, Miss Poller," said the nurse.

Celia dragged her eyes open. "How am I?"

"Everything looks good. Better than good, actually. I'm impressed." The other woman clicked her pen, then tucked it into her pocket and patted Celia's knee. "You can go ahead and get some shut-eye. The doctor will be here in the morning. Sound good?"

"Perfect."

The nurse excused herself, and Celia waited until she was gone, then counted to thirty before throwing her bedding aside. There was still no sign of Remo and Xavier, and she couldn't shake the nervous feeling that her unwanted visitor might've found them. She had to act. She swung toward the various monitors, reaching out to touch the nearest one—the automated IV drip. As she ran her finger over the buttons, it occurred to her that she knew what each one did.

Strange.

But she wasn't going to question it. Not at the moment, anyway.

She keyed in a sequence, and the IV monitor beeped once, and went silent. Carefully, Celia pulled up the tape from the infusion site on her hand, then drew out the needle. Blood beaded in its place, and she quickly swiped it away, while at the same time scanning the room for a change of clothes. It was all well and good to free herself from the tubes, but it would all be for naught if someone noticed she was walking the halls in nothing but an open-backed robe and her underwear. She heaved a relieved sigh when she spotted her jeans and T-shirt peeking out of a bag near the window. But as she started to stand, a shelf just outside the door caught her eye. It was piled with folded garments, and it brought a better idea to mind. *Scrubs.* The man who'd invaded her room had been dressed in them, and the nurse had barely blinked when she saw him. She hadn't even commented on his presence.

Celia pushed to her feet, ignored the slight bit of dizziness that occurred as a result, and moved toward the door. Following a quick, careful glance up and down the hall—neither her assailant, nor Remo and Xavier were in view—she snagged a stack of fabric at random. She tossed it on the bed, relieved to find she had everything she needed. Pants, a top, and a mask and cap.

Moving as fast as her aches and light-headed state would allow, she discarded her robe and slipped into the scrubs. She tied her hair into a knot at the nape of her neck, then snagged her purse from the nightstand. She winced, though, when she noted again how damaged the bag was. And after a quick glance revealed that there was nothing but the library card inside, she decided to simply toss it in the trash. With that done, she slid her feet into her shoes, then counted off three slow breaths. She took one more look around the room, then moved out into the hall. It was still clear.

Is that a good thing or a bad thing?

A bubble of dread made her stomach churn, but she ordered herself to stop. She had to assume the best until she had a reason to think the worst.

What had Remo said about where the pudding was? She thought he'd mentioned going down the hall and around the corner. But which way? Celia flicked a look back and forth. At one end, there was a T and an elevator. At the other, she could just see the nurses' station. Her gaze hung on the latter. Surely Remo would've mentioned having to pass it, if that'd been the direction they had to head.

No time for second guesses.

Celia swung the other way and took five self-affirming steps. But as she lifted her foot for a sixth, she very nearly tumbled over. Because the elevator doors slid open slowly, and inside were Xavier and Remo. The blue-eyed man was smiling and held two pudding cups in his big hands. Oddly, Celia's son was wrapped in a hospital blanket and seated in a child-sized wheelchair with a book in his hands. But it wasn't that concerning fact that made her nearly fall. It was something far more frightening.

Coming into view and approaching them at a leisurely pace from one side of the T—seemingly unaware that the kid he wanted was right there—was the man who'd threatened her.

Remo glanced down at the kid and put his hands on the wheelchair—a "special ride" offered to him by one of the kitchen staff who'd had to dig out a pudding from the depths of dry storage—and prepared to exit the elevator. Before he could make a move, though, he spied a small, female figure hurrying their way. Her quick pace gave him pause. Frowning, he watched her stop abruptly in front of the last room in the hall, grab a chart from the door, then start his way again. Her eyes came up just long enough for Remo to catch sight of them before she dropped her gaze down to the chart. She offered him the barest hint of a nod, and he did a double take.

Celia.

In spite of the different clothes and strange behavior, he was a hundred percent certain it was her. What was she doing out of bed? Why the hell was she dressed like she was about to head into surgery? And why was she darting toward the elevator like it was life-and-death?

Remo hung back, waiting for an explanation. She didn't offer him one. In fact, she said nothing as she ran through the doors, pressed her back to the rear of the car, and lifted the chart to block her face.

For a second, Remo was too surprised to say anything. He stared dumbly at the back of the chart, his mouth open a little. Before he could quite collect himself, a man's voice drew his attention back to the elevator doors.

"This your floor?" asked the newcomer.

Celia's foot came out and tapped Remo's ankle hard enough to make him wince.

What the hell? Then he clued in.

Whatever the gray-eyed woman was up to, it had everything to do with the man who was currently holding the elevator doors open. Who was dressed in scrubs and looking expectantly at Remo.

"Your floor?" the man asked again.

Remo cleared his throat and quickly formulated the most obvious lie. "Not us. Just having a little ride for fun before we head back to peds."

The man inclined his head, then stepped into the elevator and lifted a hand to press a button. He stopped when he saw that each and every one was already lit up.

"Hope you're going down," Remo joked.

"Sorry!" Xavier added immediately. "I pressed them all!"

Remo held his breath, waiting for the man to look down and notice the kid. For him to notice *anything*. But he just grunted and stepped away from the panel.

The seconds ticked by, the stop at each floor so tense it was almost painful.

Celia continued to stare at her chart, flicking the occasional page and scribbling with a pen.

Xavier stared down at the colorful book one of the nurses had given him, either unaware that they should've gotten off, or just not caring that their trip was five times as long as it should be.

Remo just kept his eyes on their companion. Who was he? Not Xavier's father, or he would've recognized his kid. So someone acting on the father's behalf? It was impossible to get a good read on the guy. The scrubs he wore obscured his clothes, and his face was expressionless. He said nothing through the entire ride, not even pulling out a cell phone for a glance. When they at last reached the lobby, and the man stepped off, it took a big chunk of

Remo's willpower to wait for the doors to shut before he rounded on Celia to demand some answers. When he did finally turn her way, though, the words stuck in his throat. Celia's face was ashen, her eyes red-rimmed with unshed tears. Automatically, Remo abandoned words and reached for her. Before his hands could get to her, she flipped the chart over. His gaze dropped to it, the words she'd scrawled there stopping him from speaking or acting.

Somewhere to talk, she'd written.

He lifted his eyes up to meet hers. She clearly didn't want to expose herself yet. Remo silently nodded his understanding—and his agreement—then turned back to the panel. He juggled the puddings, then pressed the button that would take them back to the family room he and Xavier had used before. And thankfully, without having to stop at every floor, the trip was over quickly. In under two minutes, the doors were sliding open. Remo stepped back to let Celia exit first, and she shot a grateful look in his direction as she brushed past and headed straight for a nearby bathroom.

Remo resisted an urge to watch her go. Instead, he looked away, dropped the pudding into Xavier's lap, then grasped the wheelchair handles and gave them a nudge.

"Hey," the kid said, as the chair bumped from the elevator onto the linoleum. "This is the wrong place."

"Not the wrong place," Remo corrected. "Just a different one."

"My mom's gonna worry."

"Don't worry, buddy. I think she knows where we are."

"Good. Because she *really* worries."

To that, Remo said nothing. He was starting to believe that Celia had a damned good reason for her particular brand of concern.

But what is it?

He was eager to find out, but—if he was being honest—he was getting pretty damned worried himself. He was tired as all hell, too. He'd been awake for nearly twenty hours, and the lack of sleep was starting to mix unpleasantly with the roller coaster of stress.

With a suppressed sigh and a dramatic pop-a-wheelie that made Xavier squeal, he pushed the wheelchair into the family room.

"Okay, my friend," he said. "What'll it be? Cartoons? Another puzzle? Or you just wanna read that book some more?"

Xavier's little forehead creased thoughtfully, then cleared abruptly as his face lit up. "Mommy!"

Remo looked up. Celia stood in the doorway, hesitating for only a second before she stepped in and bent down to envelop her son in a hug. Her eyes stayed on Remo, though.

"This is a nice little space," she said, her silent question clear. *Is it safe?*

"Nice, *private* little space," he amended. "This part of the floor is being renovated next week, so it's more or less a ghost town."

Celia nodded, then turned her attention to her son.

"All right," she said, her voice full of real-sounding cheer. "There has *got* to be a story behind your new wheels."

Remo stood back. He was only half listening to Xavier as the kid launched into an excited explanation that involved spilled puddings and lost puddings and new puddings. Most of his attention was on the boy's mother. She'd stripped off the top layer of her scrubs, and now wore just the wrinkled bottoms with the pale yellow T-shirt she'd had on when Remo found her on the side of the road. His heart dipped at the memory. He hoped to God yanking herself from her hospital bed and running through halls wouldn't set her back. But she seemed to be in an okay state. Better than she'd been in the elevator, for sure. As she continued to talk to the kid, her eyes were clear, her face a normal shade of pink.

"Remo?"

He blinked, realizing he'd missed something.

She smiled up at him, but it wasn't quite as cheerful as her voice. "I just told Xavier that you and I were going to talk on that couch out in the hall for a minute so we don't disturb him while he finishes his book."

He nodded. "Yeah, sounds like a fair plan."

He gave the kid's hair a tousle, then followed Celia out. She pointed to the couch she'd mentioned, and as they sat down, Remo noted immediately that it was really more of a two-seater. Or maybe a one-and-a-half-seater, factoring in a man of his size. No matter which way either of them shifted, they still touched. Shoulder against shoulder, hip against hip. When Celia sighed and lifted her fingers to brush a wayward strand of hair back from her face, her hand brushed Remo's, and a little flick of electric attraction sent his mind slipping back to the brief kiss they'd shared.

Was Celia thinking about it, too? Had she thought about it as many times as he had already? If Remo was being honest, it'd dominated his mind through the whole chocolate pudding retrieval. Her lips on his had been warm and sweet. As quick as the contact had been, it had also been heated in a way he hadn't felt in as long as he could remember. His conscience had nudged a few times, suggesting that he might be walking a line. Reminding him about ethics. Professionalism. The nudges had been surprisingly easy to override, though. Sitting so close to her right then told him why. It felt good and natural to be near her. And Remo was the kind of man who believed that what *felt* like the right thing…usually *was* the right thing.

Chapter 7

"Tell me," said Remo.

Celia drew in a breath. She still hadn't quite shaken the terrible memory that had surfaced as she stood in the elevator with the man who'd threatened her life, and she itched to reach for Remo's hand. She knew she'd feel safer if his fingers were clasping hers. Even the unintentional—but unavoidable—contact brought by the small couch was comforting. But she was well aware that in spite of the desire to draw strength from Remo, their current relationship status still bordered on "almost strangers who happened to have kissed." And she honestly wasn't sure where the boundaries were, or if there was a line she ought not to cross. So she settled on adjusting just enough that their knees stayed touching, and she clasped her hands in her own lap, then exhaled and explained what the man from the elevator had said and done.

Remo's face grew darker, his azure eyes sharpening

along with his voice. "Are you still dead set against contacting the police?"

She looked down at her hands. "Yes."

He muttered something that might've been a frustrated curse, then said, "Private security, then, if we really can't contact the police. An anonymous guard outside your room."

"No."

"It's a compromise."

"An anonymous guard wouldn't be anonymous for very long, Remo. If I know anything, it's that the man back there would find a way to go through someone in order to get to Xavier. I don't want to risk any collateral damage. I'm not taking any chances."

"So you're going to do what?" he asked. "Leave the hospital? Risk your own life by not getting the medical care you need? How does that help your son? That's nothing *but* taking a chance."

"I can't stay in one place. I told you that already. And now that they know where I am… You're right. Running might have risks, but staying here is a guaranteed loss."

"We don't know who 'they' are," Remo pointed out.

Celia couldn't help but be warmed by his use of the word *we*, but she didn't have time to sit and enjoy it. She had more to share. She inhaled again, the air burning against her lungs.

"But there's something else I *do* know," she told him.

She unclasped her hands, brought them to the edge of her T-shirt, and pulled it up to reveal the faded scar she knew was there. She didn't have to look down. Its shape was etched in her mind, and it seemed crazy that her memory would've let it go in the first place. Unconsciously, she slid her fingers over the uneven puckers.

"I might not remember who 'they' are," she said, "but

I remember getting this. I was trying to get away from... someone. Xavier's dad, I'm assuming, even though that bit's still spotty. And that man back there came after me. This scar..." She touched it again. "It's from the shot he fired at me."

She looked up and found Remo's gaze hanging on the mark in question. "That's an unusual-looking one."

"I guess you've seen your fair share of gunshot wounds."

"I don't get to see the healed version all that often, but I gotta say that this one looks pretty unique."

"How many have you seen that were on a formerly pregnant stomach?" Celia asked softly.

Remo's eyes jerked up. "What?"

"I was pregnant with Xavier when he shot me. *Very* pregnant."

"How in God's name could anyone shoot a pregnant woman?" He spoke like he couldn't help himself, his horror and anger palpable.

Celia shook her head. She didn't know, either. In the elevator, it had run over her like a race car. Fast. Unstoppable. And with an excruciating kick. Because as much as the bullet had hurt *her*, the absolute terror that it might hurt her unborn son was far worse.

"I think Xavier's father is a dangerous man," she said. "Even more dangerous than the guy in the elevator."

"It'll come back to you," Remo promised.

"I wish it didn't have to," she admitted with a glance toward the room where her son sat reading. She couldn't quite see him, but she was aware of his presence. Like an extension of herself. "In my head and my heart, I *know* I'm a good mother. But..."

"Don't second-guess yourself."

"I can't help it. What if I'm blocking things out because

I'm not…" She trailed off, fighting tears. "I mean, look at where I am now. I want your help. I'm sitting here, hoping you're going to keep offering."

"My offer stands," he assured her.

"But the problem is that I'm going to *take* your help."

"Why is that a problem if I'm giving it willingly?" he asked, sounding genuinely puzzled.

"Because I know it means you could be hurt. Because I know what my son's father and his men are capable of, but have no idea who they are. Because—"

"Celia."

She took a breath that felt like a gasp. "What?"

Remo's hand came up to cup her cheek. "I'm aware of the danger. And there's no way in hell I'm letting you face it alone."

"You already saved us once."

"I know. And what kind of man would I be if I just let that go to waste?" He said it in a low, intense voice, with his eyes fixed unwaveringly on her face.

She leaned a little more into his touch. "What kind of woman would I be if I just let you endanger yourself on behalf of a stranger?"

"You're not a stranger."

"I'm not?"

"No." He inched closer.

Her breath caught, and her eyes started to drift shut. "What am I, then?"

"The mother of my new best friend."

"The—" Her eyes flew back open. *"What?"*

A small, teasing smile made Remo's lips curl up appealingly. "Chocolate puddings are the way to the boy's heart. You can go ahead and confirm with him in a minute. Then you can ask me about my plan. But first…"

His head dipped down, and his mouth found hers. And

just as it had with the first kiss, heat leaped to life, swirling through her entire body. But unlike the last time their lips had met, this time the contact wasn't immediately cut short, and Celia had time to appreciate every bit of it.

Remo's mouth was warm and welcoming. Firm in just the right spots. Exploratory but not hesitant or overly forceful. He tasted faintly sweet—like maybe he'd helped himself to a taste of the same pudding he'd procured for Xavier. Celia might've smiled about it if not for two things. First, there was the fact that her lips were already preoccupied. And second, there was the more *important* fact that Remo deepened the kiss right then.

His tongue came out to dart along her lower lip, and her mouth dropped open in an automatic invitation. Her response earned a rumbling groan from somewhere down low in Remo's throat, and the sound made her vibrate. His tongue came out again, this time to explore her waiting mouth. Slowly. Deliciously. Toe-curling-ly. And Celia's toes *were* curling—literally scrunching up inside her shoes in an absolutely heavenly way. And her hands seemed to have their own agenda, too. They slid up Remo's well-muscled arms, reveling in the obvious strength there. They tripped along his shoulders, then found their way to the back of his neck and settled there. His dark hair was thick and soft, and the short strands tickled her fingers in a thousand, shiver-inducing licks.

Celia had been kissed before. From spin-the-bottle to passion-driven moments, she'd run the gamut. But never like this. Even with the current shoddy state of her memory, she was beyond certain that she'd never once had a moment that felt like this one did.

Not a stranger, said a voice in her head.

And it made her realize something odd. Something that should've been disconcerting, but just plain *wasn't*.

Kissing Remo really didn't feel like kissing a stranger. It was more like…coming home. If coming home were an explosion of metaphorical fireworks and a need to crawl into someone's lap, that is.

His hands were on her back now, his fingers splayed and his palms searing through the fabric of her T-shirt. The small space that had been between them before was practically nonexistent now. Chest-to-chest. And one of her knees was bent overtop of one of his. Another move, and she *would* be in his lap.

But then he slowed things down. And instead of being disappointing, it was good. Like the perfect fade-out of a song.

First, he gave her mouth a final swipe with his tongue. Next, he withdrew his tongue completely, and he pressed several slow kisses to her mouth. Finally, he gave her lower lip a little suck, then pulled back.

When he spoke, his voice was a raw-edged plea. "Let me help you."

Celia stared into his oh-so-blue eyes, her face still warm with want. "Remo…"

"Please. Don't make me be the kind of man who'd leave you and your son alone against God knows what."

And there was pretty much no way she could say no to that.

As Celia nodded, a relieved breath escaped Remo's lungs. He hadn't had any intention of letting the Pollers simply walk away no matter what she'd said, but it was going to be a hell of a lot easier to keep them safe with Celia in agreement.

"Thank you," he said.

"Do I say you're welcome to that?" she asked breathlessly.

"You say whatever you like, so long as it's something that lets me keep on helping you and Xavier."

He knew full well that the words were more emotionally charged than they should've been. But he didn't care. The kiss they'd just shared was more than enough to tell him that his mission to keep her from harm was growing more personal by the second. He *had* to keep them safe, even if just for the sake of finding out where the kiss would lead.

But we need to move cautiously, he reminded himself.

He slid his hands from her back to her forearms, then to her wrists, which he held lightly in his grip. "How about you hear me out before writing me off, hmm?"

She made a face. "I was *going* to listen, but you had other ideas."

"Did you *object* to the other ideas?" he asked, lifting a finger to trace the line of her cheek.

She swallowed. "No."

"Good." He smiled. "And speaking of me and my other ideas… I feel obligated to ask…"

"What?"

"I'm obviously aware that you and Xavier's father aren't a couple. But does that foggy memory of yours hint at a significant other?"

She shook her head. "Very definitely a single mom."

"Good," he said again, then leaned forward and dusted his lips over hers before getting down to business. "So the first thing we need is a good cover story for why you've gone AWOL from your very comfortable hospital bed. I actually think we're lucky they haven't put out the hospital version of an APB."

"Do they do that?"

"Well, yeah. How else do they track down delirious patients?"

"You're teasing me."

"A little," he admitted. "But in all seriousness, if you're not there when they come, there'll be a code yellow called, and a search. Likely a call to the police, too. So the last thing we want is to prematurely draw attention to the fact that you've discharged yourself."

"Can I just do that?" Her tone was only half-hopeful— like she already knew the answer.

He shook his head and explained, anyway. "Technically, you can release yourself against the hospital's recommendation, but it'd draw attention, too. Everyone on your floor would hear about it, and an administrator would bring you a letter to sign, and likely try to talk you out of it. Which is where I come in. The admin on-call tonight is a family friend, so with your permission, I'd like to give her a heads-up."

Her forehead wrinkled. "My permission?"

"She's a friend, but I'm still going to need to give her a damned good reason for releasing you like this." It was true; Tanya had known him for a decade and a half, but that didn't mean she would just forget she also had a job to do.

Celia's brow didn't uncrinkle. "I still don't understand why you need my—oh. You want to tell her what's going on."

"I think a hint at the truth will probably do."

He thought she might balk at having even a small part of her story shared with anyone, but she just met his eyes.

"You trust this family friend?" she asked.

He made sure his own gaze was as steady as his response. "Absolutely."

"Then I do, too."

"Perfect. Once I've settled things with her, we'll get you and Xavier to a safe place."

"I take it you've got one in mind."

"I do," he admitted. "I'm going to have to call in another favor, but I think it'll work out."

She stared at him, a mix of emotions playing across her face. She looked a little impressed, a little awed, and a little amused, too.

"Are a lot of people in your debt, or what?" she finally asked, a hint of all three feelings in her tone.

He chuckled. "Actually, the person I'm going to ask for this particular favor will probably tell you that *I* owe *her* a favor. A thousand of them. But there's a lot of 'what goes around comes around' when you've known people for as long as I've known some of the staff here. I practically grew up in this hospital."

The statement clearly piqued Celia's curiosity. "You practically grew up here?"

For a brief moment, he weighed the idea of explaining. He actually wanted Celia to know. But he didn't want to give her a syncopated version of events, so he decided to wait until time was less of an essence. He pushed to his feet and held out his hand.

"It's a long story," he said. "And I promise I'll tell it to you, but we should probably get moving before Jane or one of the other nurses *does* notice you're gone."

She studied him for a second, then nodded and let him help her to her feet.

He kept her hand in his and said, "I'm just going to slip into an office a couple doors up to make the calls, all right? Easier to use the hospital lines than to hope everyone's got their cell phones handy."

Celia nodded again. "All right. I'll wait with Xavier."

He gave her fingers a quick squeeze, then released them and turned to go. He got only a few steps, though, before he heard her feet tapping noisily on the linoleum. Concerned, he spun back, and bumped straight into her.

"Whoops!" He put his hands out to steady her. "Are you okay? Is something wrong?"

Celia quickly shook her head. "No. I just…"

He frowned at the little spots of pink under her lightly freckled skin. "What is it?"

She cleared her throat and shifted from foot to foot. "I just wanted to say thank you. For everything. For helping us. For helping me."

"No thanks necessary," he assured her, his concern easing.

"Seriously." She shook her head. "I don't know what would've happened if you hadn't been there after the accident. I don't know what would be happening now, if you weren't *still* here."

"Hey. Trust me. I'm glad, too."

"Yes, but…" Celia trailed off, her face evidencing some kind of deliberation.

Her gaze hung on his eyes for a moment, then dropped to his lips. And with no more warning than that, she pushed to her toes and pressed a firm kiss to his mouth. Remo automatically brought his hands to her waist and pulled her closer. Her body was flush with his, her curves pushed against him in a way that made him groan. Her mouth moved in rhythm with his, alive and inviting and perfect.

Third kiss, he thought. *But it feels like a habit already.*

When she pulled away and murmured his name in a vibration against his lips, it took most of his willpower not to pick her right up off the floor and carry her away, caveman-style. He forced himself to ease back.

"Any time you want to thank me like that, you go right ahead," he teased, his voice rough with desire.

She dropped to her heels and stared up at him. "That wasn't a part of the thank-you."

"No?"

"No. That was motivation."

His mouth twitched. "Motivation for what?"

"To hurry back," she replied.

Remo couldn't help but chuckle. He also cupped her cheek. "I promise that I will."

Then he made himself turn without looking back, sure that if he stole another glance, he'd have an even harder time trying to convince himself to leave.

Chapter 8

Celia watched Remo go, her heart flipping unevenly for a reason she couldn't quite pinpoint. Was she nervous about being left alone for a minute or two? She didn't think so. She was well accustomed to being the sole provider and protector for her son. Was she scared overall? Absolutely. But she was also sure her day-to-day life carried an underlying fear, and she faced it willingly because it was worth it. So whatever it was that caused the dance in her chest, it was directly related to Remo's receding back. Directly related to Remo himself.

As he took a final step, then turned and disappeared through a nearby door, Celia had to swallow against the sudden lump in her throat, and shove down an urge to chase after him again. It was then that she clued in. She wasn't scared for herself and Xavier. Not any more than usual, anyway. At the moment, she worried about *Remo*. And not just because she felt personally responsible for dragging him into the current mess, but because—even though she'd just met him—she didn't want anything to happen to him.

It was undeniably strange for Celia to feel her bubble of protectiveness grow so rapidly. She knew she always felt that way about her son. Like she wanted to shield him from even the slightest harm. She'd never experienced it for anyone else. But it was definitely there for Remo. In fact, if it hadn't been for Xavier waiting in the family room, she might not have been able to stop her feet from moving in Remo's direction. It was more difficult than it should've been to spin and walk back toward her son. But thankfully, once she was standing in front of Xavier— who'd moved out of the wheelchair and into a cozy corner of the couch—the worry over Remo's well-being faded to the back of her mind.

"How's the book?" she asked.

"Good." He closed the item in question and peered past her shoulder. "Where's Remo?"

Celia stepped into the room and sank down beside him. "You like him, huh?"

"I asked him to be my best grown-up friend, and he said yes. Is that okay?" He frowned, then added, "Don't *you* like him?"

"Of course I do. Kinda hard not to like someone who rescued us from a car crash, right?"

"Yep. But I think I'd like him anyway."

"Yeah, me, too, kiddo," Celia admitted.

Xavier snuggled a little closer. "Mommy?"

She looked down at the top of her son's head, surprised. The moment he'd started kindergarten, he'd dropped into calling her "Mom" unless he was sick.

"What's wrong, baby?" she asked.

He twirled his thumb into her pants, making the cotton pucker as he answered in a small voice, "My dad was there."

Celia's heart dropped. "What?"

"At the accident," he said.

"You've never met your dad, bud." As soon as she said it, she was unequivocally sure it was true. "How do you know he was there?"

"I heard you."

She worked to keep calm. "You did? What did I say?"

"You told me to pull down the back seat and hide in the trunk. And I did. There were some bumpity-bumps, and you were saying something about my dad. Then the car went *BOOM* and everything was spinny and I was stuck until Remo got me."

With the mini flood of words, a fuzzy memory trickled in and Celia closed her eyes and rested her chin on her son's head while trying to grasp it. She could recall spying the flash of headlights. The fact that she knew the encroaching car and its driver. The fear as the vehicle bumped hers. And then came the patch of slick road. Oil mixed with water, maybe? She wasn't sure. But as her tires had hit it, she'd realized she was going to lose control of her car.

You can't have him. It doesn't matter if you're his dad or not, you don't deserve him.

She distinctly remembered thinking those exact words immediately before losing control of the car. Had she said them aloud? Yelled them with as much desperation and gusto as she'd felt them? Maybe she had, even if she hadn't meant to.

She dragged her eyes open and looked down at her son's head. He was engrossed in his book again, distracted in that easy way that kids tended to be. But Celia knew he deserved an explanation of some kind. What could she offer him at that moment, though? She'd clearly created some kind of mental block where his father was concerned. She had no recollection of his face or his name. All she had were the feelings associated with him. Dread and fear. An absolute need to stay away from him.

It was so incredibly maddening, to reach into her memory and find nothing but a black hole. Trying to do it almost *hurt*. It made her eyes burn, and she had to draw in a steadying breath to keep in the tears.

So what do I tell Xavier about his father in our everyday life?

Celia considered it. She wasn't a liar. But her son was only five. There had to be a balance, for when he asked questions. She couldn't see herself simply brushing off his concerns or trying to change the subject, but she could imagine skirting around the issue a little. Telling him that his dad wasn't in the picture because the world was full of gray areas, and in this case, the gray area was about positive role models. Was it a cop-out? Maybe a little. But she could practically hear herself saying it, and could practically see Xavier's solemn nod in response.

Swallowing, she opened her mouth to offer a similar excuse now. But whatever she'd been about to say stayed stuck in her mouth. Because—quite suddenly—they weren't alone. In the doorway stood a statuesque, sixtyish woman. Her dark eyes were both shrewd and kind, and she had them directed at Celia, who was momentarily too surprised by her presence to react properly.

And why does she look so familiar?

Puzzled, Celia stared at her for a second. The woman's hair was long and gray, and hung in two braids that nearly hit her waist. She wore a uniform emblazoned with the hospital logo and a lanyard hung from her neck. There was a card fastened to it, and when it swung sideways the name Wendy flashed into view.

Do I even know a Wendy?

Before she could mentally posit an answer, the woman—Wendy—stepped into the room, speaking as she moved.

"Well…" She greeted her with a smile. "As my grandma used to say…look what the cat drug in."

Belatedly, Celia realized that in spite of the apparent friendliness, the woman's familiarity might stem from another blocked memory. And if that were true, then there was a strong possibility that her presence was a bad thing.

She started to stand, planning to make herself a human shield if she had to. But she didn't make it all the way to her feet before her son looked up, noticed the woman, too, then let out a decidedly un-Xavier-like noise—something pretty close to a squeal of excitement.

"Nana Wendy!" he said excitedly, then tugged on Celia's arm. "Mom, Mom! That's the lady who got me the extra pudding from the secret room!"

"Nana Wendy? Xavier, what…" Celia trailed off as Remo appeared behind the woman.

His expression was as puzzling as everything else. He looked…sheepish. Almost embarrassed. He seemed to be deliberately avoiding Celia's gaze. Even after Xavier tossed back his hospital blanket and sprung out to throw himself at Remo's legs, and the big man scooped him up for a bear hug, he addressed the older woman without a word of introduction. And the resulting conversation made Celia even more curious than she'd been in the moments leading up to it.

"I told you I'd meet you here," Remo stated, his voice tinged with the same feelings that were reflected on his face. "I didn't tell you to ambush my new friend and his mom. In fact, I think I might've specifically said, '*Don't ambush them.*' Maybe I even added in a please."

"Oh, Remo. You know I always do the opposite of what you want."

"Yeah, and that's precisely why I added the please."

Wendy dismissed the comment with a wave. "That only made me nosier. And now I see that my nosiness was warranted. Your new friend's mom is extraordinarily pretty. Interesting that you didn't mention that."

"Didn't seem relevant." As he said it, Remo brought one of his hands up to the back of his neck, his cheeks ruddy.

Celia's own face was warm. And she still felt a little clueless. Wendy was obviously someone Remo had recruited for assistance, and she was also clearly someone who knew him well.

"A pretty woman is always relevant, dear," the older woman said.

And then it hit Celia. As she looked from Remo to Wendy, she actually kicked herself a little for not immediately clueing in.

They had the same squarish jaw. The same defined cheekbones. And even though her irises were coffee-colored rather than azure, there was no denying that the shape of them was identical. The matching height and strong, hold-the-weight-of-the-world shoulders were a dead giveaway, too. "Nana Wendy" absolutely had to be Remo's mother.

Remo spied the sudden understanding in Celia's face, and for some inexplicable reason, knowing that *she* knew made his neck heat. He had an urge to loosen a tie he wasn't even wearing.

It wasn't that asking his own mother for help was embarrassing. He wasn't the kind of man who thought relying on family was a source of shame.

It also wasn't the fact that his mom had pointed out Celia's good looks. Twice. Remo was already more than acquainted with that particular fact.

This was something else. He felt like a teenager, about to introduce his high school crush to his mom. Which he supposed he *was* doing. Minus the teenager part, of course.

Remo shifted Xavier from one hip to the other, and noted that his mom was staring at him with a single raised eyebrow. It was a look Remo knew well. She was waiting. With impatient mom-patience. It made him realize that he hadn't actually *done* any introducing yet.

He cleared his throat. "Celia, this is my mother, Wendy. Mom, this is Celia Poller."

His mom's eyebrow went up a little more—a final chastisement—and then dropped as she smiled widely and stuck her palm out. "It's absolutely lovely to meet you, even under the circumstances."

Celia's face was flushed, but she took his mom's proffered handshake. "Nice to meet you, too."

"And you met my new buddy earlier," Remo added.

His mom shot a wink toward Xavier. "The pudding monster."

"That's me!" the kid agreed enthusiastically. "Are you *really* Remo's mom?"

"I sure am."

"But you're not that old!"

"I like you better every second." She poked him in the stomach, prompting the kid to let out a giggle. Then she turned her attention back to Celia. "Are me and the little guy ready to get going to my place?"

"You and the little guy?" Celia echoed, turning a concerned look toward Remo. "What's she talking about?"

"I didn't get quite that far, Mom," Remo said.

"Quite what far?" his mom replied. "You mean as far as letting her know that I'm the resident getaway car?"

Celia drew in a sharp breath, and Remo fought a groan.

"Mom, seriously," he said. "My goal is to make her feel *safe*. Not like an escaped convict. I was going to explain the plan *before* you got here, then you were going to arrive and be your kind and sweet self."

His mom lifted her eyebrow again. "Oh. You wanted me to turn on my grandmotherly charm?"

"It couldn't hurt," he replied.

She let out a sigh, then dropped her voice into a phony-sounding quaver. "All right, sonny boy. Hand over the kid."

Rolling his eyes, Remo lifted a giggling Xavier off his hip and held him out toward his mom, who took him with a grin.

"Well, thank you muchly," she said, then spun to carry Xavier to the couch, speaking in a pseudo whisper as she moved. "I think your mom and my son need to have a chat out in the hall."

"They already talked for a *long* time in the hallway," Xavier informed her. "What else can they *say*?"

"Who knows? Grown-ups are weird."

Remo fought another eye roll, then gestured for Celia to follow him out the door. Once they were safely out of earshot, she spoke first.

"You want me to let your *mom* take Xavier?" she said.

"It's our best option."

"I can probably think of six better ones off the top of my head."

"But how many are you sure would work while still

making sure no one gets hurt? You said no collateral damage, remember?"

"And you think your mom isn't collateral?" she replied, her voice shaking. "And you *also* think that separating from my son is something I'd even consider?"

He reached for her hands, and was grateful when she let him clasp both rather than pulling away. "I think you'd do whatever needed to be done to keep him safe. And this is it. Your ex or his men or whoever's watching the hospital…they don't know who Xavier is, do they?"

She bit her lip, then exhaled. "No, I don't think so. Xavier's never met his dad."

"Which means they're looking for *you.* They won't notice a grandmother and her grandson. Especially since they're just going to walk out the front door like they've got nothing to hide. Trust me on this, Celia. Nothing— no one—could be a safer choice for getting Xavier out of here without incident."

"How can you be so sure?"

Remo closed his eyes for a long beat, then sighed and opened them again. "Do you remember when I told you about my father?"

Celia's gaze softened. "Yes, of course."

"The day that it happened, my mom brought me here. We went through Emergency, got my arm set in a cast, and then…we stayed."

"What do you mean?"

"We had nowhere to go. My mom's parents died when she was younger, and she had no siblings and no aunts or uncles. We sure as hell couldn't go anywhere near my dad's side of the family. My mom told me later that she thought about going to a shelter, but she was so tired, and she had access to everything she needed here. Stolen, of course, but still…" He smiled; he couldn't help it.

Celia's expression, though, was incredulous. "You stowed away in a *hospital*?"

"It was easier than you'd think. Although that might've been because my mom was—still is—pretty resourceful. She found a resident's room and rigged it so she was the only one who could open it, then stuck an out-of-order sign on the door."

"But…how long did you live like that?"

"If you ask my mom, she'll tell you a couple of days, but I'm sure it was weeks. I swear we were here long enough for me to actually get my cast taken off."

"So what happened? You didn't get caught?"

His nodded. "Oh, we *did* get caught. A doctor found us. But lucky for us, she'd been in the emergency room when we came in, and she'd seen the havoc wreaked by my father. So she didn't turn us in. She helped my mom get a job in the cafeteria, where she still works now. She put us up in a room in her house until we could afford our own place. She's an admin here now, actually."

"That's pretty incredible," Celia said.

"Things could've turned out worse," he agreed.

"And what happens after they leave?"

Remo didn't let his relief at her implicit agreement show. "We stay here for another half hour while a misdirect is created on our behalf. Tanya—the administrator I mentioned before—is giving us a hand. She's 'officially' moving you to a different room, and in thirty minutes, she's going to make an announcement over the speaker on your floor that will tell anyone who's listening that's what happened. But a little bit after that, she'll let your new nurses know she made a mistake, and that you were actually discharged. And I've got a doctor friend coming by with a round of antibiotics and some bandages and stuff so I can keep you from keeling over."

"I'm not going to keel over."

"Yet. But if you get an infection…"

She made a face, then sighed. "It's all so complicated."

"And it will work," he assured her.

"So then we walk out the front door, too?"

"Not exactly."

She narrowed her eyes. "Should I be worried?"

"Not unless you hate riding on a gurney," he replied. "You become a body under a sheet, I become your transporting attendant."

"Great. So in order to avoid death, I pretend to be dead."

"Oldest trick in the how-to-escape-a-hospital book."

Her gaze dropped to their still-clasped hands, and when she spoke again, her voice was nearly a whisper. "I'm scared, Remo."

He let her hands go and pulled her into an embrace instead. "I know you are. And my mom knows, too. That's how you can be sure that she won't take a risk."

Celia continued to rest her head against his chest for a long moment before she leaned back and looked up at him. "All right. Let's get it over with before I change my mind and decide your mom's plan to live in hiding in the hospital is a better idea."

He bent and gave her a light kiss, then released her. "Ready when you are."

She smiled and turned back toward the room where her son waited. Before she could get more than a step away, though, Remo called out to her.

"Celia?"

She paused and swung her face his way. "Yes?"

"Please don't ever tell anyone that story about us living in the hospital. The only people who're aware of it are me, my mom, and Tanya. And now you."

"Your secret is safe with me." She put her hand over

her heart in a seemingly unconscious gesture, then turned away again.

Remo watched her for a moment, then lifted his own hand to his chest in a move that mirrored hers. There was a warmth there, just under his rib cage. And he was strangely certain it was only going to grow.

Chapter 9

Celia would've been lying if she didn't admit that sending her son away with a stranger—or an almost stranger's mother, in this case—didn't make her nervous. She trusted Remo. More than she should have, maybe. And what he'd told her about his childhood in the hospital reinforced the fact that Wendy would know just how to get Xavier safely out. But when it came down to it, he was *her* son, and Celia didn't like being separated from him, especially under the current circumstance.

I miss him when he goes to kindergarten, she thought. *How am I expected to feel at a moment like this one?*

But as she gave him a twelfth kiss goodbye—he'd counted them and made an announcement about it—Wendy shuffled Xavier to Remo one more time, then pulled Celia aside. Feeling awkward and defensive at the same time, Celia waited for a speech. What she got instead was a hug. The older woman pulled her into an embrace and gave her a squeeze. It was strange only for a moment. Then Celia leaned in and took the offered comfort. It was different to receive it from another woman. From another mom. There was an understanding in the hug. Palpable empathy. And that alone was enough to ease some of Celia's discomfort.

"I know you're going through hell," said Wendy as she finally let her go and stepped back. "And to top off your unpleasant circumstances, my son told me that you've got a memory block."

Celia nodded, then answered in a soft voice. "I think my mind is trying to protect me. Except it's just making things worse."

"I get it," the other woman replied. "There are times when I wish I could forget everything Remo's dad put me through. It would feel so good not to have that heartbreak always on the periphery of my past. But the thought of the memories not being there is scarier. As counterintuitive as it might seem, I think the memories might *be* the safety net."

"Exactly." A slightly bitter laugh escaped Celia's lips. "Now could you convince my brain that's true?"

Wendy reached out and swiped a thumb over Celia's forehead. "I wish I could, sweetheart. For your sake, and for your son's. But being patient might be your only choice."

"That. And sending Xavier with you is a choice, too."

"Yes, it is. And I appreciated the trust. I'll take good care of him, and in a half hour or so, we'll all be eating breakfast in my kitchen."

Celia closed in for another hug, then called Xavier over for a thirteenth kiss. Then a fourteenth, just for superstition's sake. She made a joke about it to cover her worry, then promised to see him soon, and with a heavy heart and a thick, knotted lump in her throat, watched him and Wendy disappear into the elevator. Tears threatened. Then became an inevitability. But as they came, Remo wrapped his arms around her and guided her back to the family room. He closed the door, pulled her to the couch, and held her while she shook with the sobs she couldn't quite control. And he didn't let go until it had all tapered off into shaky breaths.

"I'm sorry," Celia said, when she was at last able to speak. "You were just driving along, minding your own business tonight—or is it last night, now? God. I don't even know. But somehow, I dragged you into this mess."

His hand slid back and forth over her shoulder. "You didn't drag me. I dragged myself."

She sat up a little and tried to smile, but it felt watery. "Sure. If you call pulling over to the side of the road at the scene of an accident dragging yourself into something. I don't even know where you were going."

"I'd actually just finished the somewhat embarrassing task of watching a movie at the theater."

"Why is that embarrassing?"

"It wasn't, until you forced me to admit that I was alone."

Celia's smile became genuine. "I did *not* force you to admit that."

He winked. "You see it your way, I see it mine."

"What did you see?"

"Action flick?"

"Is that a question?"

He sighed. "See? Now you're forcing me to tell you *another* embarrassing thing."

"What is it?" Celia asked. "I'm dying to know."

"It wasn't an action flick at all." His expression was

one part sheepish and one part amused. "It was that movie about the dog with the missing leg."

In spite of everything, a laugh burst from Celia's lips. "You're kidding. Xavier has been begging me to take him. You really went to see it?"

"What can I say? I'm a sucker for puppies."

"And you couldn't, like…borrow a friend's kid?"

"Honestly?" He trailed a finger up her arm, his eyes dropping to follow the motion. "I don't have all that many friends."

"Says the man who's *best* friends with my kid," she replied.

He lifted his gaze, and Celia was surprised to see true uncertainty and sadness there as he spoke again. "Kids are easy. It's grown-ups who're hard."

"What do you mean?"

"When you meet another adult…start to get to know them…they think they want to know all the gory, complicated details. But when they hear those details…they realize they didn't want complicated, after all."

Celia leaned her head against his chest. "Actually, Mr. DeLuca…you don't get to tell me what I want."

His responding chuckle vibrated pleasantly through her whole body. "Is that right?"

"A hundred percent. I don't buy your excuse, and I demand a messy, complicated explanation."

"Okay. But when you hear it all and you run screaming in the opposite direction, don't say that I didn't warn you."

His tone was light, but under the lightness was a strain, and Celia wondered if she should backpedal and tell him he didn't have to share anything he didn't want to. The last thing she wanted was to make him feel uncomfortable or pressured. Especially considering just how much he'd done for her and Xavier in the last few hours. But he started to speak before she could retract her request.

"I probably owe you a bit of an apology," he said.

Puzzled, she tipped her head back, trying to see his face. "For what?"

"A lie of omission. I left something out before when I was telling you about me and my mom."

"I'll forgive you for not disclosing all of your secrets in the first five minutes of knowing me if you'll forgive me for not even knowing my own secrets."

"Deal." He kissed her forehead, then smoothed back her hair, and she settled against his chest again, and he went on with his story, his voice low. "Seven and a half months after my mom finally left my dad, on my eighth birthday, my sister was born here in the hospital. I only had the most basic thoughts about where a baby came from. But I knew a man had to be involved somewhere. I thought Indigo was a miracle."

He went on, explaining how she was a hellion from the beginning. Colicky as a newborn, and a Tasmanian devil as a toddler. Their mom was constantly at a loss for what to do with Remo's little sister. Indigo didn't care if she was given a time-out, or if her toys were taken away, or if she was banned from watching *Sesame Street*.

"You know how some people have a zest for life?" he asked.

She nodded against his chest. "Yes."

"Indigo had that zest, so long as her life included getting into trouble. And the older she got, the more wild she got, too."

Celia listened as Remo described an increase in the severity of her antics. How his sister practically lived in the principal's office through elementary school. How she was kicked out of first one high school, then another, before she was finally sent to a remedial school.

"My mom used to wonder if it was really a good idea to send a kid like Indigo to a place where she'd be surrounded by like-minded kids," Remo said. "But I don't think it affected her in the slightest. She acted the way she did because she *wanted* to act that way, not because anyone influenced her. She hit her most dangerous moment when she was fourteen."

He told her about how Indigo stole their mom's car and totaled it. Then he added that the theft and the accident weren't even the biggest problem. Because just three days before it happened, Wendy had decided to let the insurance lapse in order to save a bit of money. Then the bills rolled in. And there were plenty. There was their wrecked car and the fence Indigo had destroyed. There were the vet fees for the dog who'd had the misfortune of having a paw crushed under a tire as the car rolled to a stop. And last, but by no means even close to least, there were medical costs. Indigo's broken arm and concussion and three days in the hospital. Eighteen stitches for the guy who was joyriding beside her.

"I was away at school. On my way to becoming a doctor. Or I hoped so, anyway." Remo's voice was full of regret, and Celia reached out to squeeze his hand.

"Your sister's accident wasn't your fault," she said.

"I know. It was her own reckless behavior. And I knew it then, too." He shook his head. "But I still felt responsible. I came back. Cut my college career short. I took two jobs to help cover the money we owed."

He paused there, his fingers toying with her hair, and Celia had a feeling he was building up to something even harder. She almost held her breath, waiting. Marveling over his self-sacrifice. Wondering just how much more intense his story could get.

"You did want the messy and complicated," Remo said after a few silent moments.

"I'm still here, aren't I?" she replied.

"True enough. But then again…you're kind of stuck with me for the moment, aren't you?"

She twisted herself around so she was facing him. "I'm not stuck, Remo. I could've said no to letting your mom take Xavier. I could've insisted on doing it on my own. I think I *have* been doing it on my own for five years. But I chose to stay with you."

"Didn't know what you were getting into, did you?"

"All I can say to that is *ditto*."

He laughed, and his palm found her cheek, and the contact made the air shift. It heated. It sparked. And when Remo leaned in and pressed his lips to Celia's…it ignited.

Remo kissed Celia hard, pouring the strange mix of emotions into the contact.

Just a moment earlier, he had been on edge. Worried about what she would think of his personal truth. Puzzled by how badly he wanted to tell her everything—even the things he never shared with anyone. Or maybe it was the fact that he *especially* wanted to share the things he never shared with anyone. Either way, he'd been uncharacteristically nervous. He didn't want to scare her off before he even got a chance to really know her.

With his lips on hers, all the concern lifted, unseated by desire. Overruled by the eager way her mouth moved in time with his, swept aside by her hands, which pulled him in instead of pushing him away.

Everything about Celia fit just right. *Felt* just right. Her soft, warm mouth. Her curves pushed against his body.

How his hand rested perfectly on the swell of her hips, and the light scent that emanated from her skin and made him want to inhale deeper and deeper.

But Remo didn't have to dig very deep to conclude that the rightness applied to more than the physical. There was the easy way she listened, not an ounce of judgment apparent in her responses. The trust she afforded him, even though her life had obviously worked her over enough to wring out any ease in doing so. And the fierce protectiveness for her son. Remo admired it. He respected it. He was even a little envious of that aspect of her life.

Which brought him back to the rest of his story. The part that hurt the most, and that he rarely spoke aloud, because most people didn't want to hear about true loss. Or if they did, it was in a voyeuristic way that made Remo's stomach churn. And well-meaning, sympathetic words did little to ease the residual ache that marked his soul. So he kept it inside. With Celia, though, something made him sure he could tell her everything, and not fear losing her before she truly became his.

His.

The word was powerful and unexpected. Undoubtedly premature in its implications. But it didn't matter, because it made a burst of warmth hit Remo's gut.

He broke off the kiss, abruptly more interested in figuratively baring it all than taking the kiss to the next level. He pulled back and brought both his hands to her face.

She opened her eyes and smiled. "Hi there."

"Hi," he said back, unable to resist a need to give her another quick, soft kiss.

"Is our thirty minutes up?"

"Getting close. But that's not why I stopped."

Her forehead creased. "What's wrong?"

He let his hands drop to her shoulders, then slid them

down her arms until they reached her fingers, which he threaded with his own. "I didn't quite finish telling you about Indigo."

Her expression became hesitant, but when she spoke, Remo could tell that the hint of reluctance was about him rather than about her. "You don't have to, if you don't want to."

"The funny thing is, I *do* want to. And the funnier thing… I *don't* normally want to. In fact, I usually try to keep things to myself."

"So what's different?"

Remo studied her for a moment. It was a valid question. And he had only one answer.

"You are," he said.

She blinked. "Me?"

He shrugged. "I know. It's kind of a lame answer. I pulled you from that wreck tonight, and I looked into your eyes, and…"

"And what?"

"Either I was lined up to be there at that exact moment, or you're a witch."

Her eyes widened, and her mouth dropped open as she blurted, *"What?"*

"Yeah, I'm leaning toward the former, as well," he teased.

She made a face, then turned serious. "Do you believe in that kind of thing?"

He lifted an eyebrow. "In witchcraft?"

She snorted. "In fate."

"You want an honest answer?"

"Always."

"Then I have to be very decisive and say 'sort of.'" He chuckled at her wry expression. "I believe that life gives us moments of perfect opportunity. All we have to do is fight through the bad stuff so we see those good ones."

She stared at him, then shook her head a little. "Then I guess you'd better hit me with the worst, because I think I'd really like to get a look at the best."

In spite of what he was about to disclose, Remo smiled, and started to tell her he was a give-it-his-all type of guy, but the sound of someone clearing his throat halted him. For a heart-stopping moment, he thought their hiding place had been exposed. But when he turned—defense on the ready—he found a familiar face instead of an attacker. The man had his hands on a gurney that was stacked with supplies, and his expression was noticeably curious.

"New treatment technique, DeLuca?" the man asked.

Remo exhaled. "Kent. Your timing is impeccable."

"Impeccably bad?" the doctor replied.

"You said it, not me," Remo stated.

"I save real lives, not love lives," Kent quipped, then stepped forward to hold his hand out to Celia. "Kent Fresh. I'm an *actual* doctor, in case you're ever looking for an upgrade."

A surge of unexpected possessiveness crept in, and it surprised Remo so much that he couldn't come up with a quick, clever response. Thankfully, Celia was more on the ball. She gave the other man a brief handshake, but then let go and slid her fingers back to grab Remo's— like it was an old habit more than a new venture—and she smiled up at Kent.

"I'll remember that in case I ever get a particularly bad eye infection," she said.

The doctor let out a loud laugh, then gestured to the gurney. "You wanna have a look? Make sure I got everything for your not-so-standard first aid kit?"

Remo pushed to his feet and stepped closer, eyeing each thing as his colleague pointed to it.

"Good dose of antibiotics and some painkillers," said the other man. "Both pulled from her chart, so no need to worry about a contraindication. Heavy-duty bandages for that leg of hers. Everything you need for a good old-fashioned suturing. And of course, the discharge papers." He lifted the paper-clipped stack and held it out. "Though in my humble, medical opinion, if you need all this crap, you probably could stand to stay in the hospital another night."

Remo took the papers and gave Kent a look. "Funny. I don't remember *asking* for your opinion to be added to my list."

"Yeah, well. Sometimes these things are necessary, too." As Kent said it, genuine concern played over his features, and Remo sighed.

"You know my work ethic," he stated. "I wouldn't endanger a patient's life."

The other man's eyebrows went up, and it didn't take a genius to know what he was thinking. *Sure. But I don't think you'd normally be holding a "patient's" hand, either, so maybe all bets are off?*

He said nothing aloud, though, so Remo just offered him a nod. "I appreciate the help, Kent."

The doctor reached out his hand for a shake. "Just leave my name out of the police report when they come looking for you and your stowaway."

Celia drew in an audible breath, and Remo knew the other man's joke had struck a little too close to home. He moved closer and put a reassuring hand on her shoulder, and her fingers immediately closed overtop of his, squeezing tightly.

Remo addressed Kent, but his words were intended for

Celia's ears, as well. "Don't worry. We're far too slick to let the cops catch us."

The other man laughed again. "All right. Say no more. I'd hate to be an accessory, and I have to get back to doing some actual doctoring. But try not to get in too much trouble."

"Will do."

Kent gave them a smile and a little salute, then turned up the hall. Remo waited until he was fully out of sight before releasing Celia's shoulder and offering her his hand.

"We've reached our thirty minutes. Wanna do this now and hear more of my deep, dark secrets later?" he asked.

Her eyes flicked to the gurney. "Oldest trick, right?"

"Exactly."

"Okay."

He pulled her to her feet, locked the wheels on the gurney, then said, "Can I offer you a boost onto your chariot?"

She smiled. "How could I say no to that?"

He stepped forward and put his hands on her waist. But before he could lift her up, the overhead speakers crackled, and a too-calm voice came to life. Remo paused to listen.

"Attention staff," said the voice. "We have a code black in area four. That's a code black in area four. Commence code black protocol."

The words made Remo's feet stick to the floor, and it wasn't until Celia spoke that he realized he'd frozen.

"What's wrong?" she asked. "Is it something bad?"

Remo met her eyes. He wished he could lie just to protect her. But he had to tell her the truth.

"Code black," he said grimly. "It's a bomb threat. The hospital's going on lockdown."

Chapter 10

Remo's statement sent Celia's thoughts spiraling. There was no doubt that a bomb threat right then, at that exact moment, was related to her situation. But she wasn't sure what scared her more—the idea of the bomb itself, or the thought of not being able to get out. Her heart was leaning toward the fear of being trapped. Of being away from her son.

"Xavier," she said, hearing how small her own voice sounded.

Remo's hands were still on her hips, and he quickly pulled her into an embrace, then spoke into her hair. "He's safe."

"I know," she replied. "Really. Your mom has him, and she'll take good care of him. But…"

"But he's not with you," he filled in.

"Exactly. And I know how selfish and backward that sounds."

"It doesn't."

"It feels like it."

"Then I guess we're going to have to fix that." He pulled back, let her go and faced the hall. After staring up the empty corridor for a second, he ran a hand over his hair, then turned her way again. "Here are the basics on how the lockdown works. The code and the cops are called at essentially the same time. The area where the threat is identified is cleared of staff and patients in as wide a berth as possible, with as little disruption as possible. No one comes in or out until the ERTs arrive and assess the situation. Unfortunately, there isn't much that's subtle about it."

The more he said, the drier Celia's throat became, and she had to swallow twice before she could answer. "So we're stuck?"

"Technically. But this wing is undergoing some remodeling, so even if we *are* stuck, we're not exactly under the microscope. And if that's not good enough…" Remo's eyes flicked up the hall in the direction of the elevators. "There's a literal construction zone two floors down from us. They're putting in an enclosed walkway that goes from the hospital to the long-term care facility."

"A walkway we can use to get through?"

"It's not complete."

"That wasn't really an answer."

He sighed like he didn't *want* to answer, then said, "It's probably usable, but it's not enclosed yet, and even though it's only one floor up, it's still not the safest choice."

"We have to at least go look, though, right?" Celia replied. "Because if there's a chance we can get out without being caught…" Her voice broke a little at the end, forcing her to stop.

Remo put his hands on her forearms. "We can go look,

but it'll be a climb, Celia. And you're still recovering from your accident. The blood loss will have made you weaker than you think, and that leg of yours just needs an excuse to come unstitched."

"Isn't that why you had Dr. Fresh bring you the supplies?"

"I wanted to be prepared for any scenario, yes. But I also thought you'd be tucked under a sheet on a gurney, where the only worry would be my ability to steer the damned thing."

Celia lifted her chin, stubbornness and determination setting in. "You just said 'any scenario.' And I can't not try, Remo."

He nodded and dropped his hands to his sides, but made no move to lead the way. There was something in his stance that stopped her from making another plea.

"What is it?" she asked instead.

He shifted from one foot to the other. "Nothing. Just thinking."

"Tell me."

"That code black was called in section four. Your room is—*was*—in section five. More or less adjacent."

"I figured the two things had to be related," she said.

He nodded. "Yes, no doubt about that. But my mind is arguing that the threat's a diversion. A ploy to create chaos so they can smoke you out. Everyone from section four will be moved *to* section five. It'll be crowded. Twice the staff, twice the patients. Plus the police presence. It would be the perfect setup for taking a patient against her will."

He stopped talking for a moment, and Celia knew something else was coming. Unconsciously, she inhaled a breath and held it as she waited. And Remo's next statements made her lungs burn.

"Whoever your ex is…" he said. "He's pretty damned

determined to get to you. A bomb threat in a hospital? That's a serious leap to just get access to a son he's never met. I think this guy might be more dangerous—and more powerful—than we were assuming."

Celia was starting to see stars, and she had to force herself to release the air she'd been holding in. "I wish I could remember."

"At least we're on the same page about that." Remo smiled, softening the statement. "Are you sure I can't talk you into waiting it out? If it *is* a ruse, it won't take long for them to figure out that you're not where they think you are."

She shook her head. "And then what? It will only make them look harder. And you said the chaos is the perfect moment for a kidnapping, right? Doesn't that mean it could work in *our* favor, too?"

"I don't suppose I could get you to promise me that if we get to the walkway, and it's not reasonable, you won't push it?"

"I wouldn't want to lie to you."

"No. I wouldn't want that, either." He gently touched her face, then dropped his hands to her hips and lifted her a little unceremoniously straight onto the gurney.

"Hey," she protested. "I thought the gurney wasn't a viable option."

"It isn't. Not for the walkway itself, anyway. But we have to get there, which means we have to use the elevator and risk running into any number of people."

He grabbed the bag of supplies and slung it over his shoulder, then gestured for her to lie down. Celia made a face, but leaned back and settled in. And she had to admit that it wasn't entirely unenjoyable to have Remo pull the sheet up over her body, then lean down and kiss each of her cheeks, then her mouth.

"Cozy?" he asked.

She wiggled a little. "I've slept in worse spots."

"Good," he said, then yanked the sheet completely over her face.

"Hey!" she protested automatically.

"Dead bodies don't complain," he teased.

"Fine. I guess I really *will* just take a nap."

"Go ahead. But remember that dead bodies don't snore, either."

He chuckled, and a moment later, the cart under Celia's back started rolling. She closed her eyes, but there was little chance of any actual sleep happening. And not just because she knew she'd be playing dead for only a few minutes. It was unnerving to be wheeled along without her sight to tell her where they were headed. She felt helpless. Like some unseen danger might jump out at any moment to take advantage of the situation. She balled her hands into fists and forcefully reminded herself that Remo was acting as her eyes, and that he was more than capable. But it didn't stop her from tensing up when the gurney stopped abruptly and an unknown voice called out.

"Hey, man!" The greeting was distinctly masculine, and Celia's throat closed up in anticipation of the worst. "Aren't you that paramedic?"

Remo's reply was calm and casual—like he wasn't in any kind of hurry and there was no pressing danger whatsoever. "Guess that depends on what I'm in trouble for."

The newcomer laughed. "Oh, man. I'm the *last* guy who's going to give you trouble. I'm a hospital orderly trying to sneak out for a smoke. Elm Peterson."

"Remo DeLuca."

"Good to meet you," said Elm. "Were you aiming for the elevators?"

"Yeah," Remo replied, giving the gurney a light shake. "Trying to get this guy where he needs to be."

"Morgue?"

"You bet. Pretty packed through the regular route. I was looking for a shortcut."

"Picked the wrong spot for that. You heard about the lockdown?" There was a pause, and Celia pictured Remo nodding in agreement before Elm added, "They shut down all the elevators except the central ones. Trying to limit people from coming and going."

"Damn," Remo swore.

"I could give you a hand."

"A hand?"

"Sure. We could carry your guy down. It's only a couple of floors, and God knows it's better than making the poor dude wait."

Celia tensed even more. *He'll say no. He* has *to say no. He'll tell him that dead bodies don't mind waiting, just like they don't snore or complain.*

But a heartbeat later, Remo was agreeing. "Sure. I'll take that offer. Help me get the wheels up."

And another few moments after that, Celia felt her gurney being lifted from the ground, and she squeezed her eyes shut and willed the universe to make her the most realistic fake-dead person ever.

Remo had almost a decade of practice at being calm on the outside while his insides knotted up with worry. His work made it a necessity. Unflappable exterior was a basic job requirement. But as he and the orderly trucked toward the stairs, the gurney hanging between them and the other man's mouth running on about some nurse who'd been caught with his pants down, Remo thought he might lose it for the first time if something went wrong.

One wrong bump, one slip of the sheet...

There'd be no reasonable explanation for it if Celia—alive, injured, and still wearing her hospital bracelet—was suddenly exposed, and Elm Peterson wasn't a man of discretion, Remo was sure. By the time they arrived at the stairwell, the cheerful orderly had already moved on from the pants-less nurse to a story about one of the older admins and his extended bathroom breaks. He wasn't unpleasant in his recounting, but there was no doubt that the man wouldn't keep Celia's presence a secret for long. Remo could practically hear the anecdote already. If it wouldn't have sounded odd to refuse help, he would've simply turned down the other man's offer.

Can't be done with this fast enough.

Telling himself it was only a minor setback, he gritted his teeth and forced a laugh as Elm finished with the admin discussion, then switched to talking about some guy his sister was dating.

Thankfully, aside from the orderly's voice, the only other sound in the stairwell was the bang of their feet on concrete. When they hit the final landing on the basement floor, Remo at last inhaled an easier breath.

"Thanks, Elm," he said, as they clicked the gurney's legs back into place, a little surprised by the fact that his voice came out perfectly even. "I owe you one."

"I'll put a note in my book," the orderly joked as he locked the wheels, then stood back and glanced around. "Always creepy quiet down here, isn't it?"

Remo resisted an urge to tell the guy to just hurry up and leave, and instead replied, "I'd have more questions if there was a lot of noise."

Elm laughed. "True enough. Help you with anything else?"

"I think I'm good from here."

"Then I'm off to indulge in my nasty habit. Good luck with your body, man." He stuck out his hand for a shake, and Remo took it, grateful that the exchange was over.

"See you around, Elm. Thanks again."

"Any time."

The moment the other man was out of sight, Remo grabbed the sheet and pulled it down, speaking as he did. "See? *That* is the reason why everyone owes everyone a favor in this—"

The rest of his sentence didn't make it out. From behind him—in the general direction of the stairwell they'd just vacated—came the barely discernible echo of feet hitting the floor. He exchanged a look with Celia, then put his finger to his lips and went still, listening. There was no doubt that whoever was on the other end of the sound was headed down toward them.

Not willing to risk that the new arrival might not be as amicable as Elm the orderly, Remo took hold of the gurney and pushed it blindly into the closest room. He just barely managed to grab the handle and quietly press the door shut before an angry slam and an angrier voice filled the air.

"I did exactly what I said I would do," the unseen man said.

Feet slapped against the floor, and Remo was 99.9 percent sure the guy attached to the voice was pacing as he talked on his phone.

The man went on. "My friend at social services confirmed that not only was no kid matching our description taken in or assessed tonight, but no kid at *all* was taken in. My friend was adamant."

Xavier.

He exchanged another glance with Celia. She was sitting up now, her hands tight on the edge of the gurney, her eyes wide with worry. She had her lips parted like she had something important she wanted to say, and Remo wished he could read her mind. After a moment, she just shook her head and turned toward the door, where the angry man was speaking again.

"Yeah, well, she lied. And I bought it, didn't I? So that's on me," he snapped.

Remo saw Celia swallow, and he put the pieces together. The angry talker was the man who'd come to her room and threatened her. And he'd figured out that Xavier wasn't where she'd told him he was. Bad news, all around.

Remo slid sideways and closed his fingers overtop of Celia's in silent comfort. She sent him a grateful look, but the way she sucked her lower lip in gave away the fact that her worry hadn't eased. He wished he could do more. Say a word. Pull her close. Kiss away the obvious fear in her eyes. But out in the hall, the one-sided conversation went on.

"I think they've already figured out that my bomb threat was a hoax. Overheard the boss tell one of the guys that they'd probably be able to clear out within the hour," the man was saying now. "It's not great, considering that Poller's gone AWOL." There was a pause. "How the hell should I know if someone's helping her?" Another break. "Yeah, yeah. You're right. I'll ask around. But in the meantime…it might be worthwhile to launch something official." A few moments of silence. "No, I mean official *official*. Missing person's report or an amber alert for the kid. She won't be able to hide him if the whole damned city is on the lookout."

Remo could feel Celia's whole-body shiver, and he stepped even closer and slung an arm over her shoulder. The man on the other side of the door was arguing now, pointing out how many more resources would be available if they went through the proper channels. Then his words stalled, except for the odd grunt. As if he was listening to a rant on the other end.

The whole thing made Remo frown. Why would this guy and his cohorts *want* to involve the authorities? How would it be beneficial? And why did his subconscious holler that it was most definitely not for any *good* reason?

Before he could think about it any further, the conversation started up again, distracting him. Because it was no longer one-sided. A recently familiar voice had joined in. Initiated it, actually, by mistaking the unseen man for Remo himself.

"Hey, man," said Elm. "I thought you would've done your thing and—oh, hey. Sorry. You're not Remo."

"No, I'm not," agreed the other man. "Were you eavesdropping for long?"

"Uh, what? No, man. No eavesdropping. Just thought you were someone else."

"Remo."

"Yeah. Sorry about that."

"Not a problem," corrected the other man. "I'm Teller."

For some reason, the name disclosure made Remo uneasy. He started to turn to gauge Celia's reaction, wondering if she felt the same, or if the name had been familiar to her, but he didn't make it as far as looking her way, because the man—Teller—asked a question that made him freeze once more, all of his attention on the conversation.

"Who's Remo?"

Elm's response was hesitant—like he was uneasy now, too. "Just a dude who works here."

"Is he down in the morgue?" Teller asked.

"I'm not sure."

"You're not sure, or you don't want to tell me?"

"I'm not sure," Elm repeated, now sounding both puzzled and guarded.

"How long ago was he here?" Teller wanted to know.

"A few minutes ago."

"Any idea where he went?"

"Nah, man. He was just delivering a body. Why all the questions?"

Teller ignored him. "What about anyone else? Were the two of you alone down here?"

"Just him, me, and the stiff." Elm laughed, and it sounded forced. "This is starting to feel like an interrogation."

"Is it?" The tone of the simple, two-word reply was somehow neutral and deadly at the same time.

Remo tensed. He had a feeling that something bad was about it happen. Worse than that, he *knew* he wasn't going to be able to stop it.

Elm let out another, even more forced laugh. "Sure does. I just don't know if you're the good cop or the bad cop."

"I suspect, if that were the appropriate description, then I would be bad."

A bang—somehow both muted and amplified at the same time—followed the statement, and the source of the sound was obvious. Out there, in the hall, Teller had shot Elm.

Chapter 11

Celia didn't know whether she was going to scream, throw up, or just plain keel over. She clapped one of her hands over her mouth to quell the need to do the first two, and held tightly to the gurney in hopes of staving off the need for the third. But she still felt herself sway. Her stomach still churned. And her throat burned as if the terror and shock were trying to force their way out in spite of her efforts.

Elm Peterson is dead. He's someone's son. Someone's brother. Or dad. And he's dead. *Because of me. Because he needed to smoke. Because he helped us. Because he was in the wrong place at the wrong time, and—*

Remo's whisper cut off the threatening downward spiral. "We have to go."

Celia looked up. She tried to answer. To move. To respond in any way. But both her body and her brain had other ideas. They kept her immobilized. Physically. And mentally.

Elm Peterson is dead, her mind repeated. *Oh, God. He's dead, and it's—*

"Celia," Remo said, still under his breath, but his voice was underlined with urgency now. "That guy out there is moving up and down the hall, opening every door. He started on the other side, but he's going to be here any second. We need to *move*."

At last his words got through—if they didn't vacate the room, Teller and his gun would find them. The man whose name meant nothing, but who she knew had shot her in the past. Who she could picture on the other end of a gun. Who'd just shot Elm Peterson.

Celia grabbed Remo's elbow and started to pull herself off the gurney. But her reaction came a little too late. Footsteps were already headed in their direction. Terrified, Celia met Remo's eyes. She saw fear reflected in his gaze, too. But unlike her, he seemed to have retained his ability to plan an escape.

Wordlessly, he slid his hands under her and scooped her up. He cradled her to his chest and strode purposefully across the room. Without stopping, he bent down, grasped the handle on a door Celia hadn't noticed before, then pushed it open. Just as smoothly, he turned and closed it behind them, then moved on.

Celia hadn't even truly noted what type of room they'd been hiding in, and their quick pace didn't let her take much stock of where they were going, either. It flew by. Cold air. Metal furnishings. A door. Then white walls and the scent of disinfectant. Another door. More ascetic decor. With each new space, the pressure of being followed mounted. Teller might not be able to hear them or see them, or even really know they were there, but his pursuit was relentless, anyway. As quiet as *they* were, the man with the gun and the malicious intent did little to cover his own noise. Celia could hear each door he opened, and his footsteps, too. He was falling a little behind them as he perused the rooms, but unless they found a route out, the man would eventually have them cornered.

And Remo pushed on.

How many adjacent rooms can there be? Celia wondered.

But the question no sooner popped to mind than it got an answer in the form of an office. It was a dead end. As was evidenced by the fact that Remo stopped abruptly, spun, then growled a curse. Unlike the other rooms, this one had only two doors—the one they'd come through, and the one that led out to Teller.

Celia's gaze raked over the small, untidy space, her mind trying to churn out an idea. How many more moments did they have until the armed man caught up? Just how thorough was he being in his search? Could they attack instead of hiding? And under all her thoughts was concern for her son's well-being. Would Teller really kill them if it meant maybe never finding Xavier?

Her subconscious tossed out the dark answer to the last question. *He won't kill* you. *But Remo...*

She wanted to dismiss the idea, but it refused to go, and she had to acknowledge that the more seconds ticked by, the more likely it was to become a reality. And as much as facing down a murderer terrified her, she was far more afraid that Remo would lose his life trying to protect her.

"Hide!" she gasped.

Remo stopped abruptly, midway through his second, futile spin. "What?"

Celia swallowed, then whispered her conclusion aloud. "He won't kill me."

"He just killed a stranger, and he's already threatened

you once. And that doesn't even factor in what you told me about the bullet you took when you were pregnant."

"I know all of that. But this is a whole different situation. Elm didn't know where my son is. And that's what Teller wants. He won't shoot me until he has Xavier." She inhaled. "But you…"

Remo's blue eyes darkened. "Even if I were willing, it's not like there's anywhere to hide."

"Under the desk," Celia said right away.

"I wouldn't fit under there." His gaze moved toward the piece of furniture in question, and then his feet followed. "But *you* will."

She tried to wriggle out of his grasp. "Me hiding does nothing but put you right in the line of fire."

Remo's grip only tightened, and he managed to retain his hold while pushing the chair out of the way and bending down, too.

"That's not true at all," he said. "In fact, it's better if it's me doing the talking. Because when it comes down to technicalities, *I'm* the one who knows where Xavier is. Unless you somehow managed to get my mom's address when I wasn't looking."

"I…" Her argument trailed off as the truth of his words sunk in.

He *was* the one who knew where Xavier was at the moment. And there was no doubt that he'd go with Teller under the guise of revealing that location. He'd compromise his own life for Celia's son, and nothing could've made her appreciate him more. But she still didn't want him to. Just the thought of it made her throat close up. She needed a solution that would let her have it both ways—keeping Xavier *and* Remo safe.

Maybe I can negotiate a deal with Teller.

"I know what you're thinking," said Remo. "And the answer is no. A man like that doesn't make deals."

"There has to be something," Celia insisted, fighting tears.

"There is."

"Something *other* than you leaving with Teller."

"Celia."

If he'd been about to say more than her name, he was cut off by the rattle of the door handle. This time, panic didn't make Celia freeze—it made her act. Grabbing Remo's arm with enough strength that she surprised herself, she turned and shoved the big man against the underside of the desk. Surprisingly—maybe because he was off balance—he folded into the spot without protest. He almost fit. One of his legs stuck out, but Celia saw an immediate solution. She didn't waste time wondering if it would work. Instead, she made herself as small as possible, then squeezed into his lap, grabbed his outside knee, then yanked it against her. Remo didn't fight the process, either. He just grabbed the rolling chair and pulled it in, effectively blocking their position from view of anyone who wasn't already looking directly at the spot. It wasn't perfect. But it would do. Because it had to.

Celia would've held her breath if she'd been able to, but the space was too cramped to let her do more than suck in the smallest amount of air. She settled for closing her eyes and praying that Teller would opt for a less-than-thorough look around.

Please, please, she thought. *Let this go in our favor.*

And her prayers seemed to receive an answer. As a light squeak gave away the fact that the door was opening, a cell phone chimed to life. A moment later, the tap of Teller's feet filled the air at the same time as his voice.

He greeted his caller without preamble. "Still down here, and I'm gonna need a cleanup."

Celia's muscles tensed impossibly tighter. The gunman was only a few feet from where they sat huddled. His shoes and calves were visible from their hiding space.

If he looks down...

Thankfully, a moment later, he stepped out of view. His voice, though, remained close.

"How long?" he asked. "Yeah, okay. Try to cut it to ten if you can." He paused. "Okay. Once you've done that, can you do me another favor? Look up a guy named Remo. Hospital employee, I think." There was a second pause, this one longer. "I admit that it's a little vague, but how many Remos do you think there are hanging around here?" Another pause. "No. Call it instinct. If it doesn't pan out, it doesn't pan out. But I didn't come this far because I'm in the habit of making mistakes."

Just like he hadn't issued a greeting at the beginning of the call, Teller also didn't officially sign off. But after his last statement, silence hung in the air long enough for Celia to conclude that he'd ended the call. And a few moments later, the thump of his feet on the linoleum, followed by the door creaking shut, signaled that the man had finally left the room. Relieved, Celia closed her eyes. She didn't dare move too early and risk bringing Teller back. But she did let herself relax as much as the small space allowed, and when she felt Remo's arms tighten in a reassuring hug, most of the pressure in her chest released. She counted off ten somewhat normal breaths, then slid out from the small place and extended her hand to help pry Remo's big body free.

"Ten minutes until the cleanup guys get here," she whispered as she gripped the edge of the desk and pulled herself to her feet. "Do you think that's long enough to..."

Her words died off, and her heart seized. Teller stood at the closed door, a wickedly self-satisfied smile on his face, and his gun pointed in their direction.

When Celia stopped speaking and froze with her eyes fixed forward, Remo was puzzled only momentarily before quickly coming to the sole logical conclusion. Teller's exit had been a ruse.

Remo cursed himself for assuming the best, and he jumped up from his position on the ground with the intention of shielding Celia from harm. His cramped muscles screamed a protest, though, and before he could properly position himself, he stumbled. The awkward movement had one benefit—it drew the armed man's attention. Teller swung his way instead of Celia's, his expression dark.

"Don't move," he ordered, his voice laced with assurance that he'd be obeyed. "Put your hands on your head, and I'll—"

Teller's words were cut off as something—a heavy-looking, old-fashioned desk phone, Remo realized—came flying at him. It hit the other man hard enough to make his head snap to the side, and before he could recover, Celia darted around the desk and knocked into his gut, shoulder first. As Teller stumbled, Celia then lifted her elbow and jabbed up toward his throat.

Remo was sure the moves had a practiced look, but he didn't take the time to wonder where she'd learned them. He threw himself into the fray instead. Or tried to. His intervention turned out to be unnecessary. Celia's lightning-quick maneuvers had sent the already off balance gunman toppling over. Before Remo could deliver a single blow, Teller's temple hit the corner of the desk. The weapon dropped from his hand, he let out a groan, then collapsed in an unmoving heap on the ground.

Celia immediately sprang toward the gun, snagged it from the floor, and quickly—almost expertly—tucked it into her waistband. Then, with her chest heaving with exertion, she lifted her eyes and met Remo's gaze.

"I think we're down to T-minus eight minutes," she breathed, and held out her hand. "Assuming Teller's cleanup crew are on the ball."

Remo nodded, then clasped her fingers and started to let her tug him out the door, but paused as a thought occurred to him.

"Hang on," he said.

"T-minus seven and a half minutes," Celia warned.

"Give me ten seconds," he replied.

He freed himself from her warm grasp before she could argue, then stepped back into the room and moved toward the unconscious man. Quickly, he knelt and gave the guy a rushed pat down. His search came to fruition in the form of a leather wallet, which he tugged out of Teller's lapel pocket.

"Three more seconds," Celia called softly. "Hurry, Remo."

"Hurrying," he called back.

He wanted to know more about who Teller was, but he also wanted to get out of the hospital in one piece. So he stood up and shoved the procured ID into his own pocket without looking, then turned back to Celia. But once again, he saw a reason to delay. A red splotch a little bigger than a quarter had appeared on Celia's pants. He knew without checking that her stitches had to have come loose.

Dammit.

She followed his concerned gaze, then let out a little gasp. But she also immediately lifted her eyes and shook her head.

"We don't have time to worry about it," she said.

"We don't have the luxury of *not* worrying about it. You won't be any good to your son if you bleed out, and we have to go past the room where we left the first aid kit, anyway. Come on."

Ignoring her attempt to protest, he grabbed her hand and gently pulled her up the hall to the room where they'd first taken cover from Teller. There, he paused, kissed her lightly, and sprinted through the door. He grabbed the bag from the gurney, then hurried back out again.

"See?" he said. "Future crisis averted, and still T-minus six minutes."

Celia rolled her eyes. "Less talking, more running for our lives."

"Happy to oblige."

This time it was she who did the hand-grabbing, tugging him to the stairwell, then opening the door wide so that they could step through together. As they started up the first flight of stairs, Remo expected to see some sign of strain on her part. He was ready to swoop in and carry her up if need be, but she didn't seem affected by the reopened wound. She took the steps as easily as he did. But when they'd nearly reached the first-floor landing, a new problem presented itself. From above them—maybe two or three levels up—a door whooshed open, and they both went still as two men's voices filtered down.

"You ever get tired of doing his dirty work?" said Man One.

Man Two laughed. "It's *all* dirty work. That's why we get the pay upgrade."

That was all Remo stopped long enough to hear. Silently, he pointed at the door on the first-floor landing. Celia nodded back. They took the final two steps, and Remo reached out and gave the door handle as gentle a tug as he could. A rush of air still filled the stairwell, and he tensed, ready to run out at full speed if necessary. Thankfully, the men above were too involved in their own debate to notice. Breathing out, Remo gestured for Celia to go first. He tossed a final glance up—the men still hadn't come into sight yet—then followed her through the door. Then stopped abruptly at the chaos all around them.

It was just a hallway, but it was filled to capacity. Beds lined the walls, people sat in randomly placed chairs, and medical personnel swirled through it all.

"What's going on?" Celia asked, her voice low.

"This is the emergency overflow area. Nobody in or out, so they can't discharge people, and anyone who needed to be admitted might've been delayed. Busy night in the ER, and it could easily pile up like this," he explained, then added, "At least the crowd will help keep us hidden. Speaking of which…we should get moving. Make our way to another set of stairs and get up to that second floor walkway so we can get out before things settle down."

He started to walk, but Celia didn't move when he did, and their hands slid apart. He turned to face her, surprised that she no longer seemed to be in a rush. Her expression was pained, and concern flooded in.

"What's wrong?" Remo asked. "Is it your leg?"

"No, not that. It's just such a waste. Of resources. Of time. All these people…stuck here and scared and probably not really knowing what's going on. Some of them are probably really sick, or hurt, too. And I don't like it one bit." She shook her head. "Whoever Teller is, I hope he gets caught and has to answer for this, just as much as he has to answer for Elm's murder."

Remo studied her for a moment. There was more than a hint of vehemence in her voice, and he couldn't help but wonder if it was completely related to the current situation, or if it had something to do with the bits of her past she couldn't remember. He opened his mouth to ask, but stopped abruptly as he remembered that he had at least a partial answer to her concerns. Right in his pocket, in fact.

"Let's find somewhere a little quieter," he said. "We can have a quick look at his ID and check that leg of yours before we go."

"His ID?" Celia replied. "What do you mean?"

He patted the spot where he'd stored it. "In here. What did you think I went back for?"

"I don't know?" She said it like a question. "But...you stole his wallet?"

She sounded so incredulous that Remo couldn't stop a chuckle from escaping his lips. "You're worried about me, stealing from Teller?"

Her cheeks went a little pink. "No."

"Liar," he teased. "Come on. I'll find us a spot."

She sighed, but let him take her hand and lead her through the crowd. Remo made sure to walk with purpose so that no one would look twice at them as they passed. But it wasn't until they were clear of the overflow area and halfway there that he realized his goal wasn't just a random, more secluded space. He had a specific destination in mind.

Chapter 12

A few quick turns took them away from the stiflingly busy emergency overflow hall—there was no sense in pretending it was a room of any sort—and they were alone. A few *more* turns, and they were standing in front of an unmarked door.

Celia turned her head to look at Remo, and was surprised to see that he had his free hand on the back of his neck and a strange expression on his face. Not quite sheepish. Not quite embarrassed. Something else. Something she couldn't quite pinpoint. And when he spoke, his voice had a matching timbre. A little rough, a little awkward. A little indefinable.

"So…" he said, gesturing toward the door. "This is it."

"This is *it*?" Celia echoed, puzzled by the fact that he seemed to have chosen somewhere specific rather than just a promised quiet spot.

She eyed the door again. It was literally just plain. The

same tan color as the walls. A brushed steel handle. Nothing else. She turned back to Remo. And then it struck her. His look was boyish and shy. It was the same expression her son got on *his* face when he wanted to show Celia something he was kind of proud of, but not utterly confident in. And she almost gasped.

"This is it," she repeated, but this time, she knew what the words meant—this room was the one where he and his mother had hidden out.

Remo nodded, then released her hand and twisted the handle. The door opened easily, and an automatic light flickered on overhead, revealing a room as nondescript as the exterior. There was a bunk bed—no sheets or pillows—and a sink. The walls were beige, and devoid of decoration. And it wasn't any bigger than a closet.

Celia's throat constricted, and time seemed to slow as she thought about what it would be like to live in the space. It was all too easy to relate to. She could almost feel the quiet desperation. The circumstances that would drive Wendy DeLuca to see this tiny room as a haven rather than as a trap. And as she stood on the threshold, not quite ready to step inside, she realized it was more than empathy. If she hadn't chosen to break free when she did, her own life—hers and Xavier's—might've paralleled this exact trajectory.

She could see her son, sitting on the top bunk with his game console in his hand.

She could picture herself, lying awake at night, fearing that any moment she'd be caught and flung back out into the world.

Not just the world, she thought. *Back at the mercy of the man from my recurring dream. Back into my nightmare.*

Because he was real. Quite abruptly, she knew it. He was Xavier's father, and now she could picture his face.

A salt-and-pepper-haired man with dark eyes and deceptively friendly crinkles around his lids. The friendliness masked his true temperament. And his quick fists. Celia wished the last bit didn't come to mind so vividly. But it made her understand why her mind sought to block it out. Who would *want* to remember the way those fingers and their cruelty felt? What lesson did it serve?

Just a warning to outrun his smooth voice and expensive suits.

Feeling light-headed and nauseous, Celia braced herself against the door frame. And Remo immediately came toward her, his shy little-boy side gone and his confident paramedic side taking its place.

"Here," he said, guiding her into the small room. "Sit down."

Celia sank gratefully onto the lower bunk, and even more gratefully leaned against Remo when he joined her. He slung an arm over her shoulder and pulled her closer, supporting her until her head cleared and she straightened up again.

"Thanks," she said. "Sorry about that."

"Don't be sorry," he replied. "I'm just not sure if I should hope that you're not woozy from blood loss, or if I should worry that it's something worse."

"I don't think it's blood loss. My leg feels okay."

"I should still probably take a look." He smiled. "And this isn't some clever ploy to get your pants off, either."

Celia's face warmed, but she stood up and loosened the drawstring on the borrowed scrubs anyway, then pulled them down like it didn't bother her. As if Remo—the man who'd given her the best kisses she'd ever had—wasn't about to get up close and personal with her bare skin for a decidedly unsexy reason. But as he took charge, his expertise quickly wiped away any bit of awkwardness. In moments, he had her lying flat on her back, the pants off completely, and the first aid supplies out.

"So…" Remo said, as he dabbed the wound with an antiseptic. "You wanna talk about it?"

Celia exhaled at the slight sting. "You caught that, huh?"

He gave a small shrug. "I'm well acquainted with what fainting from physical trauma looks like. Your particular shade of pale seemed different."

"I wasn't going to faint," she protested. "But you're right about it being mental. I remembered something about Xavier's dad, and it overwhelmed me for a second."

"His name?" Remo asked hopefully, as he continued with his attention to the cut.

She shook her head. "No. Just the way he looks."

"Tell me."

"He's older than I am. Maybe early to midforties? And he looks like the kind of man who people like, if that makes sense."

"Puts on a good front."

"Yes. Exactly that. And well-dressed, too. So maybe he has money?"

"Or wants people to think he does," Remo suggested.

Celia considered it for a moment, then shook her head again. "I don't know why, but I don't think so. I can picture his hands." She closed her eyes to do it, then opened them with a shiver. "They're *manicured.* And not that there's anything wrong with that, but it's kind of an indulgence, isn't it?"

"A man can't have nice hands?" Remo replied, then leaned back and lifted his own up and held them a couple feet from her face.

Celia could see that they were clean and well-groomed. His nails were short, and there was no sign of dirt anywhere. But it wasn't the same. Celia reached up and grabbed his fingers, running her thumbs over his nails.

"You've got cuticles," she told him.

He raised an eyebrow. "People generally do."

"It's often one of the first things to go during a manicure. And he doesn't have any. Plus, his nails are too perfect." She sighed. "I know that's not very helpful."

"Of course it is. We'll just go around demanding to see everyone's hands." Remo winked.

"Ha-ha."

"But seriously. It *is* good. Your memories are coming back." He pulled his hands free and gave one of her bare knees a squeeze. "And in more good news, your leg is looking okay."

"Does that mean I'm *not* dying of blood loss?"

"Nope. It was just a loose stitch on one end. Might not even have bled at all if we weren't so busy orchestrating all the narrow escapes. But I cleaned you up, put on a bit of tape stitch, and you're good to go. So if you're done sitting around in your underwear…" He trailed off with a cheeky grin.

Celia felt the blush creep back up as the reality of their current pose set in again. She was still lying down, the T-shirt she wore barely covering her rear end. Remo was seated beside her, his hip resting against her thigh. And in spite of the patchy memory issue, Celia was sure it'd been a very long time since she'd been this close to naked with a man.

She cleared her throat and shot for sounding as casual as possible. "Do you, uh…have the pants in question?"

His grin didn't fade in the slightest as he reached across her lap, snagged her folded-up scrubs, then held them out. "Here. I won't even watch you put them on."

"So helpful," she muttered, her cheeks not cooling in

the slightest, even when Remo dutifully stood up and turned away as he'd said he would.

Trying to move in a not-frantic, not-horrifically-embarrassed way, Celia swung her legs over the bed and sat up and shook out the pants. There was something strangely sexy about the soft, crinkly sound of getting redressed. Something intimate. And it was far too loud, and far too obvious in the small space, and Celia felt a sudden need to say something to cover it up.

"You know what?" she said. "I'm not actually convinced that getting my memory back is what I'd call a 'good' thing."

"Haven't you ever heard someone say that knowledge is power?" he replied.

"Sure. Unless you know too much." Celia cinched up the drawstring on the pants and exhaled. "Okay. I'm ready."

Remo turned, his mouth quirking up. "Is finding out a bit more about Teller going to fall into the 'too much' category?"

Celia made a face. "No. Let's see the wallet."

He reached into his pocket, but before he even had the palm-sized item all the way out, she knew it wasn't exactly what he'd thought it was. It *was* a wallet, all right. But the kind meant for holding a police badge.

As the front of the wallet flapped open, Remo was a bit startled to see the shiny, gold-tinted piece of metal come into view. After the briefest moment of staring down at it, though, he realized it made sense. It lined up with Celia's adamant need to *not* contact the police. Teller's comments about making things "official." His lackeys' comments about dirty money.

"'Detective Quentin Teller, Vancouver Police Department,'" Remo read aloud, then looked up at Celia. "I guess this means you're off the hook for being involved in some kind of criminal activity."

She smiled weakly. "Unless I'm a dirty cop, too."

"Or the mastermind behind a whole ring of dirty cops."

"Or the ex-wife of one."

Remo met her eyes. "It could be true. Does that description feel right?"

She cast a quick glance down toward her left hand, then brought her gaze back up and shook her head. "No. But *none* of this feels right. And it doesn't make sense, either. If Xavier's father is so dangerous—and if he's a policeman, or even had strong police ties and resources—then why would I be anywhere near him? Why wouldn't I stay as far away as humanly possible?"

"I can't answer that any better than you can, but I do know that if coming to the city where he lives was a choice, then I'm damned sure you must have a reason. You wouldn't put Xavier in harm's way if you could avoid it."

She let out a frustrated sigh. "No, I wouldn't."

He pulled her in for a quick, reassuring embrace, then said, "We'll figure it out, Celia."

She pulled back and looked up at him. "But I guess we can't do it very well from in here."

"Not so much."

He slid his fingers to hers, noting that it already felt like second nature to hold her hand at any given moment, then moved toward the door. He inched it open and took a peek out into the hall.

"Clear," he said softly.

"Ready when you are," she replied.

Together, they stepped out of the small room, and Remo guided her through the hospital, careful to once again maintain a purposeful stride while also not looking too rushed. Slow, steady, and unobtrusive was the name of the game.

"Tell me what else you remember," Remo suggested after a few silent moments.

"About anything in particular?" Celia asked. "How much I like Chinese food, maybe?"

He laughed. "Yeah, that works. It'll help me narrow down the choices when I ask you out for dinner."

"Are you going to do that?"

"Provided I don't get shot first."

She stopped so abruptly that he almost slingshot forward.

"Not funny, Remo," she said.

"You're right. Not funny." He released her hand, stepped closer, then tipped up her chin and planted a kiss on her lips. "Forgive me."

"Forgiven," she said immediately. "But just in case… you'd better ask me out *now*."

He smiled and kissed her again. "I thought it wasn't funny."

"It's not. It's very serious."

"Then I guess I'd better do it."

"And fast."

Remo started to ask lightly—to make a joke about dating under pressure—but he found himself quickly becoming earnest instead. "Miss Celia Poller, when we're done with this very unusual, very dangerous situation, I would really love it if you'd let me take you out for Chinese food. Or for any food, really, so long as it's you and me and that kid of yours."

She stared up at him, her gray eyes full of so much intensity that they pinned him to the spot. "Thank you."

"Is that a yes?"

"Of course it is."

He bent to kiss her once more, but stopped when he realized that a fresh tear was making its way down one of her cheeks. He ran a thumb over the damp path it left behind.

"Hey, now…why you crying?" he said. "That wasn't part of my plan, dammit."

Her hand came up to cup his. "It's not on purpose. And it's not in a bad way. But I just asked you to ask me out, and you invited my *son* to join us."

Remo frowned. "Was that wrong? I just assumed—"

"No," she said vehemently. "It wasn't wrong. It was perfect."

"Oh, great. Now the bar is going to be way too high."

"You're right."

"I am? Aren't you going to argue with me? Tell me I don't have to worry about messing up the first date? Maybe point out that it can only go up from here?"

She shook her head. "No way."

"Dammit. Always setting myself up for failure," Remo joked, then took her hand so they could resume their walk.

They made it smoothly to the other side of the hospital, and then without incident to a heavy door that was blocked off with caution tape. Remo took a quick glance around, and when he found no one in view, he reached through the tape to push down the handle.

"It's blocked off for the construction site," he told Celia. "Fortunately, the tape's enough of a deterrent for most people, and locking it would be a fire hazard."

He stepped back, and Celia crouched down to climb effortlessly under the strips of yellow.

"I'm guessing you'd win if we went head-to-head in a limbo contest," he said dryly as he followed behind her with far less grace, taking out two pieces of tape in the process.

She smiled. "Maybe we can put that on our to-do list. Right after Chinese food."

"Request noted. But if karaoke comes into play, prepare to be bested." Remo smiled back, then pointed to the stairs. "One floor up, and we'll be almost home free."

"Do you think he's worried?" Celia asked as they started their climb.

"Your son?" Remo replied.

"Yes. We've been gone way longer than we said we'd be. And he already worries more than a five-year-old should."

"I'm sure he's anxious to see you. But probably not as anxious as you are to see him. Which I'm pretty sure is a mom thing."

"Yeah, you're probably right," she said, then groaned and added, "But it means I should actually be asking if you think *your* mom is worried."

"*My* mom? Worried?" Remo scoffed good-naturedly. "She's probably having the time of her life. She's had toys and games stashed away since I was a kid, and she's been silently dying for someone to come and use them. I think she asks me every second week when she can expect some grandchildren."

"That's a mom thing, too," Celia told him.

"Oh, I see. You regularly ask Xavier when he's going to meet a nice girl and settle down?" he teased.

She snorted. "No. But I can't say I don't think about what it'll be like when he grows up."

They paused on the landing then, and Remo pulled the door open for her. She stepped out, then stopped, her eyes on the mess of construction material. She swallowed audibly, and Remo followed her gaze. The wall across from where they stood had been ripped away and temporarily replaced with heavy plastic sheeting. Through the slightly opaque material, the walkway itself was visible. It spanned from the second floor on the hospital side down to a winding ramp on the long-term care facility side. When it was done, it was going to be a contained bridge—glass sides and metal ceiling—and it was already wide enough to wheel at least two hospital beds past one another. But right now, it was just a precarious-looking piece of floor with a rail and some scaffolding on each side. It was enough of a barrier that no one would be able to see them as they crossed, but to say it would offer a feeling of security would be a gross exaggeration.

"Didn't you say it was almost done?" Celia asked in a small voice.

"I guess it's not quite as far along as I thought," Remo replied.

"I think I might've forgotten to mention my fear of heights."

"I won't let you fall."

"That's all well and good, but what if *you* fall?"

"Then I'll make sure I land in a way to break *your* fall."

"You just said you wouldn't *let* me fall."

"I won't."

"But it can't be both ways," she pointed out.

Remo put his hand in the small of her back. "You can do this."

"I think you're going to have to distract me."

"Okay. What should we talk about?"

She inched forward. "Tell me why you don't have kids."

Remo almost stumbled, but caught himself before she could notice. "Not pulling any punches, huh?"

She took a full step. "You're the one who brought it up a second ago. And I figure if I'm going to plummet to my death, I might as well know the gory details."

"No one is plummeting."

"Says you."

They reached the walkway and stepped onto it, and even though it was utterly solid beneath their feet, Remo felt Celia start to shake.

"Maybe I never met the right woman," he announced quickly.

Her body relaxed marginally. "That's a cop-out."

He nudged her forward, and her feet kept going. Slowly, but moving nonetheless.

"Why is it a cop-out?" he replied.

"Because it's the thing guys say to make a girl feel 'special.' And I don't think you're that kind of guy."

"No? Hmm. Then maybe no self-respecting woman would put up with me long enough to figure out what an awesome husband I'd be."

"I have a hard time believing that," she said.

Another glib reply slipped to the front of his mind—*yes, a cop-out*, he acknowledged—but when he opened his mouth, something else came out instead. "When I told you that my mom asked about grandkids every second week…that was a bit of a lie."

"What?" Celia sounded surprised and a little confused, but she didn't stop walking. "Why would you lie about that?"

"Because—if every other thirtyish, childless single man is to be believed—that's what mothers do. You even said yourself that it was a mom thing."

"So you were doing what? Caving to peer pressure? Trying to fit in with all the other thirtyish dudes hanging around here?"

She swept her hand out over the empty walkway—they were smack-dab in the middle—then drew in a sharp breath and stopped walking abruptly as her gaze followed her hand. There was a gap in the scaffolding, and a cordoned off area—full of power tools and bits of wood and steel bars—loomed threateningly below.

"Have I mentioned that I *really* don't like being up here?" said Celia, her voice weak.

"We're halfway," Remo told her. "All downhill from here."

"Poor choice of words."

He slid his hand from her back to her hip, then pulled her a little closer and started walking again, gently forcing her to move, too.

"There's a reason my mom doesn't ask me about having kids," he said, trying to distract her again. "And it's probably the same reason I *don't* have any. You remember I was telling you about Indigo?"

"Yes. Your wild and crazy sister."

"After that stuff with the car, she calmed down a lot. And for three years, things were pretty normal. We lived at my mom's apartment. I got a job as a building maintenance worker, Indigo decided to finish her high school diploma online…she told me she wanted to help *me* get back to school." Remo paused, his throat tightening a little at the hard memories, and he had to clear it before he went on. "But a little while after her seventeenth birthday, she came to me with another problem. She was pregnant. Four months along already. The father was a twenty-year-old drug dealer who she said had no interest in sticking around."

They'd made their way fully across the walkway now, and were starting their descent to the care facility. Remo's heart was squeezing in his chest, nervous about what he was sharing. But Celia's hand held his tightly, and he knew that in spite of her silence, she was listening intently. It was enough reassurance—the exact right thing, actually—to make him keep going.

"It turned out to be a lie," he said, his words full of rough emotion. "The drug dealer was *very* interested in sticking around. Not for the baby. For Indigo. She owed him money. Quite a bit of it, I guess. Enough that he spent two months tracking her down. He broke into the house. And when she wouldn't pay—or *couldn't*—he attacked and left her to die. And she *did* die. She and the baby both did."

He finished just as they got to the bottom of the ramp, and Celia turned to him, her face full of sympathy and heartbreak.

"I'm so sorry, Remo," she said.

He closed his eyes for a second, then opened them and told her the final piece. "They caught him. The scumbag told the police that he was so high that he thought Indigo's pregnancy was a hallucination. He said he wouldn't have done it if he'd known. He must've known that didn't make it any better, because he committed suicide while he was awaiting trial."

Celia stared up at him for another moment, then threw her arms over his shoulders and tugged him into a hard embrace. And even though he probably had eighty pounds and a good foot on her, strength flowed from her body into his. It dulled the powerful hold the bad memories had on him, and he drew in a deep breath—like he could suck in more of the feeling.

"Celia," he said, her name a strangely reverent plea.

He didn't know what he was asking for, but when she inched back and lifted her face to meet his eyes, he saw a matching desire in her gaze. He opened his mouth to say something else, but her attention was abruptly stolen by something over his shoulder.

"Remo," she said. "We have to *run*. Right now."

Chapter 13

Without asking for an explanation, Remo took Celia's hand and sprinted. She didn't take time to note the blind trust that she was right. She didn't *have* time. From across the courtyard, she'd spotted Teller.

Not Teller. Detective *Teller.*

The silent, self-directed correction might've rubbed her the wrong way—or made her fear worse—but she didn't have time for that, either. Because Teller had seen her, too. His eyes had locked with hers, and she'd stared back for just long enough to see the surprise on his face morph into determination. He'd be coming after them. Alone, or with an entourage of police. She didn't want to find out which. She pushed to keep pace with Remo.

Along the temporary fence, then past it.

Around the exterior of the long-term care home.

Through a group of startled, wheelchair-bound seniors who'd sneaked out for a few cigarettes.

Into a tranquil garden of flowers.

It all blurred by in a haze. And to top it off, the wound on Celia's leg hurt more than it had since she'd got it. The painkillers were probably wearing off, and they couldn't have picked a worse time for it.

Each time her foot on the injured side hit the ground, a stabbing pain emanated out from the stitched area. Each time she lifted the same foot, her quad burned. But she refused to let on that it was bothering her, and she didn't dare slow down.

Not now.

She turned the two-word command into a mantra, chanting silently in time with the slap of her shoes on the pavement, and used it to keep going.

Not now, not now, not now.

Into an open-air parking lot.

Not now.

Weaving between minivans and coupes and compact trucks.

Not now.

Nearly knocking over a young couple pushing a stroller.

Not now.

Past the bold, red Emergency sign and onto the sidewalk.

Not-now, not-now.

At last, they reached a footpath that cut between an outbuilding and the first house in the adjoining residential area. There, they paused, breaths coming in matching, heaving time. Celia's lungs burned almost as badly as her thigh. Her arms and legs were like jelly. Blood rushed through her head so hard that she could hear it thumping against her skull, and if Remo's hand hadn't been anchoring her to the spot, she might've collapsed. Maybe she'd collapse in spite of his strong grip. But then—like he could sense her imminent demise—the big man pulled her to his side. Celia closed her eyes and leaned gratefully against his reassuringly solid body.

"Guess I can cross 'running a half marathon' off my list of goals for the year," he joked.

"Sorry," she said breathlessly. "It was Teller. He saw us, Remo."

"Figured you had a damned good reason," he replied.

She pulled away as a new worry hit her, and she didn't bother to disguise the desperate note in her voice. "Xavier. What if Teller tracks you to your mom, and finds your mom's house, and—"

Remo cut her off, his tone as firm as it was reassuring. "She's not that easy to find. Even for the police. Trust me. She's very good at keeping a low public profile. Unlisted address. Doesn't keep a home phone. Old habits, I guess. I promise you that we're fine to rest here for a minute or two. I wouldn't say it if it weren't true."

Celia nodded and sank back into him, waiting for her breaths and heart rate to even out. But she no sooner settled comfortably than she remembered the conversation they'd been having immediately before the start of their frantic escape. Her heart dropped down to her knees as she thought of it. She had no siblings of her own, but she'd lost her mom at a young age, and there was still an ache in her heart every time she thought of her. She couldn't imagine what it must've felt like for Remo's mother. What it must *still* feel like. And she understood why the woman wouldn't be in the habit of asking when her son would give her grandchildren.

She drew in a breath, prepared to reiterate her sympathy. But Remo spoke first, clearly reading the turn of her thoughts.

"Was that more than you bargained for?" he asked.

There was a hint of insecurity under the question, and Celia pulled back to face him. She firmly shook her head, then dragged his palm to her chest and pressed it flat between her breasts.

"My heart hurts for you," she said, "but I'm glad you told me."

"Are you? The few people I've told have cringed, pretended it wasn't too much to handle, then made a concentrated effort to avoid me."

"Those women were obviously insane."

His mouth twitched up. "I didn't say *women*."

Celia's face warmed. "I just assumed…"

"Three *people* over the last half decade," he said with a head shake. "That's how many I've told the partial story to. One was a buddy I'd known for years before. One was a guy from work. The third…okay, well. She *was* a woman, but not in *that* way. She was just some poor, ninety-year-old nurse who got stuck sitting beside me at her retirement party after I'd had a couple of beers. But that's a whole other story."

Celia stared at Remo, processing his words. He'd said them in a light tone, especially considering the subject matter. But they had that same bit of hesitation as his initial question, and she suddenly understood why. He held it in. All the negative experience and the emotions that went along with it. And on the few occasions he'd chosen to let it out, it'd backfired.

But he took a chance with me, she thought, *and I'm not going to let him down.*

She reached up and touched his stubble-heavy cheek. "Thank you for trusting me."

His face relaxed. "Thank *you* for not screaming and running in the other direction." He smiled a slightly crooked smile. "Or I guess technically... Thank you for taking me *with* you while you screamed and ran."

"It's the least I could do for the man who keeps saving my life."

They stood still for a moment, her hand on his cheek, and his on her chest. Celia could feel her heart thrumming under his palm, perfectly in time with the slight throb of his pulse under her pinkie. Then Remo's hand curved. It slid up. It crossed the V-neck of her T-shirt and made its way over her neck, leaving a trail of heat in its path and making her breath catch. His fingers continued to her face, where they unfurled to cup her cheek. But the heat that bloomed from his touch wasn't just physical. It was taking root somewhere inside. She liked it. But she also wondered if it was entirely unreasonable. And the mom in her—the no-nonsense, tell-it-like-it-is part of herself— felt compelled to ask.

She leaned into Remo's hand a little more. "Do you think this is a transference thing?"

His mouth turned up in the corners. "You mean that thing where the kidnap victim falls for the kidnapper?"

"Yes. Only with less kidnapping."

"Why are you asking? Are you falling for me?" His smile—soft and hopeful—took away any embarrassment that might've come as a result of the teasing question.

Celia met his eyes, her mouth a little dry. "My life doesn't leave a lot of room for wasting time, so I try to always say what I mean."

His thumb caressed her cheekbone. "So say it now."

"Things are obviously...complicated for me. And even with the bits of memory I've blocked out, and even if I didn't factor in my son...it's easy to see that the whole being-in-hiding thing would make it impossible to even *think* about pursuing some kind of dating life. There'd be too many secrets. Too many things I'd have to lie about."

"But you don't have to lie to me about any of it," he replied.

She almost laughed. "I didn't really have much of a choice in telling *you* the truth, did I? Between the rescuing and the running."

"There's always a choice," he said, his tone serious. "You could've lied to me at the hospital. Or told me to take my help and shove it." He pressed his forehead to hers, and when he spoke again, his warm breath tickled her lips. "But I'm grateful that you didn't."

"*You're* the grateful one?" Her words were breathy again, and this time it had nothing to do with exertion.

"Mmm. Grateful you trust me. Grateful I drove by when I did. Grateful that you *are* factoring your son in. And extra grateful that if your choice was going to be limited, it was limited to me. Gives me a distinct advantage over all the other guys."

"Didn't we already establish that there *are* no other guys?"

"It's good to be reminded."

"There *are* no other guys, Remo."

"Perfect."

Celia tipped her mouth up expectantly. But instead of him dropping his lips down to meet hers in a fervent kiss, he spoke again.

"It's not transference," he told her, his words thick with restrained desire.

She blinked, surprised that he hadn't taken advantage of her tilted mouth. "No?"

"No. Not unless it's a reciprocal transference."

The all-over heat spiked even more.

"Does that mean *you're* falling for *me*?" she asked.

"As it so happens, I'm not a time waster, either." Then he *did* drop his mouth to hers—slowly and tenderly, toe-curling and possessive, laying a claim to Celia's lips in a way she hadn't even known she was looking for, but half wondered how she'd ever lived without.

If Remo could have, he would've let the kiss go on for a lot longer. Or he would've dragged Celia to some secluded spot and kissed her a hundred more times in a hundred more places. But he knew that in spite of his claim that his mom's home was a secure location, they had a pressing need to get there. It was true that it would take Teller and his cop buddies—corrupt *or* clean—time to track them. His mother's little ranch would also be a secondary target, sought out only when Remo's own town house was found empty. That didn't mean they had infinite hours. Leaving Xavier in one place might endanger him, and it put Remo's mother at risk, too. So he regretfully cut the kiss short, and settled for holding Celia's hand as he guided her through the residential streets.

He briefly outlined his plan—since he'd left his car at the scene of the accident, and Celia's car *was* the accident, their best bet was public transit. On the off chance that Teller and his men were patrolling the nearby streets, he wanted to go to a more out-of-the-way bus stop. From there, they could ride to the connection loop and find the bus that would take them just a block from his mom's place.

Celia agreed easily, and their walk was quiet, but not overly pensive. Remo was sure that anyone who happened to be up early enough to see them would assume they were just a couple out for an early morning stroll. The sun was just about to come up, and the horizon was already marked with a mottled purple-and-orange glow. Very romantic.

As long as anyone they passed didn't look too closely, the simple explanation would hold up. If someone took note of the fact that neither of them was dressed for the weather, then spied the bloodstain on Celia's pants, they might have a problem in the form of some Good Samaritan making a cautionary call in to the local PD. The last thing he wanted was for some call to get routed through to Teller. The thought of it happening made him pull Celia a little closer and move a little faster, too.

"Any more of those holes in your memory getting filled in?" he asked.

She shook her head. "Honestly? I keep forgetting that I'm forgetting. I think if I wasn't aware that I had the mental block, I wouldn't even know it." She let out a little laugh. "That was a pretty redundant thing to say, wasn't it?"

"Yep. Not that I'm judging."

"It's hard to explain exactly what I mean."

"Try me. We've got about three more blocks of time to kill."

She sighed, her fingers opening and closing around his as her face scrunched up in concentration. "Okay. So there's a logical part of my brain that tells me Xavier has a father. But if I ask myself who his father is…it's like the question slips over the answer and just comes up blank."

"Like when you're trying to remember a particular actor's name?" Remo asked.

Celia shrugged. "Sort of. If the actor was someone whose name you didn't know, whose face you'd never seen, and whose movies you'd never heard of."

He laughed. "So…not at all the same, then."

"No," she said ruefully, "I guess not. Maybe it's more like…if someone handed you a scalpel, told you that you knew how to do open-heart surgery when you didn't, then immediately told you that you were going to have to perform it right that second."

"That sounds decidedly unpleasant."

"Doesn't it?" She sighed again. "I remember my mom, and that she died when I was eighteen. I remember that I didn't know my dad at all. I remember going to college on a scholarship, but…"

He looked down at her. "What?"

Her forehead creased into a frown. "I remember little things. My professors' names. Dr. Huntley was one. And a female TA called Isla. I can picture the buildings. But when I think about what I was taking, or what I was doing for work after that, it's a blank."

He thought about that for a second, then snapped the fingers of his free hand. "Ten bucks says your work has something to do with Xavier's dad."

Her eyes widened. "I won't take that bet because I think you're right. It makes sense. I started college right after high school, and I had to take the second semester off when my mom died, but I was there for a two-year program. I was twenty-one when Xavier was born. Almost twenty-two. So if I met his dad either *in* school, or right after, the dates would line up perfectly."

"You said he was older. Could he have been a teacher?"

"I don't know. I want to say that I don't think I'm the kind of person who would have an affair with her teacher, but the truth is…I could be, right?" She lifted her free hand and pushed her hair behind her ear, visibly agitated. "I'm sorry. This is so unbelievably frustrating."

Remo's reply was cut off by the fact that they'd reached the final turn, and a bus was just chugging into view. Instead of speaking, he gave Celia's hand a tug, and they jogged together toward the approaching vehicle. They made it with a heartbeat to spare, and a few moments later, they were catching their breath at the very back of the nearly empty bus. And Remo's brain was churning as noisily as the engine that rumbled under them.

"You said it was a two-year program?" he asked. "You're sure about that?"

Celia nodded. "It was a free-ride scholarship. I remember opening the envelope."

"So it was probably a vocational college or trade school of some kind." Thinking of what she'd said about Xavier's father's manicured hands, Remo lightly took her fingers into his and examined them. "No polish," he mused. "Not even clear. Your nails are short. Practical. But your hands aren't rough like they do manual labor."

She tapped her fingertips on his palm. "Yeah, I don't think I'm the auto-mechanic type. And I once short-circuited my apartment while running the dishwasher and I had to call a plumber *and* an electrician in to fix it, so I think that I can rule out anything too trades-y, too."

Remo pretended to study her hand a little longer, but really he was more interested in the way her memories came out naturally as she talked. He wondered if she noticed it herself, but decided not to point it out in case it staunched the flow.

"Maybe *you're* the teacher," he suggested instead. "Special education? I can see that."

She let out a little laugh. "Actually, before I found out I was pregnant, I thought I didn't want kids. Not that there's anything bad about being a mom, but until I had Xavier I always preferred the company of adults. Seniors, in particular. I think it started when I was six, and we lived beside a nursing home. There was this seventy-year-old woman named Lily who I would always say was my best friend. I even invited her to my birthday party. My mom used to joke that—oh, my God." Her gaze flicked up from their joined hands to Remo's face.

"What?" he prodded.

"She used to say that I should get paid for how much time I spent over there."

"You think maybe you *did* get paid to be there?"

"I can see it. I can see myself going to school for it. And when I was, um…breaking myself out of the hospital bed, I knew exactly how to bypass the alarms on the IV monitor." Her hand closed on his and tightened, her face brimming with hope. "I don't *remember* it. But it feels right." Then her expression fell. "I don't know what it has to do with Xavier's dad, though. And the only stuff I can't remember has everything to do with him."

Remo pulled his hand free, then draped his arm over her shoulder and tucked her against his side.

"Hey," he said. "We have a lot to go on, and when we get to my mom's place, we can dig a little deeper, too. We can probably find out a bit more about Teller, and maybe even find a way to confirm your employment."

"You're pretty good with the optimism."

"I've got every reason to be. When I found you, you weren't even sure about your own name. Look at how much has changed in the last few hours."

"Yes," she agreed. "That's true."

Then she wriggled a little closer and put her head on his chest, a companionable silence settling over them.

Chapter 14

It didn't take long for the bus to reach the transfer loop, and they hopped on the next bus—a little busier now that it was nearing commute time for many Vancouver residents—without much fuss. Remo made brief small talk with the driver, ensuring that they were on the right route, but once they were settled into their new seats, he went quiet once more. And Celia was thankful for the reprieve. It gave her a chance to reset her brain and to process everything that had happened since she'd opened her eyes on the side of the road. It was mere hours ago, but it felt like a lifetime. And Remo couldn't have been more right in his observation. Except for one thing. It wasn't just that *a lot* had changed; it was that *everything* had changed.

Though it was true that she'd woken at the scene of the accident devoid of her name, she'd known who she was on the inside. She was Xavier's mother. A woman who had enough strength to protect her son at all costs. The edges around that had been fuzzy. They were *still* fuzzy, as was evidenced by the fact that she couldn't remember what she did for a living. But that didn't matter. She had a core, and she could feel it.

Celia stole the quickest glance down at their hands. His big fingers were entwined around hers like they were meant to be there. His olive-toned skin was a sharp contrast to her fair hand. But in a yin-yang kind of way. Different. But whole when together.

And already, knowing Remo had shifted that small, sure voice in her head that told her who she was. Instead of thinking in terms of what *her* next move would be, she was thinking in terms of what *they* would do next.

She was envisioning an end to the constant running. To the perpetual feeling of having to look over her shoulder, worrying whether or not the roots she put down should be allowed to flourish, or if they should be planted loosely enough to move at any given moment. She was sure it was a brand-new feeling. As much as her memories might be blocked, she was a hundred percent sure that she'd spent the last half of a decade thinking she'd be hiding for the rest of her life. So she welcomed the idea that an end might be a real possibility. Because it would mean the chance for a beginning, too.

As she sat on the bus, with its engine growling under her and its stifling heat blasting into her, Celia let herself imagine it. She could picture Xavier sitting in Remo's lap while the two of them perused a book. She allowed herself to see the close of a long evening. Tucking her son into bed, then arguing with the big, blue-eyed man over which movie to watch. Letting him get his way because she wanted him to smile. Under any other circumstances, it should've been ridiculous to even think about things like that. She was a grown woman. And her life didn't have room for fantasies. She'd never even considered making room for one. When she lay in bed at night, her dreams were of making it, day to day. Of finding Xavier's favorite yogurt on sale. Last-minute escape routes. It wasn't that she was boring or didn't want more for herself and her son. It was just that she'd been through a lot, and the end result was a solid footing in realism.

But now...

She closed her eyes. The unexpected fantasy was there, alive and well. It had somehow seeped into the corners of her heart and mind, and seemed to be taking up permanent residence. And strangely, it felt real. As solid as Remo's body. As firm as his grip. So if it wasn't some kind of mutual transference, then what was it? There had to be a reasonable explanation.

Because I don't believe in love at first sight.

The thought made Celia's heart flutter nervously against her rib cage, so hard that she had to draw in a deep pull of air to steady its staccato rhythm. And even that wasn't quite enough to calm it down. Then Remo's deep voice rumbled against her, startling her so badly that she almost jumped.

"Hey," he said.

Celia breathed out, reminded herself that he couldn't read her mind, and made herself answer in a calm voice, repeating his own greeting back to him. "Hey."

He smiled down at her in a way that made her heart race even more. "Wasn't sure if you were awake. We're almost there. Two more stops."

"I'm awake."

She sat up a little straighter and took a look out the window. The area was residential, just like the one they'd left behind near the hospital. But here, the houses were a little farther apart, and the yards were more spacious. There was evidence of family life nearly everywhere. Swing sets and slides. Bikes and scooters set aside for later use. It made her both envious of the outwardly easy lives on display and more eager to see her own son. So much so that when they coasted to a stop and Remo gestured toward the exit, she had to restrain herself from running straight out the door. Thankfully, he appeared to be in almost as much of a hurry as she was. As soon as they'd stepped from the transit vehicle to the street, he tucked her hand into the crook of his elbow and moved quickly along. In under two minutes, they were standing in front of a waist-high fence. The whitewashed wood panels framed a short, squat structure with cream-colored stucco siding and cheerful blue shutters. It was easy to see that the building was more than just a house. It was a home.

Flower patches lined the path that led past the gate and up to the front steps. The little porch was also covered in flowers—they were in long boxes and stubby planters, and even an empty cottage cheese container. A dozen or so colorful wind chimes hung from the soffits, and a hand-made sign heralding a welcome to visitors.

Warmth filled Celia's chest. Even if she hadn't already had good reasons to appreciate Wendy DeLuca, this added another one. She was glad that if her son was forced to run off with a stranger, it was with the woman who owned a place that looked like this. Smiling at Remo, Celia reached for the latch on the gate. But then went still with shock as a familiar shriek filled the air, carrying from somewhere around the back of the small house.

Xavier.

Thoughts of coziness gave way to fear, but panic delayed her for only a moment. Then protectiveness kicked in, and she shoved the gate so hard that it slammed against the fence on the other side. As her feet beat against the stone walkway, she was vaguely aware of Remo calling out to her. Urging her to wait. She ignored him, afraid he'd try to stop her altogether if he was given the chance. A second scream made her move even faster.

Please, no! Celia begged silently.

She pushed past the side of the house, crushed rock crunching under her shoes and her mind racing with terrible thoughts. Xavier, being dragged into an unknown car. The salt-and-pepper-haired man glancing into the rearview as his tires spun. Or worse.

But when she rounded the rear corner, there was no car. No man. And no Xavier. There was just Wendy, sitting in a lawn chair with a book in one hand and a mug in the other.

Celia was so startled that she stopped short, sending Remo crashing into her back. As a result, she lost her balance and went tumbling over. Her fall brought the big man down with her. Together, they fell against the ground, and she was sure that the only thing that stopped her from breaking an arm was the fact that Remo made a last-minute adjustment, putting him underneath her.

"Well," said Wendy with a laugh. "You two sure know how to make an entrance, don't you?"

Celia was relieved that there wasn't any worry at all in the other woman's voice, and she knew it meant her son was fine. But it didn't quite quell her anxiety. Her pulse still pounded a little, and she knew it wouldn't stop until she had Xavier wrapped in a hug. She started to push to a sitting position, but stopped halfway as her son's body suddenly appeared. Up high. Seemingly suspended in the air.

"Mooooooo-oooooom!" he yelled, his voice full of delight. He disappeared, then reappeared again. "Look at meeeeeeee!"

"Sorry," said Wendy, her voice easy. "The little guy next door has a trampoline."

Celia collapsed back, not sure whether to laugh or cry. Was she really so tightly wound that she couldn't tell the difference between her own son's shrieks of fun and his shrieks of fear? The thought horrified her. But the sweeping relief that he was okay set that on the backburner.

"A trampoline," she repeated.

"Mooooo-oooooom!" Xavier called again.

"I see you, baby!" she yelled back, watching as he disappeared once more, and a black-haired boy took his place.

"That's my neighbor's son, Danny," Wendy explained with just a touch of ruefulness. "I know it's early, but Xavier took a nap for about an hour, and when he woke up and spotted Danny out there, he begged to have a look. How could I say no?"

Deciding it was best to let her fear go, Celia made a second effort—this time successfully—to sit up. "I would've said yes, too. Doesn't Danny have school today?"

"He's not quite five," Remo said, standing up and holding out his hand to help her to her feet. "Kindergarten in the fall."

A pang of envy hit Celia. She made an effort to keep a low profile in the apartment where she and Xavier lived. As a result, she barely knew her neighbors' names, let alone the details of their kids' lives. Unexpectedly, tears stung her eyes. But before she could reach up to brush them away, Remo's palm pressed to the small of her back.

"Mom," he said, "is there coffee inside?"

"Full pot," Wendy replied.

Suddenly, Celia desperately wanted a cup. It seemed imperative that she get to sit with a mug clasped between her hands, and the pleasant aroma wafting up. Ten minutes of not thinking about anything. Just enough time to let go of the frantic pace of the last twelve hours.

Twelve hours. How can it have only been that long?

"Do we have time?" she asked, unable to keep the hope from her question.

Remo's fingers flexed. "We'll make time. Come on. I know where Mom keeps her secret, vanilla-flavored creamer, and I'm sure she'll let us know if she sees anything we need to worry about."

Celia cast a glance back toward her bouncing, laughing son, and then let Remo lead her to the house.

Remo could tell that Celia needed a minute or two to decompress, so he poured her coffee first, then kissed her cheek and excused himself to grab his mom's laptop from the den. When he came back, she was hunched over her mug, eyes closed, silent tears streaking her cheeks.

"You wanna talk about it?" he asked gently.

She didn't lift her head as she answered. "I'm envious of this life."

"This life? What do you mean?"

"The cozy house. The best friend for Xavier next door. We live in a decent apartment. Two bedrooms. Cute little window seat in the living room. But I don't send him on playdates. I don't give the other moms my number. I keep a burner cell, for crying out loud."

Remo's heart squeezed, and he bent down to fold her into an embrace. "You know it's not your fault."

"I *do* know. I'm just keeping him safe." She sounded like she meant it, but there was a desperate edge to her voice. "But it doesn't make the life we have anything like the life I'd like for us. When I heard him yelling out there... God. I can't even describe the panic. And now I'm sitting here, asking myself what kind of mother assumes her child is being kidnapped when he's just out having fun."

Remo leaned back and used his thumb to tip up her chin. "The kind who would run straight into danger to protect her son. You thought the worst, just then, and you still went running."

She sighed. "Can I admit something to you?"

"Anything."

"Part of me wants to just grab Xavier and make a run for it right now."

"And then do what? Hide again? Never recover your memories? Feel like this for the next twenty years?"

"I don't even want to feel like this for another twenty *minutes*," she replied.

"So let's look for some answers and a permanent solution," he suggested.

He didn't add his other, selfish thoughts. *What about me? What about that date I promised you? What about exploring the idea of an 'us'?* Instead, he dropped his hand and dragged the laptop over so that the screen faced her.

"Here," he said. "Instead of running, we can start with tracking down the not-so-nice detective, and see if it jars anything for you."

Quickly, he typed in the corrupt cop's name, and was pleased when the effort was rewarded right away. A dozen newspaper articles popped. Arrests and interviews. Accompanying thumbnail photographs that confirmed they had the right man. There was even a feature on Teller, dating back about two years. When Remo clicked on it, a quick scroll through it showed a teeth-grindingly perfect record. So squeaky that the person writing the piece referred to the man as "Midas."

Celia shook her head, clearly having read the line at the

same time as Remo. "I somehow doubt that everything he touches turns to *real* gold. Maybe more like gold-plating."

"At best," Remo agreed, clicking back to the search results. "Any of those stand out to you?"

She leaned forward, but shook her head again. "None of the headlines are familiar. Maybe the image search?"

He switched screens, and the man's face filled the screen in another dozen poses.

"Sure likes to have his picture taken, doesn't he?" Remo said, scrolling down.

"Staying above scrutiny by staying in the spotlight," Celia murmured.

"But still nothing?"

"No. Unfortunately."

Remo ran his hand over his hair and started to close the laptop, but Celia's hand shot out, stopping him.

"Wait," she said, a tremor in her voice and her finger stretched out to point at the screen. "What's that?"

Remo followed her gesture with his eyes. "Mom's live news app. Why?"

"Can you make it bigger?"

"Sure."

He complied, clicking on the small square. The breaking story immediately came to life, and even though the sound was down, the ticker across the bottom gave away the subject matter—the bomb threat at the hospital. A local councilman—who'd recently become well-known because of his bid for mayor—was giving an interview in front of a crowd. The camera panned out, giving a view of the construction area they'd fled just a short time ago. Celia's sharp inhale was immediate, and Remo moved to turn it off.

"You don't need to watch this," he said. "It's just going to—"

Her whisper cut him off. "That's him."

"That's who?"

"Xavier's father."

"Who is?"

"What do you mean, 'who is'? That man, right there." This time, her finger actually hit the screen, smacking into the councilman's head.

"That's Neil Price."

"Should that name mean something to me?"

"He announced his bid for mayor just a week or two ago."

"I'm a hundred percent sure he's Xavier's dad."

Remo still found himself frowning. "Are you sure you couldn't have seen him on TV? Somehow mixed that up with your memories?"

He felt bad as soon as he asked it, but Celia just met his eyes, her gaze unwavering. The only hint of nerves was in the way she sucked in her lower lip before speaking again.

"I don't remember the relationship, Remo, but I remember *things*. He has a scar on the inside of his left elbow," she told him softly. "It's diamond-shaped, and I can remember the way it *feels*. When his beard starts to grow in, it's such a dark shade of brown that it's almost black, but he has a patch just under his chin that's almost completely white. Should I go on?"

Remo stared at her. There was no denying her conviction. No denying that the details were intimate and believable.

But it doesn't make sense.

He didn't realize he'd spoken aloud until she answered him.

"Why not?" Celia asked, her expression more guarded than he'd seen it since she first awoke in the hospital, and he immediately felt guilty.

"I'm not doubting you," he said quickly. "It's just that Neil Price is Mr. Good Guy. Hard stance on local crime, good..." He trailed off as he felt something click.

"What is it?" Celia asked, reading his expression.

"I was going to say that he has a well-known, well-established connection with the local PD. But if his connection is with the corrupt side of things..."

"You mean like a tag team effort between Midas and Mr. Good Guy?" In spite of the way it sounded, there was nothing humorous about the question.

Remo nodded grimly, then pulled the laptop closer again. His fingers flew over the keyboard, opening the search engine again and plugging in both Teller's and Price's names. This time, the relevant result was singular. A news article that featured the two men. The caption announced the dawning of a new day—a crackdown on petty crime and the promise of more to come. There was a photo in the middle of the article, too. A black-and-white shot of Teller and Price that showcased their smiling faces and a handshake. Beneath their clasped palms was a bench, embossed with a dedication to the City of Vancouver itself.

Before Remo could scan the contents of the article, Celia sucked in another breath.

"He's married," she said. "And it says that putting family first is one of his main campaign points."

Remo pulled his attention from the laptop to her face, and he nodded reluctantly. "Yes. That's right."

Her eyes held his. "What else?"

He inhaled a breath of his own and decided it was better to come out and say what he knew. "His wife is expecting a baby."

The color drained from Celia's face so fast that Remo's

hand shot to her waist to hold her up in case she fainted. She leaned into his touch, but her eyes stayed open.

"How long?" Her two-word question was laced with an emotion he couldn't quite pinpoint, but which made him want to pull her closer nonetheless.

"How long to which part?" he asked.

She swallowed. "How long has he been married? Did he... Did we..."

Then he clued in to what she meant. "No. You didn't have an affair. He's only been married to his wife for two years, and this is his first marriage."

Celia sagged hard against him, and now her eyes did sink shut. "I know I've said this ten times before, but this is so incredibly frustrating. I keep second-guessing myself, again and again."

Keeping his hand on her hip, Remo adjusted so that he was facing her. "And I know *I've* said *this* ten times before. You're a good mother. Tough as hell. I'll tell you that a thousand times again, if I need to."

Her lids lifted, and her gray eyes held him just as they seemed to every time she looked at him. The smallest smile tipped up her kissable lips.

"It'll probably get tiresome," she said.

"I can be a patient man."

"Yeah?"

"Yeah."

He leaned forward, and her knees parted to let him press his hips between her thighs. A pinpointed want washed through him, and it wasn't the physical one he would've expected. It was much more than that. It was that yesterday morning, he'd woken up having no clue that Celia Poller existed, while today he couldn't stand the thought of going back to not knowing her. It was the way she protected her son so fiercely. That she fit so perfectly against him. The way she tipped her lips up to his, welcoming and ready, trusting and demanding. It was *everything* about Celia that made him want her even more.

He tightened his arm on her, pushed his fingers to the narrow space between her T-shirt and her pants, then lowered his mouth to hers. He barely got in a brush of a kiss, though, before the sound of a throat being cleared pulled him back again.

"Remo," said his mom. "We've got a little bit of a problem."

He turned to face her, every muscle in his body tensed for bad news.

Chapter 15

Too worried to be embarrassed at being caught in the slightly compromising position, Celia grasped Remo's wrist tightly, and her gaze darted around his mother, searching. When she didn't immediately spy her son, she brought her eyes up to the older woman's face.

Wendy lifted her hand right away. "Xavier's fine. I asked Danny's mom to take them in and give them some juice."

Celia relaxed her hand, and Remo gave her knee a squeeze, then stood up and said, "You probably should've led with that, Mom. What's wrong?"

She offered an apologetic shrug, then launched into a quick, concerned explanation. "A navy blue car pulled up to the barricade at the back alley. I wasn't too worried until a second, almost identical one pulled up, too, and both drivers got out."

Celia's heart jumped nervously, and Remo spoke up, voicing her own foremost concern.

"Did they see Xavier?" he asked.

Wendy shook her head. "Not the right angle to see into the neighbor's yard. Doubt they even saw me."

"And where are the two guys now?"

"I only watched until Xavier was safely in Danny's house, but I did see the second man get back into his car. Far as I know, the first car is still there."

Fighting full-fledged panic, Celia pushed up from the stool. "We need to get to Xavier before they do."

Remo put his hand on her elbow. "Hang on."

Before she could argue, he slipped out of the kitchen at a light jog. Celia scrunched up her toes in an attempt to keep herself from chasing after him.

If whoever's out there is anything like Detective Teller...

Remo would sacrifice himself. She knew it. And the thought didn't just make her chest compress; it made her whole *body* compress. She'd barely had a chance to find out what life might be like with Remo, but the idea that she might not get any more time was almost more than she could bear.

"He'll be fine, sweetheart. Him and Xavier both." Wendy's voice gave her a start, and she was embarrassed to admit that in the last ten seconds, the other woman's presence had slipped her mind.

Celia shot a rueful look her way and tried to reply in a strong voice. "I'm so sorry that I brought this into your home."

"You didn't. I volunteered."

"What?"

"When my son brought yours down to the cafeteria, I knew straight away that I—that *we*—were meant to help you. So I volunteered. No woman and child should have to go through what you're going through." Wendy paused, then nodded. "I can see from your face that Remo told you why I feel so strongly about it."

Celia nodded. "He did."

The other woman studied her for a moment. "My son is an excellent paramedic and the kindest man I know. Bit of a hero complex, but I'm proud of who he is. And he's always been too good at holding things in. I've been waiting five years for him to open up. If he does that with you…then count me in for all of it."

By the end of the short speech, a lump had built up in the back of Celia's throat, but she didn't get a chance to clear and answer, because Remo reappeared just then, shaking his head.

"I checked the front," he said. "One unmarked car, sitting three houses up. Driver sat there for a second on his phone, but he's getting out now. Headed our way. I think he and the guy in the back are trying to box us in. We've got about sixty seconds to come up with a plan."

His mother jumped in right away. "You can go out through the window in my en suite. It's big enough. And there's a space about four feet wide between the houses. If you head toward the front, a shrub blocks you in the whole way. I don't see why you wouldn't be able to sneak onto the porch from there. I can text Danny's mom to let her know to expect you."

Celia noted that Wendy hadn't included herself in the suggestion, and the omission didn't get by Remo, either.

"You mean 'we,' Mom," he said. "*We* can go through the window."

She gave him a look Celia knew well—the no-argument mom stare—and shook her head. "My car's in the driveway, and my neighbors know I'm home. It's safer and less suspicious for me to answer the door and play dumb."

Remo's jaw set stubbornly, but Wendy was quick to speak again.

"Your sixty seconds are down to thirty," she told him. "And you've got a little boy waiting next door. My pepper spray and I can handle this."

Remo muttered something about stubbornness under his breath, then pulled his mom in for a quick kiss on the cheek.

"We'll be back for you," he promised.

Then he grabbed Celia's hand. He tugged her from the kitchen to the hall, then into the master suite. It was the kind of room she would normally have taken a few minutes to appreciate. As it was, she barely had time to note the basics. Hardwood floors and a cozy nook with a reading chair. A built-in, floor-to-ceiling bookshelf and a big window with the blinds drawn. Remo pulled her past it all and into the spacious bathroom. He barely paused before stepping around the toilet and sliding up the window.

"I'll go first to make sure it's clear," he said, stepping up onto the closed lid. "If anything goes wrong—"

She cut him off. "It won't go wrong. It *can't.*"

He looked like he wanted to argue, but he didn't do it. He just bent down, pressed his mouth to hers, then turned and used his long legs to climb through the window frame. There was a soft rattle on the other side, and Celia knew his feet had hit gravel. She held her breath, and mentally crossed her fingers for his safety. And after a moment, his voice carried up through the window.

"You're good to go," he said. "And Mom was right. There's complete coverage from curious eyes out here."

Exhaling, Celia climbed with the intention of following the same motions he had—one leg, then the other, a quick grab of the frame overhead, and a jump out. But as soon as she got up onto the toilet, she realized she didn't have the same height advantage. She was going to need to get a bit higher, and there was only one place to do it. Up on the tank.

With a slight cringe at the anticipated instability, she grabbed hold of the window ledge and boosted herself up. The ceramic tank lid immediately wobbled in protest, and at the same time, a doorbell chimed loudly from elsewhere in the house.

"Celia?" Remo called, his voice tinged with concern.

"I'm coming," she replied.

But she got only one foot up and out before realizing she had a problem. She couldn't quite lift herself up enough to bring the other foot through, too. She was stuck straddling the bottom of the window with her torso still in the bathroom.

"Duck through and jump," Remo urged.

"I'll fall face-first," she whispered.

"I'll catch you."

"I mentioned my fear, right?"

"Of heights, not of falling," he reminded her. "We're on the first floor, remember?"

"I think it's psychological," she replied.

"You're only six feet up." She felt his hand land on her ankle. "See? When you jump out, it'll be straight into my arms. Win-win."

His fingers dropped away, but the reassurance that they were there—that *he* was there—lingered enough that Celia felt a little more confident. And a new motivation propelled her, anyway. She could hear Wendy talking to someone in the house, and their voices were far closer than was comfortable. With Remo's touch held in her mind, she bent herself in half like a contortionist, then more or less dived through the window. As promised, she landed against the big man's chest, his strong arms stopping her from even touching the gravel under her feet.

"Good?" he asked, setting her down, but not releasing her.

"Still breathing," she confirmed.

He planted a quick kiss on her lips, then dropped his hand to hers and said, "Okay. Let's go get that kid of yours."

Even though they were hidden from view, they moved in unison to press their backs to the exterior of the house, and maneuvered cautiously toward the bushes that blocked the way to the front yard. The closer they got, the quieter they got, too. Being out of sight didn't mean being out of hearing range.

When they reached the thick greenery, Remo put his finger to his lips, then pointed to the narrow space where the shrubs wrapped around the neighbor's porch. Celia nodded, but her heart was racing. She made herself let go of his hand in spite of her trepidation, and watched as he crept forward, then slipped in between the tall bush and the house next door. She started a slow count to ten—*one one-thousand, two one-thousand, three one-thousand*—and tried to stave off the fear that the man in Wendy's house would see Remo in spite of the cover. She hit *ten one-thousand*, and silence still reigned. She bit her lip to keep from calling to him, and started the count over again. She willed him to be safe and hurry at the same time, then immediately followed that with a prayer that the two things weren't mutually exclusive.

When she hit *nine one-thousand* a second time, tears threatened. She wasn't sure she could make it through the count once more without going after him.

C'mon, Remo.

Then, as though the direct thought prompted it, the

bushes in front of her shuddered, then parted, and the big man's body pushed back into view. And he wasn't alone. Xavier was glued to his side, fear evident in the way his lower lip trembled. It made Celia want to cry, too. Even more so when he pulled from Remo's grasp and stepped toward her, silent, but with his arms outstretched. She bent down and lifted him up, folding his familiar little body against her. When his skinny arms snaked around her neck, grasping her tightly, it was almost impossible to keep the tears in.

"I'm sorry, baby," she whispered.

He squeezed her even harder, and she wished like crazy that she could just magically whisk him away. But she had to settle for meeting Remo's eyes instead, sending him a silent query as to what their next move would be. In response, he put his hand on Xavier's back for a moment, then pointed toward the rear of the house. Celia nodded her understanding, then turned without setting down her son, and started to move in the direction he'd indicated. But she made it only halfway along before Remo touched her elbow and stopped her from going any farther.

"Hold on for one second," he said in a low voice.

She stopped and faced him again. "What's wrong?"

He eyed Xavier like he was weighing what to say, then replied, "Small problem. The two men my mom saw are decoys."

"Decoys for what?"

"A third man who's stationed up the street, trying to look inconspicuous. Possibly a fourth one in the alley, too. I think the guy behind the house and the guy at the door let themselves be seen on purpose to try to lure us out."

Celia's pulse tripped. "So what are our options?"

"Mom said the backyard vantage point worked in her favor," Remo said. "She could see the car and the driver, but she doubted he could see her, and she was *sure* he couldn't see the boys on the trampoline. So our best bet— our only one, really—is to go through Mom's backyard and into the neighbor's, then keep going until we come out at the opposite end of the street. That route should steer us clear of where they think we'll be, and we can decide what to do from there."

The word *should* didn't exactly bolster Celia's confidence. But she nodded anyway. Because as Remo had said, there wasn't really a choice.

Remo didn't blame Celia for being worried. It was sheer luck that he'd spotted the man out front. A few seconds later and he wouldn't have noticed him as he slipped behind the large oak at the end of the street. A few seconds earlier and the guy might not have stepped into view and fixed his unwavering gaze in the direction of the house, drawing attention to the fact that his stare was a little too focused.

The seconds-long study Remo had done of the man had made his gut churn. It was long enough to note a couple of things. Like the bulge of a gun under his jacket, and the easy authority in his stance in spite of the fact that he was clearly hiding. He was a cop. Remo was sure of it. Undoubtedly one of Teller's men. So Remo was damned thankful for the fortuitous timing, and sure as hell wasn't going to look a gift horse in the mouth. He had to get Celia and Xavier to safety, then decide what to do to help his mom.

One thing at a time, he told himself. *If anyone can handle themselves, it's her.*

That much was definitely true. His mom was as tough as they came, and if a couple corrupt cops thought they could manipulate her, they had another think coming. It made him smile to imagine. Maybe he would've even laughed a little if lives hadn't been hanging in the balance.

Worry spiking at the mental reminder, Remo pressed his hand to the small of Celia's back, then silently indicated that they should turn to their left. He crouched a little as they moved from behind the bushes and out into the yard. The fence was a full six feet high, but he was four inches taller than that, and he wasn't taking any chances that the top of his head would give them away.

He pushed on, carefully unlatching the gate between his mom's place and the neighbor's. He opened it only as far as he had to in order for them to slip through, then made sure it shut silently behind them. They sneaked past the trampoline to the next fence, then out to the next yard. By the time they'd reached the fourth yard, Celia was breathing hard, and Remo kicked himself for not offering to take Xavier from her right away.

He tapped her shoulder, held out his arms, and opened his mouth to make the suggestion. His words died before they formed, though, because over Celia's shoulder he spied a bit of movement between the slats of the fence. Making a quick, keep-silent gesture, he inched forward for a closer look.

Let it be a cat. Or a kid.

But it wasn't either. Instead, it was another man, this one in a suit. He stood with his back against a garage directly across the alley, one leg bent up. Though he had a phone in his hand, his eyes were very clearly roaming the space near Remo's mom's backyard.

Dammit.

One creak. One bumped rock. One tiny sound of any sort, and the man's attention would turn their way.

Hoping for another stroke of luck, and racking his brain for a way to create his own in case one didn't naturally present itself, Remo very slowly and very quietly swung his gaze back and forth in search of an idea. He didn't get a chance to form one. Celia was quicker. Clutching Xavier to her chest, she bent down, snagged a golf-ball-sized rock from somewhere near her feet, then stood. Faster than it took Remo to clue in to what she was doing, she drew back her arm and tossed the stone in the other direction. It sailed silently through the air—above the waiting cop's sight-line, thank God—then cracked hard against the ground just outside Remo's mom's yard. A perfectly placed shot. And it had the desired effect. The cop didn't just turn his attention that way, he pushed up from his spot against the garage and took off toward it at a jog.

If Remo had thought they had a second to spare, he would've tugged Celia in for a thorough, thankful kiss. As it was, all he had time to do was relieve her of her son so she could move more easily. He reached out for the little boy, who seemed perfectly content to settle against Remo instead of his mother, then pointed toward the next house. And then they were on the move again, faster this time, but with no less regard for keeping quiet.

Thanking the universe for the fact that no nosy neighbors seemed to note their movements, Remo led the way through yards five and six. Then through yards seven and eight. At yard nine—the final one before they'd be on their way—Remo paused and realized they had a small challenge. Though every other yard had a side gate, this corner lot had one only on the alley side.

Gritting his teeth, he handed Xavier back to Celia. "One sec."

He slipped to the other side of the yard and took a peek around. The fence was a dead end. He made his way back to Celia and shook his head.

"We're going to have to go that way," he whispered, with a nod toward the back gate.

Celia gave her lower lip a nervous little suck, but nodded. Remo gave her arm a reassuring squeeze, then moved forward and cautiously opened the gate. He took a very slow, very careful look up and down the alley. The side closest to them was clear. But the other…not so much. Just outside Remo's mom's place, the man Celia had so cleverly distracted was engaged in a visibly heated discussion with another guy, presumably the one from the car his mother had noted.

Remo drew his head back into the yard and hazarded a whisper. "Company's still out there. We can wait and see what happens, or we can slip out and make a run for it. Move low and quick along the outside of the fence."

Celia met his eyes, and he expected her to pick the former. Instead, she said, "On the count of three?"

He couldn't keep the surprise from his voice. "Really?"

She answered in a quick, sure voice. "I know it's risky, but it's not like staying here is totally safe, either. A neighbor will eventually notice us and give us away. Or call the police and give Teller a legitimate reason to chase us. And at least this way, those guys out there don't know that *we* know they're here. Right now, they're trying to flush us out quietly."

"As long as you're sure."

"I'm sure."

He put a hand on Xavier's back. "You want to ride with me, buddy?"

The kid turned and stretched out his arms, and Remo took him from his mom and settled him against his hip, then reached for Celia's hand.

"One," he said softly.

"Two," she replied.

"Three," piped up Xavier in his own little whisper.

And they went for it.

Chapter 16

In spite of the fact that it was her own decision to run, Celia still managed to play out the worst-case scenarios in her head.

Getting caught.

Getting killed.

Losing Xavier.

Losing her mind.

She didn't take risks where her son was concerned. Not at all. And the bottom line was that this particular escape left them exposed, and as short as the exposure was, it was more than enough time for the arguing men to turn their way. So her pulse thumped hard, and the five-second dash took a lifetime, and her head repeated the worries in her heart.

Caught.

Killed.

Xavier.

Her mind.

But they made it. Or Celia assumed they did, because there was no outcry of recognition. No thunder of pursuit. They rounded the corner and kept going. She couldn't have estimated how far or how long they ran, but she was sure it wasn't anywhere near as long as it felt. She had no clue if they were drawing unwanted attention, or if they had a destination. She just pumped her legs. At some point, she and Remo had separated their hands so that they could move faster. But now her quads and calves were growing leaden, and she was thankful that Xavier was in Remo's arms. Houses flashed by. Street names were a blur. Maybe they went five blocks, maybe ten. At last, just when she wasn't sure she could take another step, Remo slowed, then came to a stop. Celia bent over, her breath coming in gasps.

"Mom?" Xavier's voice was full of worry.

She lifted her face to reassure him, but words failed her when she spied her son's stance. He was standing beside Remo, one of his little hands folded into the big man's palm. Although she'd seen them together a few times now, this was somehow different. They were...*united.* It was the only word she could think of to describe them. They wore matching expressions of concern, and all of it was directed at her. It made her want to laugh and cry at the same time.

"You can both stop looking at me like that," she finally managed to say, her voice punctuated by a few more heavy breaths. "I'm more than aware that I'm a little out of shape."

Remo chuckled. "Might have something to do with your short legs."

Celia shook her head. "I'm not short. You're tall."

Her son dropped Remo's hand, stepped closer, and eyed

her lower half with a serious expression on his face. "I dunno, Mom."

"Great," she replied, straightening up and reaching out to ruffle his hair. "You're *both* working against me?"

"I don't know about *this* dude," Remo said, with a wink and nod toward Xavier, "but I'm definitely Team Celia."

Xavier's eyes flicked from her to Remo. "I'm Team Celia!"

Then he winked, too, and Celia pressed her lips together to keep from laughing.

"Even though I have short legs?" she teased.

"Yes," Xavier told her with a giggle.

The joyful sound was at complete odds with everything going on, and it filled Celia's heart. She ran her fingers over her son's mess of hair again, then tugged him to her side and lifted her eyes to Remo's face. She hoped he could see the gratitude in her gaze. That he could feel how much it meant to her that Xavier could still laugh, even when faced with such an adverse situation.

The big man's mouth curved up into a half smile, and he dropped another wink. But this one wasn't jovial or conspiratorial. It was just for her. An expression of the fact that he *did* understand, and that he was keeping the mood up for Xavier's sake. Celia's insides warmed. She was suddenly sure that there was nothing sexier than a man who would put the needs of her child over all else. If she'd had any doubt before, it was gone now. She most definitely wanted the kind, sexy hero of a man. Even standing the way they were—five feet apart, not touching, just staring—sent the temperature up a few degrees. And somewhat ironically, if the child in question hadn't been there right then, she probably would've dragged Remo off somewhere to show him just how he made her feel.

Then, as if to remind her solidly that he *was* there, Xavier spoke up. "Where are we going now?"

Celia had to expel a breath before she could answer. "I'm not sure. Maybe the captain of Team Celia has an idea?"

Remo aimed his smile at her son. "How do you feel about buses?"

"The yellow kind or the other kind?"

"The other kind."

"They're okay."

"Only 'okay'?" Remo replied. "What about hotels? And don't you dare ask me if I mean yellow ones."

Xavier wrinkled his nose. "They don't make yellow hotels."

"You sure?" Remo teased.

"Yes," her son said firmly, then added, "But I like the not-yellow kind. We stayed in one when the taps exploded and made the house smelly."

"Ah, yes. Hotels are better than smelly houses." He bent down. "How do you think you'd feel about a bus that *takes* us to a hotel?"

Celia saw the little bounce her son did before offering a too-cool shrug and saying, "That sounds okay."

Once again, she wanted to laugh. She knew just how much better than "okay" everything about the suggestions were to Xavier. She'd once heard him tell a classmate that the three nights they'd spent in the hotel were the best days of his life. He'd also asked her if they might one day be rich enough to *live* in a hotel.

She aimed a smile at Remo. "I think a bus ride to a hotel sounds fun. But maybe that's just me."

The big man smiled back. "That settles it then. Team Celia is all-in. I'm just going to give a friend a call, then we'll find a bus stop and get going."

"Sure," she said, but as he pulled his phone from his pocket, worry pricked at her. "Could someone track your phone?"

"I keep my GPS off," he assured her.

"The police don't have a way around that?"

"Possibly. But we're talking about police who are doing decidedly *un*-police-like things. They can't exactly use official channels."

"Still…"

"Let me make this one call, then I'll grab a disposable cell from the first corner store we find, okay? I'll only be a sec, all right?"

"Okay."

She waited until he'd moved a few feet away and pulled his phone from his pocket before she turned her attention to Xavier.

"You hanging in there, bud?" she asked.

He nodded, then let out one of his familiar, grown-up-sounding sighs. "I'm good, Mom."

"But?"

"I was having fun on the trampoline. And Danny's mom was going to give us some juice."

Celia's throat burned. They were on a run for their lives—and she knew beyond any doubt that it had to scare her son, too—yet the only thing he complained about was that his playtime was cut short. And his next words moved the ache from her throat to her chest.

"When we're all done running away can we get a trampoline, too?" he asked. "I think one would fit in the park outside. Maybe."

Celia swallowed. "You mean in that grassy space between the swings and the sandbox?"

"Yeah!" His enthusiasm was almost heartbreaking. "Then *everyone* could use it. Even Mrs. Lutz."

This time, she couldn't contain her laugh. Michelle Lutz was the eighty-year-old woman who lived in the ground-floor apartment below them.

"That's very generous of you," Celia told him.

He fixed her with a suspicious look. "Are you making fun of me? Because I mean when Mrs. Lutz's hip gets better."

She used her hand to swipe away her immediate chuckle, and replied, "Do I ever make fun of you, my little love?"

He seemed to give it serious consideration before answering. "No."

"So there you go."

"But you don't want a trampoline?"

Celia opted for the truth, as she preferred to do whenever possible. "I would *love* a trampoline. With safety nets. And some cushions, probably. But I'm just not sure it's possible to have one set up in a common area like that."

"Oh."

"But you know you're my favorite thing ever, right? And if it was up to *me*, Mrs. Lutz and I would be bouncing on that trampoline tonight."

"Yeah."

"*Ever* ever." She bent down, kissed his head, then pulled him into a bear hug and whispered, "Ever, ever, *ever*-ever."

"Mom…!" he groaned, wriggling free just as Remo stepped back in their direction.

"Did I miss anything good?" the big man asked. "Or are we ready to go?"

"We're ready," Xavier said, so quickly that Celia had to stifle yet another laugh.

Remo lifted an eyebrow, clearly noticing her son's

haste, but he did a better job of keeping a straight face than she had done.

"Glad to hear it," he said. "My other good buddy booked us into a hotel. Under his name, just to be safe. I checked the transit website on my phone, too, and it says if we walk up a block and take the path, we can hop on a bus that'll take us right there. And if no one minds… I'm starving and would love to hurry and get some room service."

"Yay!" Xavier said. "Can we have pizza?"

"Mom's the boss," Remo replied. "But I just so happen to *love* pepperoni."

"That's our favorite, too. Right, Mom?"

"A hundred percent," Celia agreed.

Xavier's excitement was obvious in the bounce in his step as they started their walk, but after a few moments, he spoke again, his little voice serious. "Remo?"

"Yeah, bud?"

"Do *you* have a house?"

"I do."

"Is it big or small?"

Celia frowned, but Remo answered before she could get out a gentle admonishment about politeness.

"It's a pretty decent size," he told her son. "Two floors. Three bedrooms. Three bathrooms. And a pretty awesome place to hang out, if I do say so myself."

"What about the backyard?" Xavier asked, and Celia suppressed a groan as she realized where he was leading.

"The backyard?" Remo echoed. "Well, let me see. I've got a garden because I like to grow my own tomatoes. And I've been thinking about adding a gazebo because I want somewhere to sit on hot summer nights. So, yeah. It's not too small."

"Would it fit a trampoline?"

"Yeah, I think it would, buddy."

"Good."

As soon as he said it, Xavier slipped his hand into hers, then reached out and took Remo's, too. And it was strange. Because in spite of what they'd been through in the last day, Celia had never felt more content or complete than she did in right that moment.

Except for the kid pointing out the odd phenomena he spied through the window—a house with a slide at the front in lieu of steps, a porch crowded with a dozen cats, the big bridge that took them over the Fraser River and out into the suburbs, and a dozen other things—the bus ride was quiet. Remo wasn't sure whether he preferred it that way, or if he'd rather have had a little more adult conversation. He'd left out a small detail when telling Celia and her son about the plans he'd made. In addition to calling his friend, he'd tried to call his mom. It was a little risky, but he'd made sure to block his number before dialing. But the phone had rung only once on the other end before abruptly kicking over to voice mail.

Remo's first thought was a bit of a panicked one—that the corrupt cops had her and had the phone, and were deliberately intercepting the call. After the briefest consideration, though, he realized that if the cops had the phone, they would've answered. Or made her answer. From that, he concluded his mom had ended the call herself. Probably tapped the button the moment it rang in order to stop anyone else from hearing it.

But did *they hear it?*

He strummed his fingers nervously on his thigh. His knee-jerk reaction was to call back right away, but he'd resisted the urge. If they *hadn't* heard the phone, he didn't want them to. And if they *had* already, then he didn't want to give them the chance to pick up and make any threats or use his mom as leverage. So he held off. But he knew he wouldn't manage to much longer. He *needed* to know that she was all right. The moment he had Celia and Xavier safely settled at the hotel, he'd slip away and call again. Pretend to be somebody else if he had to. Whatever it took.

That doesn't mean I'm happy about it.

Unconscious that he was doing it until his fingernails dug too hard into his palm, Remo clenched his hand into a fist. When he realized it, he forced his hand to open again and took a few breaths. He wasn't typically an angry man, but a situation like this one, where the people he cared about were in danger, did make him mad. If he could have, he would've hopped off the bus somewhere around City Hall, stalked up to Neil Price and demanded to know just who the hell he thought he was. Threatening the lives of innocent women and children. Killing hospital orderlies as a matter of collateral damage. And for what? His hand started to curl again, but Celia's fingers closed overtop of his, then threaded between them.

"Whatever was happening before with his dad..." she said, her voice too low to carry any farther than his ears, "I wouldn't trade it away if it meant I couldn't have my son anymore."

Remo's instinct was to argue. To say that it didn't have to be one way or the other. His words stalled, though, when he looked down at their clasped hands. He lifted his gaze and tried again, but this time Xavier caught his eye. The little guy was in the bench seat across from them, his hands pressed to the window, a delighted smile turning up his mouth as the scenery flashed by. It filled Remo's heart in a way he'd never experienced, and he realized that Celia was right. Sometimes, something good came out of the worst situation. He wouldn't wish one like hers on anyone, but he also wouldn't undo it if it meant never meeting her and her son.

He dragged his thumb back and forth over her hand. "I want to fix this mess."

She leaned against his shoulder. "Your mom did say you have a bit of a hero complex."

He smiled and rested his chin on the top of her head. "She took the time to tell you that, hmm? Does that mean you're worried that I'm just helping you to satisfy that hero complex?"

"No."

"No?"

"No. Because your mom *also* told me that you don't share your secrets."

"But I shared them with you."

"Exactly." She tipped her face up, smiling.

He laughed at her cheeky expression, then started to kiss her, before remembering that they had a five-year-old audience, and instead settled for running his knuckles over her cheek.

"Just in case you *were* worried," he said softly, "this time, my hero complex is personal."

Her smile widened and softened at the same time, and her gray eyes pulled him in and held him the way they had every time she looked at him since the second they'd met. Warmth filled his chest again. Only now it was all about her. The soft skin under his touch. The way she needed his help right then, but had made it through the last five years on her own. Her curves and her lips.

Her lips.

Remo inched forward, knowing that if he didn't find a way to distract himself, he might not be able to pull away. Who had that kind of willpower? And what harm would one small kiss do, no matter who could see? Thankfully—or maybe *not* so thankfully, if he was being honest—Xavier picked that moment to let out an excited exclamation.

"There's a castle, you guys!" he almost yelled. "Mom, Mom. Look. Remo! *Look*."

Remo leaned away from Celia and brought his attention to the window, knowing already what he'd find.

"I see it, buddy," he said.

It would've been impossible to miss. The four spire-like corners of the building pointed up to the sky, a Canadian flag flicked cheerfully atop the nearest one, and a big sign welcomed people to Ye Old Medieval Inn. There was no denying that it looked out of place. It was a monstrosity that stuck up over the horizon. And it would be even *more* conspicuous once they got closer, because it was sandwiched between a gas station and a little house that belonged to a man who refused to sell and let his land be turned into commercial property.

Celia turned a twitching mouth Remo's way. "A castle."

He kept a straight face as he shrugged. "An inn."

"I suppose it was the only hotel option."

"The only one that has suits of armor guarding the lobby, serves root beer in wooden chalices at its restaurant *and* has free movie channels."

"Of course it is. Do you think they know 'medieval' makes the 'old' kind of redundant?"

He laughed, then sat back to watch Xavier's eyes go wide as the bus slowed, then wound its way up the ramp, bringing them closer to the oversize structure.

"Is it *our* hotel?" the kid finally asked, as they turned up the street toward the inn.

Remo reached over Celia's head to press the stop signal. "*May*be."

Xavier practically flew from his seat to throw himself

at Remo, his skinny little arms flinging around his neck and squeezing.

"Oh, sure," said Celia. "You'll let *him* hug you."

"It's a *castle*, Mom," Xavier replied, disentangling himself just as the bus chugged to a stop.

"And it's *awesome*," Remo added. "You'll see."

Celia rolled her pretty gray eyes, but when they'd finished with their quick stop at the neighboring gas station to grab the disposable phone he'd promised—paying cash, just to be sure—and made their way to the lobby, she was clearly not immune to the deliberate splendor of the hotel, either. She paused to look around. And he didn't blame her. Though the hotel really *was* old—it'd been around for a couple decades before Remo was even born—it was well-kept, and its medieval vibe was on point. Swords and flags hung from the walls. No less than six full suits of armor guarded the space. The young guy behind the counter who checked them in even handed over an old-fashioned, iron-heavy key.

"You've really never been here?" Remo asked Celia as they made their way to their assigned room.

"I didn't even know it *existed*," she told him. "Unless my memory blocked this out, too."

"No way," he replied. "This would be the first thing you remembered."

She laughed, and her hand found his, her palm meeting his in that meant-to-be way that he liked so much. He couldn't help eyeing Xavier. The kid was running ahead, stopping at each new decoration to admire it, then running ahead again.

"Do you think this is okay with him?" Remo asked, giving her fingers a squeeze.

"The hand-holding?" she replied.

"His *mom* hand-holding. With a stranger."

"You brought him to a castle. I think you should be more worried about whether or not he's going to demote *me* to the role of stranger."

He gave her shoulder a nudge. "I'm serious."

She sighed. "I know. It's just that I'm not sure what the answer is. I don't date, so I don't have a quick comparison. But if I had to reason through it, I'd say that if I *was* going to bring a man into Xavier's life, I'd wait until I was sure it had the potential to be serious. Then ease into an introduction. Maybe a visit to the park. A dinner. Then get a feel for his thoughts before jumping into the PDA. I think maybe that's single mom 101. But since none of it applies, I don't have any idea what I should do."

"Hmm."

"What?"

"*One* of those things applies," he said.

She turned her head and frowned. "Which one?"

"I most definitely have the potential to be serious."

Chapter 17

As Celia got Xavier settled on the couch with cartoons and a package of complimentary cookies, Remo set up a much-needed pot of coffee, then slipped to the bedroom—another perk of Ye Old Medieval Inn was that every unit was a suite—to try his mom again. He took the new phone from its package, booted it up quickly, then dialed. This time, the call didn't go to voice mail. But his mom's greeting was nowhere near its usual cheerful self.

"Wendy DeLuca speaking," she said, her voice curt.

Relief hit Remo in the gut, so hard that he had to sit down. He hadn't realized how truly worried he was until right that second. He didn't get a chance to respond and tell her, though, before she spoke again.

"Oh!" she said. "Scotty Armitage. Is that you?"

Surprised, Remo answered carefully. "Yes. It's me."

Scotty Armitage had been his best friend in high school, and had moved to Toronto right after graduation.

His mom let out the smallest of breaths. He knew she'd recognized his voice.

"Not that it's not nice to hear from you," she said. "I just wasn't expecting it. But I guess you've been watching the news, like everyone else."

"A little," Remo replied cautiously.

"Well, yes. And before you ask, what you saw is true. The police *are* looking for Remo."

"Are they." His words came out flatly—an unimpressed statement rather than a question—but his throat was tightening with concern.

"That's right," his mom said. "So if he calls, please, please ask him to do the right thing."

"I will."

"Thanks, Scotty. I can't say much else about it."

"I understand."

"Talk to you soon."

Remo dropped his hand to his lap and stared down at the phone. Obviously, someone—undoubtedly the same men who'd been there when they'd made their escape—had been listening in on her end. Equally obviously, they were using his mom to find *him*. It meant her life wasn't directly in danger, and that was a good thing. The comment about watching the news, though…that worried him.

Eyeing the TV that sat atop the dresser, he stood up, then moved over to it and flicked it on. He didn't have to try hard—or at all, really—to find what he was looking for. The screen zapped to life, and his own image immediately filled it. An unseen female broadcaster spoke overtop of it.

"…and later died in hospital. Now, in connection with the fatal hit-and-run, police are seeking *this* man, Remo DeLuca. He's described as six foot four, a hundred and ninety pounds, with dark hair and blue eyes. And now we go to our on-scene correspondent."

With dread building in his gut, Remo watched as the news channel cut to a live feed of two men standing in front of the hospital. One was obviously the reporter, microphone in hand. The other was someone Remo knew just enough to make him grit his teeth.

"Thanks, Carrie," said the reporter to the disembodied broadcaster. "I'm here with paramedic Isaac White, who both attended the victim and works with the alleged perpetrator. What can you tell us about the situation, Mr. White?"

Remo gritted his teeth even harder as his coworker opened his mouth. He knew the man had likely been selected by the board to give a statement. Isaac's penchant for following rules often made him the "correct" choice for representing the everyday hospital worker. He was also sure he wouldn't like what his fellow EMT would have to say. Sure enough, his little speech didn't disappoint. Isaac described Remo's presence at the car accident as a "weird coincidence," and also gave a nice outline of Remo's lack of ability to play by the rules. He described the whole thing as tragic. His words were matter-of-fact and disappointed rather than accusatory, and no one but Remo himself would know the whole thing was a dig.

"Thank you very much, Mr. White," said the reporter. "Back to you, Carrie."

Now an overhead picture of the car accident took the place of the hospital exterior, and the unseen woman spoke a little more, describing the probable sequence of events. Remo stared at the screen, his fists clenched. The horrific pieces of Celia's shattered car were on display. So was his own vehicle, fully intact, set at a strange angle, with skid marks trailing out behind it.

As the announcer again said how tragic the loss of life was, and asked for anyone with information regarding Mr. DeLuca's whereabouts to call the tip line, Remo reached over to turn the TV off. As he did, a little gasp cut through the air. He turned and found Celia standing in the doorway, her horrified gaze fixed on the now-silent television.

"They think I'm dead," she said, stepping into the room. "And they think *you* did it. They think you forced me off the road."

"They do," he agreed grimly.

"What about Xavier?" she asked.

"No mention."

"What does that mean?"

"It could mean the so-called cops are keeping it quiet." He shook his head, not really wanting to say what his thoughts were.

She came to her own conclusion, anyway. "They don't *want* anyone to know about him, because that way his father can just..." She swallowed, panic filling her eyes. "We have to go. We have to hide better. People know we're here. Your friend. And if someone saw you and saw the news...oh, God. The front desk guy. Or the bus driver."

She turned back to the door, but Remo quickly put his hand on her arm. "Wait, Celia. They're telling people you're dead. Think about that. It means they're going to make sure you are. That they're confident they *can* make it happen."

"I'm not just going to sit around, waiting to let them do it."

"I wouldn't ask you to. But I think we're safe here for the moment. The front desk guy was more interested in his phone than he was in us, and if anyone asked, he'd probably describe us as a family. That's not who they're looking for."

She didn't let it go. "What about everyone else who saw us at the hospital? Any one of them could turn you in."

He slid his fingers to her palm and gripped it reassuringly. "They won't."

She opened her mouth, closed it again, then sank down onto the bed, still holding his hand. After a moment, he joined her. He didn't mention his concern for the lives of the people who were aware of Xavier. He knew she'd figure it out on her own, but he didn't want to add guilt to her already heavy burden.

"We're stuck, aren't we?" she finally said.

"A little," he admitted. "But that doesn't mean we can't keep figuring things out."

"How?"

"Technology." He nodded toward the TV. "That thing's equipped with the internet. We'll look you up. We'll dig a little more about Neil Price. We're not going to give up just because we're backed into a corner."

Her eyes came up. "You know…before you came along, I was taking care of us on my own."

He touched her cheek. "I know you were. If I'm trying to do too much or stepping on your toes…"

"No. It's not that."

"What, then?"

"I just can't imagine doing it without you now."

He offered her a little smile. "The beauty of it is that you don't have to."

"It's crazy, though, isn't it?" she asked.

"Maybe."

"Maybe? You're not going to tell me it's *not* crazy? Maybe try to argue that it's normal?"

"Normal and crazy aren't mutually exclusive."

"They're not?"

"Not when you're talking about falling in love."

"Is that what this is?"

"That's what I want it to be. In spite of the crazy. Or maybe because of it? I don't know. But since the second I found you on the side of the road, my whole life has been flipped over."

"That was only yesterday," she reminded him.

His smile widened. "Okay. Crazy it is, then."

"Remo." She brought her hand to the back of his neck and tipped up her face, expectation and desire clear in her eyes.

Remo dipped his mouth and gave her the lightest dusting of a kiss before pulling back and murmuring, "Xavier?"

She brought her mouth up and ran her tongue over the edge of his lower lip. "Sound asleep. And once he's out…he's out."

It was all Remo needed to hear. He jumped up, padded silently across the floor to lock the door, then turned back to Celia and took her in his arms.

Falling in love.

The phrase ran through Celia's mind, again and again. Like a song stuck on Repeat. Only the song was somehow both brand-new and her favorite at the same time. And she never wanted it to stop.

Falling in love.

As they peeled off each other's clothes.

Falling in love.

As they kissed—hard and soft, and everything in between. As they murmured about risk and life being short.

Falling in love.

As they gave in to recklessness and quickness for the sake of not losing the chance. As he filled her, physically and emotionally. As she bit back a need to call out his name at full volume, and settled for a whisper instead. And as they collapsed onto the bed together, breathing heavily and laughing a little. And finally, as he propped himself up on one elbow and stared down at her, his eyes shining with warmth.

Falling in love.

It was crazy and unrealistic and utterly true at the same time. If Celia could have formed a coherent sentence, she would've told Remo as much. But instead she had to settle for simply watching him as he watched her. And it was he who spoke first—not breaking the spell, but just putting it on hold.

"I think I've found my new favorite way to spend the afternoon," he teased, running his fingers over her arm in a way that warmed her and made her shiver at the same time. "But…"

She sighed. "But with less bad guys, cops, and newscasters hunting us down?"

"Yes. All of that. So…we should probably put on some pants."

"Okay. But for the record? At this exact moment, I *hate* pants."

He laughed, low and sexy, then lightly kissed her mouth. "Same. And I'd gladly dive into the research rabbit hole without them, but there's a little boy on the other side of the door who *might* have some questions if he knocks and we answer in a pants-less state."

"Right," Celia said, pulling the sheet to her chin and studying the long, muscular lines of Remo's back as he sat up, then bent over and snagged his clothes from the floor. "Remo…"

"Yeah, sweetheart?"

"Should I feel bad?"

"About what?" He cast a little frown over his shoulder, then stuck his feet into his boxers, stood up, and pulled.

"Xavier."

"Why would you feel bad about Xavier?"

She gave him a look, and he flopped back onto the bed beside her, shirtless and so breathtaking that she almost forget her worries. Again.

"Which part are you feeling bad about?" he asked. "What we just did? What's happening between us in general? Mom-guilt over starting a relationship without discussing it with your son?"

"Yes to all of that," she replied, then shook her head. "But I *don't* feel bad. Well. Except for feeling bad about not feeling bad."

He chuckled. "I can't argue with you about it. I feel too damned *good* myself."

She gave him a lighthearted swat. "I mean emotionally bad."

His face abruptly turned serious, and so did his tone. "So do I, Celia. You know that, right? I don't want some quick fix. Or something that's going to end before it can even really get started. And if having your son in the other room made you uncomfortable in any way—"

"No, it's not that." She paused. "I mean, yes. It *is* that. But I don't have any regrets. And if someone asked me to go back in time to an hour ago, I'd make the same choice. I just… I don't know. How can something so fresh already feel so permanent? How come I think that if I were to walk out there, wake up my kid, and tell him that you—a man we both only just met—are now my boyfriend, he'd just give me one of his 'no duh, Mom' looks and ask when the pizza's coming?"

Remo's oh-so-blue eyes brightened, and he leaned over and gave her a slow, heated kiss, then pulled back and said,

"I'm going to assume that it's because your son is a genius who knows when something is meant to be."

"Very funny," Celia responded breathlessly.

"Oh, I'm deadly serious," he said. "That doesn't mean we can't take things as slow as you want. Tell him whatever you think he needs to be told, whenever you think is the right time." He kissed her once more, then swung his legs to the side and sat up again. "But right now, I'm going to order room service, then indulge in some cyber stalking. Care to join me?"

"I'm starving. And Xavier will be, too, when he wakes up."

"Perfect," Remo said, tugging his shirt over his head. "How about you boot up the TV while I get room service?"

"Sure. Sounds good."

She watched him tiptoe toward the door, then open it in practiced silence. She stared after him for a second, held captive by her own overwhelming feelings.

Falling in love.

As the thought came back again, even more forceful now than it had been before, a pleasant blush crept up her cheeks, and she had to tamp down an urge to wake up her son right then and there to tell him that Remo De-Luca was going to be a big part of their lives. She forced out a breath and distracted herself by hastily tossing on her own clothes, then grabbing the remote and flicking through until she found the internet search option. Unsure where to start, she opted for punching in her own name. It didn't surprise her when nothing familiar popped up. She was sure she wouldn't have put her and Xavier in danger by creating a traceable presence online. But she scrolled through the list anyway, searching for anything that popped out. She obviously shared the name with a few others—a number of social media profiles showed the other Celia Pollers around the globe—but there was nothing of note on the first or second page of search results. On the third one, though, a listing did catch her eye.

"'Celia Poller,'" she read aloud. "'Graduate of the Home Care Attendant Program at Vancouver Medical Career Center.'"

She clicked, and a whole row of photos filled the TV screen, her own included. Beside each was a year, a name, and a program major. There was no other information. No address, no phone number, no catchy quote. But it was a relief to know that she'd been right about what she did for a living.

"Now if only I knew how that connected to Xavier's dad," she murmured, scrolling through the other names and pictures slowly, and sighing when once again nothing looked at all familiar.

Remo stepped back into the room then, speaking in a low voice as he shut the door. "Kid's still asleep. But I ordered his pepperoni pizza anyway. And garlic bread. And wings. Possibly a salad and a lasagna. I *might* be hungry." He eyed the TV. "You find something?"

"Nothing big," she said. "It's just a list of everyone who finished school at the same time as I did."

"But that's still something." Remo joined her on the edge of the bed. "Can I see the remote?"

She shrugged and handed it over, and a second later, he'd clicked quickly through to another screen. It was pictureless, but full of names and email addresses. Another scroll, and Celia's own name was highlighted beside one of them—ccpoller@VMCC.edu, it read. Remo tapped it with the pointer, clicked, and a new window prompted the user to enter the password associated with the email address.

Remo turned her way. "Well?"

Celia shook her head. "I don't..."

She trailed off. Because suddenly she *did*. She knew. It wasn't the email she used in her daily life, but it was an email she'd used in the past. For school. For making work contacts. And for Neil Price.

She held out her hand, and when Remo placed the remote in her palm, she quickly tapped in the password, and up came the proof. The emails were all at least six years old, and Neil's name was in the From box of every one of them.

"I'll be damned," said Remo.

Celia laughed a little nervously. "Do I want you to see these?"

He met her eyes. "Can't say I'm *excited* to read love notes from him, but I'm a grown man. I can handle it."

But his possible jealousy and Celia's own worry were both unfounded, anyway. As she opened the first email on the list, it brought up a thread of back and forth messages, all related to a job. They scanned the notes together in silence—all nineteen of them, and when they were done, it was Remo who spoke first.

"So you met because you took care of his uncle," he said.

Celia nodded, wishing it was memory rather than just a logical conclusion. "At least we know I'm not making it up. Or completely insane."

He put his warm hand on her knee. "We already knew that."

"Did we?" She meant it to be a joke, but it came laced with bitterness, and she gestured toward the screen. "Shouldn't this jog *something* for me? Anything?"

"It'd be helpful if it did," Remo admitted. "But we'll just keep working with what we've got."

"You're maddeningly positive, aren't you?"

"No one likes a doomsday paramedic."

She made a face, then moved to click the email account shut. Except as she did, a line in one of the correspondences made her pause.

Great, it read. I'll get you the direct deposit information tomorrow.

That was it. Nothing huge. But it prompted her into autopilot mode. First she closed the email server. Then she opened a new browser window and typed in "West End Savings." The link to the credit union website appeared right away, and she selected the customer log-in option from one of the drop-down menus. Vaguely, she heard Remo ask what she was up to, but she ignored him in favor of typing in a user name and password that she didn't even know she knew until right then. As soon as she hit Enter an account came to life.

Available Balance: $213,475.23

As she stared at the number—an amount of money that she was a hundred percent sure she could only dream of having—a curtain lifted in Celia's mind.

She could see herself entering the bank with Detective Teller at her side. She could hear his dark-edged voice, instructing her, and she could feel her own fear as she approached the counter and made an unusually large deposit—far, far, *far* more than what her pay would typically look like.

Suddenly light-headed, Celia felt herself sway. The TV remote slipped from her fingers. Remo's hand shot out, and somewhere in the periphery of Celia's mind, she thought he was going to reach out just in time to catch it before it hit the ground. Instead, his palm found her shoulder. And it was a good thing, too. As the remote thumped against the carpet, Remo's strong grip was the only thing that kept her from actually keeling over.

Because it wasn't just the money she remembered. It was what it was for.

Chapter 18

Remo had never so thoroughly understood the term "as white as a sheet" as he did in that moment. Even Celia's freckles had paled into oblivion. Her already slightly translucent eyes had somehow managed to fade, too, their gray tone becoming washed out. She was so still and so silent that only the flutter of her eyelids gave away any sign of life.

"Celia," he said gently.

The prod got no response, and he realized her chest wasn't rising and falling as it should be. Worry sliced through him, and he slid his hand down her shoulder to her elbow and tried again.

"Hey," he said a little more urgently. "You need to breathe, sweetheart."

She didn't move, and his concern deepened, adding medical worry alongside his personal one.

"C'mon, Celia. Take a deep breath for me."

She blinked. Once. Then she finally drew in a shuddering gasp. But she held it, her chest high, her eyes a little too wide.

"Now let it out," Remo added.

On command, she forced out the exhale.

"Again," Remo said.

It took three more breaths in and out before Celia started doing it without his cues. She was still quivering a bit, and she was gripping his arm so tightly that it was probably going to leave a mark, but the color was coming back to her cheeks. And when she blinked this time, he could tell that she was back in the moment.

"Better?" he asked.

She nodded, then looked down at her fingers on his arm and cringed. "Sorry," she said, peeling them off.

"I can take it," he told her lightly. "I was once putting a blood pressure cuff on a lovely older lady and she hit me with a cane."

"Really?" she replied.

He smiled. "Nah. Just trying to make you feel better about mauling me."

In spite of the way she was still shaking a bit, she laughed. "You're terrible."

"Worked, though, didn't it?"

"A little."

He nodded toward the TV. "I take it you weren't expecting to find that there."

She rolled her shoulders like she was trying to work out a kink. "Actually, I kind of *was*. At least as soon as I started typing in the password, I was."

"You wanna talk about it?"

"No. But I guess I have to, don't I?"

"Keeping it a secret *probably* won't help us move forward."

She closed her eyes and took another breath, then exhaled it, too. "I don't remember why Neil hit me the first time. That side of thing still feels…vague. But what I *do* remember is that I thought Teller was one of the good guys. I was under police protection. Or I thought I was. And he was assigned to keep me safe. But instead, he dragged me to that bank, and he told me that if I didn't 'take care of the problem,' then he would take care of me."

Her words hit Remo with a sudden punched-in-the-gut feeling. He understood why the memory had made her react the way she did.

"They wanted you to terminate the pregnancy," he said, and saying it aloud just gave him more of a chill.

"That money was a payoff to do it," she added softly. "And I took it."

"You took it, but you obviously didn't touch it," he reminded her. "It's still in the account."

"Plus interest." She smiled wryly for a moment before her mouth drooped again. "I wasn't very far along then, but I was already completely in love with the idea of becoming a mom. Ending the pregnancy was never a consideration."

Remo brought his arm up and dragged her closer, then ran his hand over her back in small, soothing circles.

"You don't owe me an explanation," he said.

She sighed. "I know. I just wish I remember *why* I took the money, or what I was planning. There has to have been something. And I can still hear Teller, whispering in my ear while I waited with the check. He told me that if I thought about reneging on the deal, no one would believe a word that came out of my mouth once they saw that money in my account, and that if I tried to take Neil down, I'd suffer more."

"That could be helpful, though."

"How?"

"Because it means that somewhere in your head, you know of a way to take down Neil Price. All we have to do is keep working to figure out what that is."

She was silent for a few moments, then spoke quietly into his chest. "I think I should go there."

He stopped making the circles on her back. "Go where?"

"To the bank. West End Savings."

"That's a bad idea, Celia."

She pulled back and looked up at him. "Why? It's the next logical step, isn't it? Someone there might recognize me. Or remember the transaction. Or point us in the right direction."

"Or someone there might be working with Teller and Price."

"We can't know that."

"Exactly."

"You know what I mean, Remo," she grumbled.

"I do," he agreed. "And you know what *I* mean."

"That doesn't make you right," she replied.

"Are we having our first fight?" he asked.

"There's no fight," she said firmly.

"Because you're going to insist that we go, or because you're agreeing with me?"

She opened her mouth, but a tap on the door stopped her from answering.

"Mom?" said Xavier from the other side. "Someone's out there, and he smells like pizza."

"I think that's our cue," Celia said. "I should probably answer, just to make sure he doesn't recognize you from the news or something."

She jumped up, while Remo stayed in place, watching as she smiled a little too brightly, then quickly opened the door and greeted her son. There was no doubt in his mind that she was in a little too much of a hurry. He tried to brush off the worry, and for a little while, it worked. Mostly because he didn't have time to think about it. Between the pizza and a kid-friendly movie, then a hotel-supplied board game and a pillow fort and some more pizza, his mind and hands were occupied. They couldn't very well talk about things in detail with Xavier's little ears in range, so the conversation was as much of a distraction as everything else. And it was actually nice to sit and talk about less intense things.

Remo liked hearing about Celia and Xavier's life. He enjoyed the little game they created, comparing the things they had in common and contrasting the things that made them different. There was the fact that all three of them loved waterslides and cheese, and that none of them had been to Disneyland. And of course, the pepperoni pizza was a given. There was the fact that in spite of his job, gore in movies made him queasy, while Celia loved anything in the horror genre. Xavier put in his bid for "funny movies about dogs or monkeys," and they all laughed. The more they talked, the more Remo *wanted* to talk. The more he wanted to see the glow-in-the-dark stickers on Xavier's ceiling. The more he wanted to carve out a permanent place in their lives and the less he thought about Celia and the bank.

Even when the day wore into evening, and Xavier started yawning and asking for warm milk and saying on repeat that he wasn't tired, and Celia scooped her son off for a bath, Remo's earlier concerns didn't quite worm their way back in. He was too busy focusing on the needs of the moment. He dragged fresh sheets from the closet and changed the bed linen for Celia and Xavier, then made up the pull-out couch for himself. He helped settle the kid into the big bed, indulged in the request for a made-up story, and promised not to leave until Xavier had fallen asleep.

It wasn't until his own exhaustion pulled at him, and he started to drift into sleep himself—still tucked in between Celia and Xavier—that his mind at last poked at him and asked if he was still worried that she was going to push harder about going to the bank.

I am, he acknowledged sleepily, *but it can wait until morning.*

In the end, though, the morning turned out to be a little too late. Because when Remo woke from a dead sleep several hours later, he and Xavier were alone. Celia's spot was empty except for a note.

Sorry, it read in flowing handwriting. *I know you're going to be mad. But I know you'd probably have succeeded in talking me out of going, too. So...forgiveness instead of permission, right? Keep an eye on Xavier, and I'll be back soon. XXOO. C.*

Remo's instinct was to chase after her. To run down to the concierge and ask how long ago she'd passed by. But he couldn't. Not only did he risk getting recognized, but Celia had also made him responsible for her son. He was trapped, and there wasn't a thing he could do about it.

It wasn't until Celia actually climbed out of the taxi—after murmuring to the driver that he could just circle the block and come back for her—and spied her destination that the first lick of trepidation crept in. Until that moment, she'd somehow managed to convince herself that she was doing what needed to be done. But as she drew in a slightly acrid, city-tinged breath, doubt and fear tried to sweep away the resolve she'd come in with.

You can do this, she said to herself.

But instead of agreeing with the self-directed statement and stepping forward, she bit her lip, stayed planted to the spot, and asked herself if she'd completely lost it. Her mind slid back over the last forty minutes, trying to pinpoint when, exactly, she'd abandoned all sense.

When she'd first woken up, she'd felt oddly energized. Completely refreshed, and hopeful, too. Then she'd found Remo and Xavier still asleep, and the idea of sneaking away had popped up. It might have even seemed like a good one. So she'd written the note and slipped away without looking back.

Get to the bank as soon as it opened.

Get some answers.

Get back to the hotel room.

That had been the plan.

Maybe the first moment of second thoughts should've come when she stepped into the elevator. Another woman had been standing in the back corner of the small space, and there'd been no escaping the startled look she'd given Celia. Or to be more accurate…the look she gave Celia's *pants*. The same scrubs—complete with now-darkened bloodstain—she'd been wearing since escaping from her hospital room. Definitely out of place, and far too attention grabbing.

Yeah…that probably should've been enough to make you realize this was a bad idea, she thought, shifting from foot to foot.

But it hadn't been. Instead of taking it as a hint to turn around, she'd simply found a way to fix the issue. She'd made her way to the store attached to the lobby— Ye Old Gift Shop read the sign over the door—where she'd grabbed a pair of sweatpants embossed with a line of swords down own leg and a T-shirt with a shield decal across the chest. She put them on in the change room, tore off the tags, and made her way up to the till.

Then came what Celia now suspected should've been
the second red flag. The moment she realized she had no
means of paying. But being as determined as she was,
she'd found a way around that, too—by charging the purchase to their room. A tickle of guilt *had* reared its head
just then, but she'd simply told herself she would pay Remo
back as soon as they were out of the current situation. And
the next moment supplied an opposing sign, anyway. Attached to the cashier counter hung a little flyer that ad-
vertised a pay-by-room taxi service.

Celia took immediate advantage of the offer. And on
the ride over, she hadn't felt overwhelmed or scared. Just
anticipatory. So she wasn't sure why the change of heart
wanted to come *now*.

Maybe it was just the way the concrete structure
loomed up in front of her, its tall, tinted glass doors intimidatingly opaque. Or maybe it was how she could recall the way Detective Teller's hand had felt on her back
as he forced her to walk through those same doors. Or it
could've just been that reality had caught up. She was outside. Exposed. Alone. Away from her son. Away from the
only person in the world who she could truly trust. And
she had no idea what she was walking into, and all their
lives were hanging from a very frayed rope.

She almost spun on her heel. But before she could turn,
someone pushed through one of the doors, then held it
open. And the action gave Celia a full view of inside.
What she saw surprised her, even though she knew she'd
been inside before.

It didn't look like a regular bank at all. There were not
roped-off tellers, or advertisements for investments, or
visible ATMs. The decor was both understated and imbued with wealth at the same time. Dark cherry accents.
Mahogany desks. Just a hint of cream.

And suddenly Celia had a feeling that her 200K balance was probably a pittance compared to what the usual clientele brought in. It didn't exactly ease her mind—she was pretty sure Neil Price was a well-to-do man himself—but it did make her curious enough to finally take a step closer. Her forward motion caught the eye of a dark-haired woman standing just inside the door. Celia was surprised to realize that she actually recognized her. And clearly, the familiarity was mutual. The woman's eyes widened, but a moment later, she smiled, then made a "come here" motion with her hand. Celia hesitated for only a second before quickly deciding that if the friendly look on the brunette's face was put on, she was a damned near perfect actress.

And the plan was *to go in, right?*

She took a quick glance around, then lifted her hand in a small wave, and took the steps, two at a time. Walking in was like being sucked into a slightly altered reality. The sounds from outside disappeared, including the siren that had wailed to life just a second earlier. Voices were hushed, the music overhead was barely audible, and a strange, contradictory sense of relaxed busyness hung in the air. Like everyone had something to do, but no one felt harried by that fact. And the quiet wealth became even more obvious. Tailored suits and designer shoes and perfect hair. It overwhelmed Celia, and even if she hadn't been wearing hotel-themed sweats, it still would've made her feel completely out of place. And her discomfit only grew when the dark-haired woman approached and addressed her by name.

"It's Ms. Poller, isn't it?" she said, her voice low and rich and perfectly suited to the atmosphere.

Celia cleared her throat and did her best to sound confident. "Yes, that's me."

The woman let out a small, not-buying-it laugh that

was just muted enough not to carry through the rest of the bank. "Don't worry. I don't expect you to remember me. Putting names together with faces is kind of my superpower. I'm Maxine Maxwell—yes, Max Max, don't ask—safety deposit box supervisor."

"Nice to, uh…remeet you."

"Likewise. Do you have an appointment today, Ms. Poller?"

Celia was sure Maxine already knew the answer before she shook her head. "I'm afraid not."

The brunette didn't miss a beat, and Celia wondered how much of her easy congeniality was built-in, and how much was adapted to deal with finicky clients.

"Well, good news," said the other woman. "No one's in the storage room at the moment, and I can take you right in. I *am* the boss, after all." She let out another of her soft laughs, then gestured toward the other side of the room. "Right this way."

Celia followed nervously, trying not to draw any extra attention. And to the credit of both the bank employees and the customers inside, not one person looked askance at her—or her sore thumb of an outfit—as they made their way past desks and offices and cubicles that somehow passed themselves off as stylish and chic. When they reached a closed door, a suited man with an earpiece offered them a nod, but it was the only acknowledgment they received. Maxine smiled at the man, punched a code into the keypad below the knob, then pressed the door open. She led Celia into a long hall. They passed three more doors before stopping at a fourth, where the brunette held her thumb to a little screen.

"Always makes me feel like I'm doing something top secret," she joked as the screen beeped and lit up with a green glow.

Celia forced a laugh, but her throat was dry. The security *did* reek of something far more than just safely stowed family heirlooms and important documents. And the inside of the small room looked more high-tech than expected, too. Instead of keyed lockboxes—which Celia belatedly realized she wouldn't have been able to access—there were rows of number-controlled safes. It was intense. Almost scary. And when the door shut behind them, Celia nearly jumped.

"Ms. Poller..." said Maxine, her voice abruptly switching from customer-service friendly to something that sounded like genuine concern. "I don't want to overstep, but is everything okay?"

Celia answered carefully. "Is there a reason it wouldn't be?"

"When you came in all those years ago and set up this box, you were scared. You told me that this was your insurance. I didn't know what you meant, but I always assumed it had something to do with that big, mean boyfriend of yours. I offered to help you then, and you said you were preparing for a second-to-worst-case scenario." The other woman paused, then shook her head. "Not a day's gone by that I haven't thought about you and worried a little. Maybe it wasn't as dramatic as I remember. Or maybe I'm out of line, and I should just—"

"No. It's fine. Really. You're not out of line. And I'm okay."

"The offer of help still stands," the other woman stated.

"I appreciate it. Truly. But I think I just need to do what I came to do."

"Okay. Then I'll let you get to it. Box eighty-two. Just in case."

"Thank you," Celia replied.

She waited until the other woman slipped out, then

sagged against the table in the center of the room. Her eyes sank closed. She was sure that when Maxine had said "big, mean boyfriend," she had to have meant Detective Teller. He'd accompanied her to the bank at least the one time. And no way would Neil Price fit the description. Not on the outside, anyway.

"But if I was so scared…" she muttered, opening her eyes again. "Why did I come back and open a safety deposit box? And what did I mean by insurance for a second-to-worst-case scenario?"

She knew she must've been truly beside herself to have told the woman—a stranger—anything at all, let alone something specific like that. For the briefest second, Celia considered calling her back. But as her gaze drifted toward the closed door, it got hung up on the numbered safe fronts instead. *Eighty-two.* It was at eye level, and the same as the rest. Yet somehow it blazed to life for her. Thoughts of asking for Maxine's assistance slid away, and Celia moved to the box instead. In autopilot mode once again, she lifted her hand and dropped her fingers over the keys in a sequence that dredged itself out of somewhere in her foggy memory. As soon as she was done, the four-inch by twelve-inch door let out a pressurized hiss, then clicked partway open. With shaking hands, Celia gave it a soft tug. She was frozen for a moment, just staring at the manila envelope that sat inside the small space.

C'mon, she urged silently. *This is why you came here.*

But the moment her fingers closed on the thick paper, she realized she didn't need to look to know what was inside. Her recollection of its contents was crystal clear.

Chapter 19

The more minutes that ticked by, the more Remo understood why lions paced in their cages. He was doing his damnedest to stay calm—and more importantly not to reveal his concern to Xavier—but it grew harder and harder. His mind kept wandering back to Celia. He itched to get out. To act. To not have to shove room-service waffles into his mouth and pretend they didn't taste like cardboard. There were only so many cartoons and games of I Spy a man could handle when the woman he was falling in love with had thrown away all pretense of safety and disappeared to God knew where.

You know where she is, he said to himself in a silent, futile attempt at reassurance.

It was true. Ish. After finding the note—then crumpling it into a ball and tossing it across the room in a decidedly unsatisfactory fit of worry and frustration—he'd taken the time to do an internet search for the bank. It wasn't far. Nowhere near the West End of Vancouver, as the name implied. Just across the bridge, no more than a twenty-five-minute drive. Presuming traffic was light. And that she *was* traveling by car. Because she could've got back on the bus. She wasn't crazy enough to have attempted the trip on foot? He scrubbed at the two-day-old stubble on his chin, then jerked his head up in surprise when Xavier's voice cut through his worried thoughts.

"Remo?"

He forced a smile. "What's up, kiddo?"

The kid pointed toward the playing-card-riddled table. "Your phone is making a noise."

Remo blinked and turned his attention to the chiming that had blended in with the TV. Frowning, he dragged the device out from under the ace of spades. Sure enough, the screen was flashing with an unknown number. Remo stared for a moment, quickly weighing the options. But really, he didn't have any. His mom was the only person who had the new number for sure, but Celia could very well have taken it with her in case of emergency. He had no choice but to answer it. So he tapped the screen, then lifted the phone to his ear, and waited for someone to greet him. Instead, the sounds of muted conversation immediately carried through. He was a heartbeat away from clicking off before realizing that he actually recognized one of the voices. It was his friend who'd booked the hotel on his behalf. *Freddy Yan.* A moment later, he placed the second voice, too. *Detective Teller.*

Cursing in his head, Remo made a lips-zipped gesture to Xavier—who nodded solemnly—then focused on listening as best he could.

"...that kind of space for a single man?" the corrupt cop was saying right then.

"I'm here, aren't I?" replied Freddy.

"And you lost your key." Even through the fuzzy line, the disbelief in the statement was clear.

"It happens." The shrug in the response was just as obvious.

"Lying and withholding information really aren't in your best interest."

"I'm not withholding anything, and I've been forthcoming about the fact that I only spoke with him once. You looked at my phone yourself."

"I did. Which is how I noted that you conveniently neglected to mention the conversation with his mother and the credit card charge."

"An oversight."

"In the police world, that's what we refer to as 'obstruction of justice,' Mr. Yan."

"In my lawyer's world, this is what he refers to as a 'courtesy.' So if you want me to call him again…"

"Not necessary. I'm simply suggesting that if there's anything else you'd like to tell me, you'd better do it in the next ten minutes."

Their voices grew more muffled again, and Remo strained to make out what was happening on the other end. Instead of distinct words, he heard only noises. The shuffle of fabric. A few rhythmic thumps. The rush of traffic. Some kind of dinging sound.

Where were they? And why was Freddy with Teller? It clearly wasn't where his friend wanted to be. Remo debated hanging up, but as he started to pull the phone away from his ear, the clues from the conversation finally came together.

Too much space for a single man. The lost key and the credit card charge.

The pocket dial wasn't a pocket dial at all. It was actually a warning. The two men were on their way to the hotel, and there were only ten minutes to spare.

"Crap," Remo muttered under his breath, tapping the phone off and stuffing it into his pocket.

"Mom says that's not a nice word," Xavier piped up.

Remo squeezed the kid's shoulder. "Sorry, little man. I promise to give myself a time-out as soon as I get the chance. But we need to go for a walk, and we need to do it fast. Can you get your stuff? Your shoes and coat?"

"What about Mom? You said she was coming back soon."

"And she is. She'll have to meet us outside."

"Are you sure?"

"I wouldn't let you down, would I?"

The kid studied him for a second, then shook his head, accepting the promise. And as Xavier moved to grab his things, Remo silently vowed to make sure he kept it.

"But first…" he murmured, with a glance around the room.

There was evidence everywhere of their presence. No way would it pass for a single man's overnight getaway. Which put his friend—who had done them the favor and who probably had no clue that his actual life was on the line—in even more danger. At least Teller had used official channels and Freddy's lawyer was involved. It offered a bit of a safety net.

Quickly, Remo moved through the suite. There was no time for a complete sweep, but a surface one was in order. He dumped the playing cards and board game pieces into a box together, then shoved the box into a free-standing cabinet. He flicked the living room TV to a news channel, then turned it and all the lights off. Finally, he slipped to the bedroom to clear the browser history from the smart

TV. By the time he was done, Xavier's shoes were laced, his jacket in place.

"You ready?" Remo asked.

The kid nodded. "Are we supposed to clean our dishes?"

Remo bit back another bad word as Xavier's question prompted him to look toward the room service tray. It was loaded with the remains of a two-person meal, and there was no way to disguise it.

"Maybe we could put it outside," Xavier suggested. "The cleanup guys could still get it then, and no one would be mad about the mess."

"That's a genius idea, kid. C'mon. Give me a hand, all right?"

Together, they pushed the cart across the room and out the door. There, Remo positioned it beside the next door down. Not much of a ruse, but hopefully just enough. Satisfied that he'd done what he could to cover their brief stay in the suite, he held out his hand. Xavier took it with no hesitation, and Remo was extra grateful for the trust the kid offered him. Moving quickly and quietly, they made their way up the hall, then to the stairs. It took them only a few seconds to get to the lobby floor, and when Remo peered out to scan the area, he was relieved to see that their timing was impeccable. Teller and Freddy were just turning away from the concierge desk. Their trajectory would take them to the elevator rather than the stairs, and in ten seconds, they'd be out of sight.

But what are the chances that Teller doesn't have some kind of backup, waiting out front?

The thought sent an unpleasant tickle of worry up Remo's spine. Not just because it put him and Xavier at greater risk of being spotted, but because he had no idea where Celia was in relation to whoever was out there. There had to be another way out. As he stepped back and let the door close, he saw that there was a possible solution right there—the stairs kept going down.

He tipped his head down to Xavier and smiled. "How do you feel about a bit more adventure before we go find your mom?"

"Is it scary?" the little boy asked.

"I sure hope not."

"Okay."

Remo took his hand again, and guided him over the landing and down the next set of stairs. About halfway down, Xavier spoke again.

"Remo?" he said. "It's okay if it *is* scary. I just like to know."

Remo tightened his grip on the kid's hand. "Anyone ever tell you that you're a little too wise for your age?"

"Is that like smart?"

"Exactly like smart. But smarter than smart."

"Mom tells me I'm smart all the time. But I think she has to, so I'm not sure if it counts."

Remo chuckled. "Maybe not. Then again, your mom could just keep quiet, right? Not say anything, if she didn't mean it?"

Xavier shrugged. "I guess."

"What about your teachers at kindergarten? You probably get a pretty nice report card."

"Mrs. Fernridge gives me smiley faces."

"Well, that's a good sign."

"Yeah."

They reached the bottom of the stairs then, and they paused. An oversize, thick-looking door loomed in front of them.

"Is that the adventure?" Xavier asked, his voice echoing off the concrete.

"Guess there's only one way to find out," Remo replied,

freeing his hand so he could turn the knob and give the heavy door a push.

He didn't know what he'd been expecting to find on the other side of the door, but it wasn't the sudden rush of air, the honk of car horns, and a direct view into a narrow, house-lined alley. And what he was expecting even less than that was to see Celia, swinging her legs out of the back door of a taxi directly across the cracked pavement.

Celia's feet no sooner touched the ground than her favorite little voice carried to her ears.

"Look!" said Xavier, his delight obvious in just the one word.

Startled, Celia stopped midexit and lifted her gaze. The big man and her son stood just on the other side of the alley, hand in hand, attention on her.

"You were *right*, Remo!" Xavier added. "She *did* find us!"

Remo dipped his head and said something she couldn't hear, then reached down and scooped her son from the ground. And before Celia could complete her exit, they were rushing across the street to join her.

"Get back in," Remo said gruffly. "Trust me. *Here* is the last place you want to be right now."

Too surprised to argue or ask why, she simply lifted her feet and slid to the other side of the back seat. Xavier clambered in beside her, quickly buckling his seat belt without being asked. Remo followed, addressing the driver as he closed the door.

"Take us out of this area and into the city," he instructed. "Don't worry about using the most direct route. In fact…avoid it. And the front of the hotel, while you're at it."

The cabbie glanced in the rearview, and Celia tensed

as she waited for a sign of recognition. But he just nodded and said, "You got it, man."

As the car eased into the road, Remo's silence was somehow louder than Xavier's chatter about how they'd spent the morning. And while Celia nodded at the enthusiastic descriptions of board games and waffles, her eyes didn't leave Remo's profile. There was no denying that his expression was just barely shy of stormy. His jaw was set stiffly, his mouth a flat line. Whether he stated it or not, his anger was palpable.

And can you blame him? Celia said to herself. *How would you feel, if he took off while you were sleeping?*

Her throat closed up at the thought, and she unconsciously clutched the envelope in her hand as guilt washed over her. It'd been a lot easier to justify the sneaking away when she didn't have to look him in the eye.

"I'm sorry," she said.

"Don't," he replied quickly.

"Remo."

His gaze flicked in her direction, then slid down to Xavier, then found the front windshield again. "This isn't really the moment for a discussion."

He was right. She knew it. And she didn't want to argue with him in front of her son, either. But the fact that he was mad at her twisted her stomach into knots. Her hands tried to tighten even more, and she had to force them to relax for fear of ruining the contents. And Remo stayed disappointingly silent until they were almost back in the city. When he did speak, it was only because the cabbie asked whether or not they had an address for him yet. But as he started to answer in the negative, the roof of a building one block over caught Celia's eyes, and she found herself interrupting.

"Can you take us to 404 Hoight Avenue?" she asked.

The driver shrugged. "You're the boss."

Remo didn't argue—or comment at all—and Celia found that strangely disappointing, too. She opened her mouth, then decided it would be ridiculous to force more of a fight, and instead focused her attention on their new destination. She knew it was going to be a four-story, brick-front structure with a set of yellow doors at the front. Just like she knew the name of the building manager was a woman named Rupinder, and that the suites inside came furnished, and that Remo's presence would make the occupants blink, just because he was a man.

There was nothing that declared the place for what it was, but Celia didn't need to be told. She'd spent the weeks after Teller shot her living there. And the weeks after that, too, when Xavier was a newborn. Their current situation might not fit the bill for the shelter's usual clientele, but as they pulled up and climbed out of the cab, she was sure that Rupinder wouldn't turn them away.

Before they went knocking on the door, though, she knew she needed to talk to Remo. Waiting would only build the bad kind of tension.

"There's a fenced playground around back," she said. "Can we stop there for a minute so Xavier can stretch his legs?"

"Please?" Xavier piped up, bouncing on his toes. "Please, please, *please*?"

It was a bit of a dirty ploy to mention the park in front of her son, but she didn't want to let things get any worse. And Remo nodded easily. He even took her hand as they made their way around the squat, reddish building toward the closed area in the back. And when Xavier ran through the gate and headed straight for the tall, twisted slide, he was the one who stopped her near a bench and spoke first.

"Please don't tell me you're sorry," he said.

"I don't want you to be mad." It was impossible to keep her voice from breaking.

He brought both of his hands up to her face and cupped her cheeks. "I'm not mad."

"How could you *not* be mad?" she replied. "You have a right to be. And I understand."

"Listen to me, Celia. You scared the hell out of me. Leaving like that…" He trailed off, his hands dropping to his sides and his voice growing even more cut up than hers.

"I'm sorry."

"No. *I'm* sorry. If you thought going to the bank was the right thing to do, then I should've agreed to go with you."

"You don't have to cater to my every whim."

"Do I seem like the kind of guy who caters to every whim?"

"Well…"

He stared at her for a second, then—like he couldn't help it—let out a laugh. "Seriously? I don't think I've ever, in my whole life, been accused of being accommodating."

"You've been pretty accommodating about everything with us," she pointed out. "And you left medical school to help your sister."

"That's because…" He trailed off again, scratched at his chin, then sighed. "I would've done anything for Indigo. That kid was my life, even when she was doing her damnedest to ruin it."

"I don't want to ruin your life all over again." The words were out before Celia could stop them.

"You are *not* going to ruin my life, Celia. You could never ruin it." He paused and muttered something that didn't quite make sense.

"Did you say 'Neil damned Price'?" she asked.

He met her eyes, his expression fierce. "I've known you

for all of a day, but I can tell you right now that he did a number on you. I don't want you to be sorry for making a decision and sticking to it. I don't want you to be walking on eggshells because you're worried that I'm going to get angry. And I think Neil Price is the reason behind the way you feel the need to do it. I'll build you up. Support you. Cater to your whims—your words, not mine— if that's what it takes."

At the end of his speech, Celia drew in a breath. "I might not remember what happened with Neil, but I *do* know you're not him, Remo. You're a good man, and I don't want to jeopardize the chance we have to become something good."

"We *are* something good." He paused. "And the reason I accommodated my sister is that I loved her more than anything. I'd do the same for you two."

Celia's cheeks burned as she realized what he was saying. And once again, she thought about how implausible it was to fall in love with someone in so short a span. Yet there Remo was, practically declaring that it was true. And she didn't want to argue or tell him that it was unrealistic. She wanted to declare it back. Maybe she *would* have, if Xavier hadn't called to her just then.

"Mom?"

He sounded just worried enough that she had to turn her attention his way. He was in a swing now, pumping his legs.

"What's up, buddy?" Celia asked.

"Is that lady a stranger?" He pointed as he swung forward, and Celia turned her head to follow the direction of his finger.

A woman stood at the end of the short path that led from the enclosed play area to the apartment building. She was dressed in traditional Indian garb—a sari and a flowing scarf—and her long, mostly gray hair was wound into a thick braid that touched her waist. She had a long, puckered scar that ran from her left eye down to her lips, but it did nothing to mar her obvious beauty. And even from the ten-foot distance, it was easy to see the kindness in her eyes, which fixed on Celia for only another second before she swept forward over the concrete and enveloped her in a hug so hard it made her eyes water.

Chapter 20

As Rupinder Dhillon, the manager of Living Hope Shelter, refilled his mug of tea, Remo wondered if he should feel out of place. After Celia's pink-cheeked introduction of him as her new "friend"—with the quotation marks as obvious as day—the Indian woman had made a point of telling him twice that the building was generally open to women only. She'd emphasized that exceptions were few and far between. Even male children were permitted only if they were under the age of sixteen. But for some reason, in spite of all that, he felt right at home.

Maybe his comfort stemmed from the fact that it had quickly become obvious that the outspoken woman had saved Celia's life six years earlier. Or maybe because the shelter was the exact kind of place he would've loved for him and his mother to have found when they made their escape two decades earlier. Either way, he found himself relaxing, enjoying the tea and the company in spite of the circumstances. Xavier was happily reading a book in an overstuffed chair in the corner, while Rupinder and Celia reminisced about the good and the bad of the time she'd spent there.

From their conversation, Remo learned that Celia had met Rupinder by chance. After Teller shot her, she'd run straight out into the street and into the Indian woman's car. Both women agreed that it was fate. Rupinder—who was a retired nurse and an abuse survivor herself—had nursed Celia back to health, and also delivered Xavier into the world. She'd also helped Celia establish a contact up north, in Prince George. At one point, Celia turned a pleased smile his way and told him she could remember all of it with fantastic clarity.

But a mug and a half of tea, plus one entire plate of cookies later, the building manager turned a shrewd eye toward Celia.

"Let's not waste any more time with the bull *c-r-a-p*, shall we?" she said, her lightly accented English somehow managing to make the suggestion sound like a pleasant one. "Why don't you tell me why you're here?"

Remo set down his tea and watched as Celia licked her top lip nervously. One hand was tight on her own mug of hot steaming liquid; the other held the envelope she'd been carrying since they climbed into the taxi. Remo glanced toward the yellow item. She hadn't yet said a word about what it contained, but the way she'd been gripping it made him sure it held something significant in spite of its innocuous appearance. She squeezed it once more, then set it on the counter and slid it toward Rupinder.

"This is my insurance," she said softly.

The other woman didn't blink before answering. "The photos."

"Yes."

"You didn't burn them like you said."

Celia shook her head. "I'm sorry for lying to you, Rupi. But how *could* I burn them?"

The gray-haired woman reached across the counter and placed her fingers on the back of Celia's hand. "I always told you that you shouldn't. It was your ticket out."

"Only if I wanted to risk losing Xavier."

"I would've helped keep you safe."

"But *I* would've been under the microscope. It would've put you at risk, too. And all of the other women here."

"That's true enough," Rupinder said with a sigh. "I don't worry about myself so much, but I would hate to see any harm come to the shelter. So what will you do now?"

"Find a way to use it, I guess," Celia replied, not sounding sure at all.

"So Neil has found you."

"Yes. Or I found him for some reason that I don't really understand."

Remo cleared his throat. "Okay, not to be *that* guy… but does anyone want to tell me what's in the envelope?"

Both women turned his way like they'd forgotten his presence altogether. Then Celia moved to pull the envelope closer again, but Rupinder stopped her.

"Why don't you two take a breather in the apartment next door?" suggested the Indian woman. "It's empty at the moment, and where Mr. Price is concerned, I have a feeling it's better for me to know less rather than more. I can keep an eye on your son, if you and he both like."

"I'm game if you are," Remo offered.

"And I want to keep reading!" Xavier called out.

"I guess that settles it," Celia said.

Rupinder stood and quickly retrieved a key ring from inside a cabinet beside the fridge, then ushered them out to the hall.

"Take as much time as you need," she said, as she unlocked the door directly next to her own. "I've got plenty more books and plenty more cookies, too."

Celia thanked the older woman, then stepped into the apartment. Remo followed, letting the door close softly behind them, taking a quick look around as they made their way from the small foyer into the living room. The space was small. Sparsely and impersonally decorated. It could've been sad or disheartening, but it mostly felt like a hopeful place. A chance at a new beginning. He could picture Celia—pregnant and scared, injured and traumatized—arriving here. Making it her own while she waited for her son to be born. The image unexpectedly overwhelmed Remo, and it compelled him to put his arms around Celia so he could draw her into a tight embrace. Her arms came up to circle around his waist, too, and she held him just as hard.

"So this was home when you made your break?" he murmured into her hair.

"It really feels like a lifetime ago," she told him.

"But you remember it."

"Every detail. It actually seems kind of bizarre to me that I would forget it at all." She sighed and pulled away enough to look around, and her eyes hung on the closed door.

"What're you thinking?" Remo asked, pushing back a loose lock of blond hair and tucking it behind her ear. "Trying to make another escape?"

She swung her gaze back to him, a smile brightening her eyes. "From you? Never. You're stuck with me. I was just considering that in the last day, I've left my son alone more times than I have in the last five years. Aside from school, that is."

"Is that a bad thing?"

"I don't know. Maybe it's a more normal thing?"

Remo lifted an eyebrow. "Normal?"

"It's a relative term," she said.

"It would have to be," he teased.

She made a face, then dropped her arms, wriggled free, and held out the envelope. "Are you ready to look?"

Her tone was light, but there was a telltale tremor in her voice, and Remo replied, "I am. Are *you*?"

She met his eyes. "I guess I have to be. I mean… I already *know* what's in here. I'm just afraid that when I look at it, everything bad will hit me all over again."

He took her hand and led her to the couch. "In the unlikely event that you can't handle it, you can lean on me. I promise."

She exhaled. "Okay. Let's do this."

He watched as she slid a finger under one corner of the envelope's unsealed flap and lifted it open. He could see that her hands were shaking as she dumped out the contents—four standard-sized photographs.

"These are them," she said, her voice laced with obvious nerves as she adjusted them on the table.

Remo leaned over to have a look. Each shot was of the same group of men—Neil Price, and three others. One of the three looked vaguely familiar, but the two others were complete unknowns. The pictures were all taken from a funny angle, and it was pretty clear that the men didn't know they were being photographed.

"I took them with my cell phone," Celia explained, reading his thoughts. "I wasn't supposed to be there that day. In fact, we'd split up about two weeks before. Neil had gotten rough with me a couple of times, and I wasn't interested in sticking around. But I'd just found out I was pregnant. I knew he wouldn't be happy, but I also knew I had to tell him right away. I wasn't expecting to walk in on the meeting. Neil shoved me into the room next door, and I don't think he realized I could see and hear."

"What was it about?" Remo asked.

Celia tapped the picture. "You already know who Neil is, obviously. The other three men are city officials. Gary White and Lewis Dieberman are the first two. And the other is—*was*—Raj Singh."

Then the recognition hit him. "Raj Singh. He died during an overpass inspection."

She swallowed. "Yes. It wasn't an accident. Before Neil was on the city council, he worked in municipal planning. And there was something *wrong* with that overpass they were building. They knew it, and they argued about it on the night that I took those pictures."

Remo snapped his fingers. "Right. There was a structural compromise. A piece of it collapsed last year. A dump truck driver was paralyzed. I think they actually blamed Singh for it."

"They did. But it wasn't him. Neil took bribes all over the place. Contractors, subcontractors, architects. The fight went on so long that I think Neil forgot I was there. I left. And I managed to avoid him for a good week. I saw the news about Raj Singh and I just *knew* that it was Neil."

Her hands pulled away from the pictures and clenched into fists in her lap. Remo reached out and placed his fingers on top of hers.

"At the time, I thought I could've stopped it somehow. If I'd gone to the police or told someone else what I knew…" She shook her head. "But it wouldn't have mattered, because Detective Teller would've intercepted anyway, just like he did later. So I just ran."

"But Neil caught up to you," he said.

"Yes." She closed her eyes. "It was a nightmare. I was just about to run. Literally getting into a taxi, when one of his thugs grabbed me and dragged me back to my apartment. I think the only reason he didn't just kill me then was because I screamed out that I was pregnant."

"He told Neil," he filled in.

She opened her eyes and met his gaze. "Yes. And things got worse. Neil came to the apartment. He ordered me to terminate the pregnancy, and when I said I wouldn't, he got violent. I was terrified—for me and for my baby—and I said I had evidence of what he'd done, and that it would come out if I died. Like I said, he'd gotten a little rough a few times. But I had no idea who he really was until that moment. He said he'd find the evidence and make sure I never took another breath. After that, I *did* try to go to the police. Which put me in contact with Teller. And you know the rest."

Remo tightened his grip. "I'm sorry he put you through that. But at least now you remember everything. And knowledge is power."

"But there's still one thing I don't know—why I came back." She sighed. "I'm ridiculously glad you're here."

"Me, too."

He leaned over and brushed her mouth with a kiss. He meant it to be gentle. A bit of loving agreement. And it did start that way. But her lips were soft, warm, and tinged with a pleasant bit of residual spiced-tea flavor. Remo couldn't help but linger for another second, enjoying it. Enjoying *her.* When he started to pull away, Celia's fingers came up to the back of his neck, twining in his hair and deepening the kiss.

The fervor in her contact immediately ignited his own need. Want coursed through him. His body took over, the envelope and its contents momentarily forgotten.

His hands slid down her shoulders and down her back. They paused briefly at the curve of her hips, then slipped around to cup her rear end so he could lift her into his lap. A little moan escaped her lips, and a responding growl built up in Remo's chest. His finger moved to the bottom of her shirt, then under it. Her skin was as soft as her lips, and just as inviting. He was losing control in the most pleasant way possible.

He pulled away. "Celia."

"Yes, Remo?" She pushed his shoulders back against the couch to trail kisses down his jaw and throat.

He groaned. "I don't know if this is what Rupinder had in mind when she gave us the space."

"Two birds, one stone," she breathed.

Her lips came back to his, and there was no way he could fight it. Even if he'd wanted to.

She arched against him, and the memory of how she'd felt lying underneath him the day before leaped to mind. He wanted her like that again. He kissed her harder, then grabbed hold of her waist and flipped her to her back. But he overshot a little, and together, they rolled off the couch. His spine hit the ground, and her side hit the coffee table. The impact sent the photos flying.

"Leave them," Celia ordered, rolling over so that she was on top of him again.

"Had no intention of retrieving them," Remo growled.

"Thank God for that." But as she dipped her face toward his, a solid knock on the door stopped her, just shy of another kiss. "That's probably Rupinder, checking to see if we fell down and cracked our heads open. And there are about a *dozen* curse words jumping around in my head right now."

He couldn't help but chuckle. "Ditto. But we should answer it."

"I know. But I don't have to like it."

She sighed, kissed him far too quickly, then rolled off

and stood up. He followed suit, but before they could make it to the door, Celia spun back.

"Promise me something," she said.

"Anything," he replied.

"As soon as we're done with all this, we'll go away for a weekend together. I don't care if it's just to a nice hotel here in town, or if you want to head up to Sechelt or over to Victoria." Her words came out faster, her enthusiasm audible. "Or across the border? But maybe we can leave Xavier with your mom and ignore everything."

Remo felt a grin build up, and she caught it—and herself—at the same time.

"What are you smiling ab—oh, God," she groaned, pink creeping up under her freckles. "That was a complete runaway train of a suggestion, wasn't it? I'm blaming the head injury."

"I think it sounds good. Better than good. And my mom would love it."

He grabbed her hand and pulled her in, but the kiss was once again cut short by a knock, this one more forceful than the first. Laughing, she tugged him along to the door, then flung it open, speaking as she did.

"Don't worry, Rupi," she said. "We're—"

Her words cut off, and Remo knew exactly why. The Indian woman's face was pinched with worry, and when she spoke, her tone matched her expression. "Come on. I think the two of you need to know something, and it's better to just show you."

Celia's heart fluttered as she and Remo followed Rupinder back to her apartment. She was sure the other woman would've immediately said if something was wrong with Xavier. In fact, Celia was certain Rupinder would've explained just about anything dire. But knowing that did nothing to ease her nerves. The ten-second walk was still enough to make sweat break out on her upper lip, and by the time they got as far as the kitchen, her stomach was fully knotted up. She actually had to silently tell her feet not to go running for Xavier—who was still immersed in his stack of books—and to pay attention to the laptop Rupinder swung toward them.

"I keep the news feed going," the older woman explained. "Paused and rewound the relevant bit for you. Subtitles on for the sake of little ears."

Her fingers tapped the keyboard, and a moment later, Remo's picture became the dominant thing on the screen.

Under the photo, words flickered, recapping the story they'd heard earlier. Of Celia's accident and subsequent death in the hospital. No mention of her son. The so-called road rage incident. The manhunt for Remo.

"No need to tell me the how and why," Rupinder murmured. "The first bit is obviously untrue, so I assume the rest is, too."

Then, right near the end of the summary, the news feed was interrupted with a breaking bulletin. A red warning flashed an apology for the interruption, and the camera view cut from the static image of Remo to a podium. Celia's stomach—which had barely come untwisted—became a hard, aching mass. Neil Price and Detective Teller stood together, the former speaking into a microphone, the latter looking like a sentinel.

Celia shivered involuntarily, but Remo's hand landed on the small of her back, steadying her body and mind. It was still hard to see Neil's sincere expression and the accompanying words on the screen, and it was downright impossible not to imagine him saying them. She was just glad she couldn't hear his voice. It would've made things so much worse.

She drew in a breath and focused on the subtitles. The first part of his speech made her bristle. He talked about how sorry he was for anyone who knew and loved Ms. Celia Poller, and added that she appeared to have no next of kin. He spoke of the injustice. He pleaded with Remo to turn himself in. And the fact that he seemed like he meant it made Celia want to shove the laptop straight off the counter. Anyone watching would believe him. But that wasn't all. When Neil stepped away from the microphone and Teller moved forward, Celia tensed.

"Something's not right," Remo stated, his voice low.

She felt it, too. And a second later, the unpleasant sense of foreboding came to fruition. The subtitles announced that Mrs. Wendy DeLuca was missing. That the police had come by her house to discuss her son with her, and found the door unlocked, and the woman herself nowhere to be found. A picture of Wendy appeared in the bottom corner of the screen, and Teller reeled off a number for people to call if they'd seen her.

Remo's fingers flexed on Celia's back, and she knew his worry was as thick as hers.

"There's just a tiny bit more," Rupinder said.

And sure enough, the two men switched spots again. This time, Neil's speech became a campaign spiel. He announced that he was taking the situation personally, adding that *his* city didn't have room for these games, and that he wouldn't rest until DeLuca was taken care of. There was no denying the ominous undertone of his words. He paused for a moment, as if to let them sink in. Then he looked directly at the camera, his gaze making Celia want to squirm, as he made another statement, this one an odd-sounding comment about how he would offer Mrs. DeLuca shelter at his own home, if necessary. In closing, he announced that he would be at the VPD's main detachment around the clock. As soon as he'd said it, the screen cut back to the news studio, and the anchor there moved on to something else.

"He has her," Remo announced, his voice grim and angry and concerned all at the same time.

Celia turned to face him, and repeated, "Has her?"

He gestured toward the laptop, his expression dark. "What do you think that nonsense was at the end? It was meant for *us*. He's taken my mom hostage, and he wants us to know it."

"I have to say that I concur," Rupinder added.

"So he's baiting us?" Celia said.

Remo nodded. "He knows I'll come."

Celia's heart dropped, and she spoke before she could stop herself. "You can't go!"

Across the room, Xavier dropped his book, drawing attention from all three adults. His little face was pinched with worry, and Celia immediately felt bad.

"It's okay, buddy," she said quickly. "You can keep reading."

"Or I can take him back out to the playground?" Rupinder suggested.

Celia nodded gratefully, and her son jumped up. She waited until the two of them were gone before addressing Remo as calmly as she could manage.

"You aren't seriously thinking about going there," she said.

"I can't just let her go when there's a chance I could save her," he replied, pacing back and forth across the kitchen. "And I'm not planning on sacrificing myself."

"Not planning it doesn't stop it from happening."

"Celia."

"You *know* they aren't going to let you come out alive. If they were, they wouldn't have done anything that could leave them publicly exposed. They probably have people watching for you to come. Neil is smart and devious and ruthless, Remo." Tears stung her eyes, and she didn't bother to wipe them away as they overflowed. "How we can even be sure that—"

She stopped short, but it was too late; Remo had already picked up on the end of her question. He ceased his pacing and faced her.

"I know she's alive," he told her, "because if Neil is as smart as you think, then he knows that with one, single shred of doubt on my part, I won't come. He *has* to keep her alive, because otherwise I won't show up."

Celia exhaled, seeing the logic in his response. "There still has to be a better way."

"Then give it to me. But in under five minutes, because that's about all I'm willing to spare before I go."

"Me."

"What?"

"It's not really *you* he's after. It's *me* he's been chasing."

"That's true. But it's *my* mother he's got."

"Then I'll call the local news instead," she said. "I'll show them that I'm alive. The whole story will fall apart. It's like Rupinder said. The first part is a lie, so the rest has to be, too. I can out myself publicly, and show everyone who Neil really is. I've got the pictures, and..." She trailed off as she realized there was a flaw in her plan. "And he has your mom. And if I expose him, then he has no reason to keep her alive."

"Which is exactly why I need to do this. Would you do any less, if it were Xavier?"

"No. Of course not."

Remo put his hands on her shoulders, then pulled her in close and pressed his chin to the top of her head. "My mom is my only living relative, sweetheart. I *have* to go. And I need to do it quickly."

"I know," she conceded, unable to keep the words from cracking as she said them.

"We've made it this far," he added.

"I know," she repeated.

"And I won't take any unnecessary risks."

"I know."

"And I'm *probably* going to use you as a bargaining chip."

"I— What?" She pulled away, startled.

He smiled. "Just working through my options in my head."

"Not funny, Remo."

"*I* know." He bent to kiss her, but she pulled back, suddenly thoughtful, and he paused, clearly sensing the change. "What?"

"It's not actually the worst idea ever."

"What?" he repeated.

"Using me and Xavier as fake bait."

"It's a terrible idea," he replied.

But Celia could tell that he was thinking about it, too.

Chapter 21

It was almost impossible not to keep track of the minutes. As much as Celia told herself it only slowed things down even more, she couldn't seem to stop herself. She'd joined Rupinder and Xavier outside after saying goodbye to Remo—who'd left in a borrowed ball cap and sunglasses—but it wasn't enough of a distraction. If anything, the playground only provided more things to measure by.

Six slides. Remo was probably done with the on-foot portion of his trip. His plan had included making a stealthy move out of the neighborhood before letting himself be seen.

Two under-ducks. Remo had probably called for a cab near the corner store Rupi had described as she half-laughingly said she'd never given a *man* runaway cash before.

Two more under-ducks. Three more slides. One game

of tag. The cab was probably there, and Remo was probably climbing in.

Celia hated the thought of it all.

She hated their plan.

She hated the thought of Remo dangling her and Xavier's location over Neil like the metaphorical carrot.

She hated that she didn't know what he was planning to do once he'd convinced her cruel-minded ex that he would trade them in for his mother.

She hated that she had no real way of knowing if he was safe, or if he'd come through.

And she *really* hated that she wasn't by his side.

Hate, hate, hate. *All of it*, she thought.

"Celia?"

At the sound of her name, she jerked her attention back to the playground. Rupinder stood in front of her, her adult-sized hand wrapped around Xavier's little one. Celia forced a smile, belatedly realizing she'd been staring blankly at the gate. The last spot where she'd seen Remo before he took off.

"Are you okay, Mom?" Xavier asked.

"I'm doing just fine, buddy," she replied.

"Your nose is wet," he said, then pointed up. "It's getting ready to rain cats and dogs."

Celia swiped the back of her hand over her face. Sure enough, there were more than a few raindrops dampening her skin. The wind had picked up, too, and the clouds overhead did look ominous.

"I think the sky's about to open up," Rupinder added. "We were just saying that we should go inside and dig into my arts and crafts box. Maybe make some lunch."

Celia made herself nod. She knew that she was just going to switch from counting games at the park to counting glitter and macaroni art, but she followed Rupi back into the apartment anyway, and even went through the motions of helping to prepare soup and sandwiches. But small talk was hard to manage, and her old friend picked up on it quickly.

"You've changed, over the last few years," the other woman observed as she laid out slices of bread.

"Five years of mothering," Celia replied ruefully. "It ages you."

Rupi shook her head. "It's not that, I think. I see more than my share of mothers come through. This is something different."

"Well…I do have that whole memory-loss thing happening," Celia joked halfheartedly.

"Maybe. But I think this is bigger."

"What do you mean?"

"When you first came to me, you were scared. Understandably so. You'd been shot. You were on the run for your life. You needed to get as far away from here as you could, but you couldn't leave without medical attention first, and you were sure that seeking it traditionally would get you killed."

"Yes," Celia agreed, unsure where Rupinder was going with the recounting of events. "All true."

"But you were resilient, underneath that," the other woman said. "Now it's the opposite."

"I'm not quite following."

"Before…your strength was hidden and fear was dominant. Now your strength is visible, and your fear is underneath. If that makes sense?"

Celia started to argue, then stopped before she even got started. She could remember how frightened she'd been when trying to break free from Neil Price and the men who worked for him.

Not just frightened, she corrected silently. *Terrified.*

And that fear had dominated every aspect of her life. Which—as Rupinder had just pointed out—was completely understandable. But it had also seemed inescapable. Even after Xavier was born and she made the move, that underlying worry of being caught didn't go away. There was a looking-over-her-shoulder kind of feeling ingrained in her. She didn't know when it had stopped. She wasn't even sure whether it was gradual, or if something had triggered it. But she was sure that Rupinder was right; she *had* changed.

She straightened her shoulders a little and glanced over at Xavier, who was happily coloring a page full of farm animals. "When I ran all those years ago, I felt like I had no other options. Everything led back to losing Xavier. And honestly…even if an easy one had presented itself, I don't know if I would've been capable of taking it. I wouldn't have risked it."

"And now?"

"I'm still scared. But I feel like I might stand a chance of coming out on top. Maybe that even has something to do with why I came back, I don't know."

Rupinder said something in reply, then excused herself when the shelter's emergency phone line rang. But Celia didn't hear her. Because the laptop caught her eye just then, and held her attention. The news channel was running its program about Remo again. Only this time, Celia noticed that Teller and Neil weren't the only ones in the frame. A woman—a tall, well-dressed brunette with a tight-lipped smile on her face—stood just to the side of the podium. She was very attractive. Model caliber for sure. She was also very, very pregnant, and a prominent diamond ring flashed on her finger. But it wasn't any of those things that made Celia almost drop the spoon she held. It was the way—when the woman turned just slightly—that her scarf billowed out, revealing an angry red mark on her throat.

That mark...

It brought it all back.

Celia sat on her couch, a steaming cup of coffee in one hand and the TV remote in the other. Xavier was at school, and she was on a late shift at the care home where she worked. She'd decided to take advantage of the rare few minutes of solitude and was flicking idly through the channels. But she stopped abruptly when Neil's face came up on the screen. It startled her just enough that she forgot to flick it off.

Over the past five years, she'd spent an equal amount of time being afraid he'd come looking for her, and trying to forget he'd ever been a part of her life. Seeing him—alive and well and carrying on as though he'd never tried to have her and their son killed—filled her with cold dread. It should've prompted her to switch channels immediately. But something about the piece drew her in. She paused. She listened. She was sickened by the fact that Neil was running for office. But it was really something about the woman standing behind him at the campaign table that had stayed her finger on the channel changer.

At first, Celia didn't see that the brunette was pregnant. She was too preoccupied with the way the woman held herself. A little nervously, maybe? Stiffly, for sure. Celia wasn't able to pinpoint what it was, exactly, that held her. But just about anything was possible, where Neil was concerned. And as much as she wanted to turn it off, watching became something close to a compulsion.

The woman wore a decorative scarf. Black, with little red flowers. Celia noticed it because she liked it. She might even have picked one like it for herself, if she'd seen it in a store. So her eyes had hung on it for a few extra seconds. And that's when the other woman bent over to speak to a boy who'd just approached the campaign table. The movement exposed both the baby belly and a horrendous mark on her neck.

Celia dropped her coffee mug, spilling the hot contents across her lap and onto the carpet. But she barely noticed. Because at the same moment, her ears had picked up what the newscaster was saying.

"And as the old saying goes..." said the anchor. "Behind every successful man is a successful woman. Neil's wife, Felicity, is a little over eight months along with their first child, but that doesn't seem to slow her down in the slightest. Her architectural firm is providing 49 percent of the financial backing for the city's brand-new Parkour Extreme. People said the permits would never come through, but Neil and Felicity have made the dream a reality, and the outdoor facility is destined to please when it opens next week..."

The newsperson's voice went on, but Celia stopped listening. She was too distracted by two sure things. One, Neil was abusing his pregnant wife. And two, the project had been pushed through. A project designed with children in mind. That put children at risk. What kind of godawful monster was he?

Autopilot took over.

Celia grabbed her phone and dialed Neil's office. God knew what she was thinking. Nothing reasonable. She was stunned that she still remembered the number and equally surprised when he picked up. But when she said nothing, and he responded to the long silence with her name, she knew she'd been fooling herself by thinking for even a single second that he'd stopped looking for her.

First came the panic and the fear.

Then came the need to act.

The memory was so real—so close—that as Celia blinked it away, she half expected to see it frozen on the laptop screen again right then. Instead, what she caught was a repeat of Neil's closing words. And that's when Celia clued in. He wasn't being metaphorical. He was being literal. When Neil had said he would open his home to Wendy DeLuca, he really meant he already had. And Celia knew exactly where in his house that "shelter" would be.

Remo was two blocks from the police station. He'd been there for a few minutes, just trying to find a viable way to approach. The rain was trying to move from a sprinkle to a solid beating, and it didn't help with his planning at all.

Teller and Price undoubtedly had a slew of lackeys watching the place. They'd be looking for him both on foot and in a car. They'd have covered the major entrances, but would be paying close attention to the less obvious ones, too. Of course, Remo had no idea where any of those were. It wasn't like he'd had time to stop by City Hall and check out the municipal plans so he could plot his way in. Everything he knew about the station was based on the few times he'd driven by, and the one time he'd gone in to pay a fine for a burned-out headlight. So basically all he had was the fact that it was an older, two-story building that sprawled the length of one corner.

"Fat lot of good that does," he muttered. "Might as well mention that it's brown, too."

But he was sure that even if he'd been armed with insider knowledge, it wouldn't have done any good. He was a suspect in a falsified fatal hit-and-run. All it would take to end it would be the addition of a falsified weapon. Remo could picture the headline.

Armed Suspect Approaching Police Station Shot by Local Officer.

It didn't mean that he could walk away. His mother was somewhere under Neil's control, and aside from Celia, he was the only one who could do anything about it. Even if he wasn't a hundred percent sure what that was yet. Frustrated, he lifted his now-soaked baseball cap and ran a hand through his hair, then stuck it back in place and took another two steps toward the end of the block.

If I were any kind of proper hero, I'd be creating a diversion right now, he thought. *Paying some guy ten bucks to pretend to be me. Or changing into a more effective disguise than sunglasses and a ball cap. Maybe hunting down one of the guys who's spying on me, knocking him out with his own gun, so I can steal his uniform, then sneak into the station.*

"And shout 'surprise' at the unsuspecting cops," he added aloud as he reached the corner.

The idea of it actually made him chuckle. With his luck, the cop he knocked out would end up being six inches shorter and fifty pounds lighter, and he'd be trying to stuff himself in a uniform five sizes too small. He just pictured how that would go. But his amusement lasted only for as long as it took to reach the crosswalk between the blocks. On the other side of the street sat a police cruiser. Its fresh-faced, uniformed driver stood outside the car, his notebook in his hand. Remo stopped abruptly, then spun back and ducked into a bus shelter.

In the reprieve from the rain, he reasoned it was more likely that the beat cop had nothing to do with Teller. There were plenty of stand-up policemen in the city. Remo came into contact with them regularly during his shifts. He knew more than a couple by name, and he was certain there were more good cops than bad kicking around in

Vancouver. The problem was, it didn't *matter* whether the kid out there was corrupt or straight. That was the devious beauty of Price's plan. Every cop in the city was looking for Remo for what they thought was a legitimate reason.

But maybe I can use that.

As soon as the idea came into his head, it expanded into a potential plan. He could sneak up on a nonspying cop, *not* knock him over the head or steal his uniform, and just announce who he was and ask to be taken in. Simple as that. Assuming the one he chose to approach wasn't affiliated with Teller.

He inched forward and poked his head out of the bus shelter. The young cop was still there, and he was starting to seem like the best option. If the kid was more than twenty-two years old, Remo would eat his borrowed baseball cap. That meant he was a rookie. Or close to it. The chances that his idealism had rubbed off were slim. Plus, the street was public. Plenty of passersby.

As the policeman tucked his notepad into his pocket, Remo decided it was a now-or-never kind of situation. He stepped back into the street and strode forward. He hit the crosswalk, took a quick side-to-side look, then jogged to the opposite corner.

"Excuse me!" he called out, careful to keep his voice friendly. "Officer?"

The cop paused with his hand on the car door handle and swung toward Remo. "Sir? Is there a problem?"

"No problem," Remo replied, giving the man's name tag a quick read. "Is it Officer Hank?"

"Constable Hank," the cop corrected. "What can I do for you, sir?"

Remo reached up to drag off his sunglasses so he could meet the other man's eyes. "I think you might be looking for me. I'm Remo DeLuca."

The recognition in the cop's gaze was immediate, but to his credit, he didn't flinch or look nervous, or reach a hand for his weapon. He just gave Remo's face a thorough once-over, then nodded.

"Mr. DeLuca," he said. "Do I need to call for backup?"

"No, sir," Remo replied. "I'd appreciate it if you could take me right in to Neil Price. And I know I'm not in a position to ask for any favors, but I'd appreciate it more than you know if you wouldn't call my arrest in ahead of time."

Constable Hank studied him for a second, then nodded. "I'd normally deny that request. But the truth is, you *are* in a position to ask for a favor, Mr. DeLuca. About a year ago, you attended a break-in on the Downtown East Side. You saved the life of an attending officer."

"I remember. Female, midfifties."

"Sergeant Constance Hank. My mom. First thing she said to me when she saw that news bulletin about you was that there had to be more to the story."

"There is," Remo replied. "But you might not want to ask me too many questions about it."

The young cop put his hands up. "I'll take your word for it."

He turned back to the car and reached for the door handle, leaving his back exposed. It was a purposeful move, Remo was sure. A sign of trust. And it was a relief to know that the constable felt it was deserved. It made climbing into the back seat of the car a little more tolerable. But the tolerability and relief didn't last long. Only the amount of time it took for them to take the one-minute drive to the station, park the car, and start to make their way up the front steps. There, a voice he recognized—but wished he didn't know at all—spoke up from behind.

"DeLuca," said Teller. "The source of both my physical headache *and* my mental one."

Remo turned, already gritting his teeth. The detective stood on the bottom stair with an umbrella in his hand and a smug expression on his face. But his real feelings were given away in the fact that he had his other hand resting on his hip. Constable Hank obviously had more guts than the man who outranked him. It turned Remo's gritted teeth into an almost smile.

"Detective," he said in greeting. "Always a pleasure. For me, anyway."

Teller's eyes narrowed, and while his gaze didn't leave Remo, he addressed the young cop. "Constable. I appreciate that you were able to apprehend this suspect, and I'll ensure that you get the recognition you deserve. But I can take this from here."

The young cop wasn't quite that willing to step away. He angled himself between Remo and the detective, and he spoke in a clear voice. "Sir. I've told Mr. DeLuca that I'll take him to Mr. Price." ·

Teller's eyebrows went up, and his attention flicked to Hank for a moment. "That's convenient, then. Because Mr. Price is actually waiting around back in his car."

Constable Hank cleared his throat, and in the split second before he added anything else, Remo realized that further argument would end badly. The kid would wind up on the wrong side of some kind of accident. Remo had zero interest in any more collateral damage.

"Guess that would resolve the problem of drawing attention to myself." He said it quickly, and after the briefest hesitation, Constable Hank cleared his throat once more.

"Then I guess it works out for everybody," he replied agreeably.

Remo wasn't sure if the kid meant it, or if he'd just picked up on the implicit threat. He didn't care, either way. So long as it meant Constable Hank walked away in one piece.

"You have a good day, Detective," the young officer added, then spun and took the stairs, two at a time.

"Could've used some cuffs, Constable," Teller called after him.

If the young policeman heard the statement over the splash of his feet in the shallow puddles on the concrete steps, he pretended not to. Remo waited until he'd disappeared into the building before facing the detective once more.

He held out his wrists. "Go for it."

"I think we both know that your mother is better than any bit of steel," Teller stated, then cocked his head to the side. "We could cut this short, you know. Just tell *me* where the ex and the kid are, and it can be over."

"I assume by 'over,' you mean my life," Remo replied dryly.

"Did I say that?"

"Did you have to? Let's just cut the crap, Teller. I'll speak to Price, and Price alone. And I'm not even giving up a *hint* of what he wants until I see my mother."

"Suit yourself." The detective shrugged, then turned and started down the stairs without even checking to see if Remo was following.

Chapter 22

Celia had asked the cabbie to drop her off at the top of the steep hill that led down to Neil's house. But now that she was there, her feet might as well have been bricks. She was feeling light-headed, too. She regretted leaving Xavier behind, even though there was no possible consideration of bringing him along. She wished she'd hugged him one more time. Told him she loved him. Again. But it would've felt an awful lot like goodbye, and that wasn't something she was willing to recognize as a possibility.

Xavier was the whole reason she needed to face Neil. Her son, and other people's sons and daughters, too. She couldn't let her money-hungry ex push through a project like Parkour Extreme. If things went wrong the way that they had with the hastily built overpass, there could be worse consequences than a solitary man being paralyzed. That by itself was bad enough. But the hundreds of children who would be at the new park…it was unacceptable in Celia's heart and mind.

Which is why you have to push through.

In spite of the firm, self-directed reminder, she still had to force her feet forward. The rain had stopped momentarily, but the sky was still blotted with dark gray clouds, leaving no doubt that the storm was just taking a break. Any moment, it would start up again. Even the streetlights were on, triggered by the premature darkness. They buzzed with their yellowish light, and the sound reminded Celia a little too vividly of the car accident, and how the water had been pouring down in sheets and making the live wires zap.

Even more reason to keep going, she told herself as she stepped closer to the hedges that lined the downward angle of the street. *You don't want to go through anything like that again.*

It was true. Now that all her memories were back in place, she was a hundred percent sure that she didn't ever want to return to running and hiding. She'd appreciated what Rupi had offered, and would never be able to adequately express her gratitude for the fact that the other woman had saved her and Xavier's lives. But she'd also hated feeling trapped in her own city. She hadn't minded living in northern BC for the last five years, but she resented that it felt like a punishment, when she was innocent of any wrongdoing. And now that she knew how easy it was for Neil to find her—one wordless call was all it took, apparently—she wouldn't ever be able to stop looking over her shoulder. So on top of the fact that she couldn't let Parkour Extreme become a reality, she needed to do this for herself, too.

Her renewed conviction drove away much of the worry and propelled her forward. She didn't pause again until she was just outside the familiar fence that surrounded Neil's palatial home. Whether or not he still lived there wasn't a question. He'd forcibly inherited the place from his father. The terminally ill old man—whom Celia had been hired to care for, and who disliked his son intensely—had tried to will the place to a charity. But Neil had wanted the sprawling lawns and the koi ponds and the manicured garden just because he couldn't have them. So he'd wrested it all away in court, and had told her on more than one occasion that he would never give it up. It was a point of bitter pride with him.

"And maybe all that should've been a clue," she said under her breath.

But as she'd so often thought before, in spite of every single awful detail, she wouldn't have undone it. Because as much as so many things about Neil were a mistake, she got Xavier out of it.

With that truth at the front of her mind, Celia paused just long enough to give the property a quick once-over. It hadn't changed a bit since she'd run from it the last time. Same ostentatious fountain just visible from the top of the driveway. Same manicured shrubs and same peaked roof jutting up to the sky. And even though the rain had started up again, blurring her view enough that she couldn't quite make it out, she was a hundred percent certain that the same shingle would be missing from the space just above the oddly placed weather vane.

It was disconcerting, to see it again. She wondered if the sight would've been less unnerving if it had changed even a little bit. Or maybe it just made it better. It certainly confirmed what she knew already; Neil Price was incapable of change.

Shaking off the last bit of uncomfortable déjà vu, she stepped the rest of the way down the driveway, then walked straight up to the coded panel and tilted her face to the security camera up above. She knew from experience that her presence would've triggered a notification inside the house. The video would be rolling. One of the three or four regular staff—or maybe Felicity Price herself, if she was in there—would be deciding whether or not to buzz the intercom to greet her. But Celia didn't bother to wait. She reached over and plugged in the code, sure that Neil wouldn't have changed that, either. And just as she anticipated, the gate let out a noisy buzz, then shuddered to an automatic open.

The moment it was wide enough, she slipped through. She made it only two steps, though, before she stopped again. Felicity Price stood at the bottom of the porch stairs with her hand on her pregnant belly. She wore no makeup, and was dressed simply in leggings and a stretch-fabric tunic. No scarf covered the angry red marks on her neck now, and those weren't the only visible injuries, either. A partially healed bruise led from her left wrist all the way up and under her three-quarter-length sleeve. The pinkie finger on the same side had been wrapped in some stiff tape, and the tip of a shattered fingernail jutted out from under it.

It all made Celia cringe with understanding, but it wasn't so much the woman's appearance or presence that made Celia pause in her approach. She'd been presuming she might see the other woman there, and she was certainly aware of the pregnancy. But what she wasn't expecting was the invisible thread of kinship that overtook her. She'd lived Felicity's life. Or part of it, anyway. She knew what it felt like to wake up and wonder how she'd gotten there. To question if it was somehow her fault, even when knowing full well it wasn't. The self-doubt was agonizing. And then to bring a baby into the mix…

Xavier's brother or sister.

The realization, which only came right then and there,

nearly made her stumble. The little life inside this stranger was Celia's own son's sibling. It left her a little breathless, to think about that. Her eyes hung on Felicity's stomach, her speech and demands forgotten. Was it a girl or a boy? Was she or he healthy? What day was the baby actually due? The questions overrode everything else for just long enough that the other woman got a chance to speak first.

"You're twenty minutes late for my appointment," Felicity stated, her tone irritated, but her eyes pleading. "Hasn't anyone ever told you that it's rude to keep clients waiting? Especially pregnant ones."

Celia didn't even blink before she replied. "I know. I'm sorry. My car broke down, and I had to catch a cab."

"A call would've been nice." The pretty brunette mouthed a thank-you, then gestured to the side of the house. "The massage table's around back, but I'd prefer not to trail mud into the house, so if you could follow me?"

"Of course."

She let the other woman lead her around the front porch, then to the grassy patch between the large home and an ivy-covered wall that shielded the space from view. But it was as far as Celia was willing to go without an explanation and some reassurance that Felicity Price was actually on her side. When she stopped moving and cleared her throat, Neil's wife spun back, her expression surprised.

"What're you doing?" she whispered, her voice urgent and concerned. "I did a temporary override on the surveillance camera back there as soon as I saw you coming. But I think the delay only lasts for fifteen minutes before it reboots itself automatically, so you'd better hurry."

"Back where?" Celia asked, her voice equally low.

"At the guesthouse. That's where he's keeping her."

"Wendy DeLuca?"

"Isn't that why you're here?"

"Yes," Celia admitted, and she could hear the hesitation in her own voice.

"But you don't trust me," the other woman filled in. "And I don't blame you. I wouldn't trust me, either, if I were you. But we *really* don't have that much time. I think that—ooh. Sorry. Braxton-Hicks all day today." She blew out a breath and placed her hand on her stomach, then spoke again. "Look. I'd love to stop and tell you everything I know and don't know, but I think the new house manager is actually some kind of spy or bodyguard, or… God. I don't even know what. Either way, the clock is ticking."

"So give me the syncopated version."

"The synco—okay, fine. When Neil and I first met, he was charming and handsome and ambitious, too. Sound familiar?"

"I wish it didn't. But yes."

Felicity took another breath, then went on in a rush. "He knew he needed a wife to get where he wanted to go. I was ambitious, too, so I agreed to marry him. Fast-forward a year, and I'm having all kinds of doubts. He doesn't like that, and he starts to get aggressive. I try to leave. I fail and wind up with a black eye. I try to be clever. Make him think we were okay, while I looked for a way out. Fast-forward another three months, and I'm pregnant. Neil informs me he's planning on running for mayor. Things are getting worse. I'm desperate to leave now. He shows me a paper trail that will implicate me in some bad things. Serious jail-time things. Does any of *that* sound familiar?"

"Yes," Celia repeated.

"After that, he stopped covering things up. I found out about you. About your son. About things I'm afraid to say out loud. So if helping you comes even *close* to helping me…" She trailed off, then straightened her shoulders. "I know I have to leave. And I will. But I haven't figured out how to do that while still keeping my daughter safe."

"A girl?" The revelation distracted Celia for a moment.

Felicity smiled. "Zoey."

"That's pretty."

"Thank you. But more importantly…does that mean you're convinced that I'm sincere?"

Celia nodded. "Yes."

"Thank God," said the other woman. "Let's go."

Felicity turned and started walking again, but Celia called after her. "Wait."

She paused. "What?"

"Come with us."

"Come with you?"

"You're looking for a way out. I'm it. You're hanging on because you're scared of what Neil might do to you and the baby. No one understands that more than I do. But he can't take down both of us. Your word and my word together will put him away for a long time, Felicity."

Tentative hope bloomed on the other woman's face. "You really believe that."

"I've had almost six years to think about it. Trust me when I say that you don't want to wait that long."

Felicity's dark brown eyes hung on Celia for a few moments before she exhaled and rubbed her stomach one more time. "Okay. Let's take the son-of-a-you-know-what down."

She spun again, and this time Celia followed. They made their way across the rest of the grass and out to the back of the main house, then over the short patio that led to the small guest home. She couldn't help but shoot a nervous look at the camera mounted on the eaves, but she had to trust that the other woman had turned it off as she'd said. And a moment later, the trust panned out. Felicity punched in a sequence of numbers on the keypad at the little house, the door sprung free, and Celia was face-to-face with Remo's bound and gagged mother.

Even though Remo was in the front seat of the car, he had no delusions about the fact that he was a prisoner rather than a guest. They'd taken a winding path out of the city, presumably to avoid detection. Now they were on the freeway, and if Neil was to be believed, they were headed toward his own home. Through the whole ride so far, Teller—who sat in the rear middle seat of the sedan—had barely moved. He was silent, but he held his weapon casually on his knee, the business end angled toward Remo's left kidney, and that said more than enough. Neil, on the other hand, had been offering his best effort at being Mr. Congenial—the perfect mayoral candidate, just chatting away with a constituent. Remo shut him down at each turn. That didn't mean the corrupt man didn't keep trying.

"Who does my boy look like?" he asked right then with a smile. "I've been wondering that for the last five years."

Remo smiled back. "Exactly like his mother."

The twitch of a finger was the only indication that Neil was bothered by the response at all. "So he has her eyes, then. Always one of my favorite features. I'm actually looking forward to seeing them again."

It was Remo's turn to twitch. He covered it with a grunt, then turned his gaze out the side window.

So far, all he'd told the older man and his detective buddy was that he was willing to negotiate information about Celia and Xavier's location. He supposed that neither of them believed he'd really do it, and he didn't blame them. He had no intention of ever letting either man get close enough to Celia that they'd be able to see her shadow, let alone the color of her eyes. But he'd face that hurdle when he got there. For the moment, what really mattered was seeing that his mother was as alive and well as they claimed she was.

God help them if she's not, he thought, just barely keeping his hand from curling into a fist.

The scenery flicked by, and he tried to use that to distract him. The sides of the road were marked with more and more evergreens, and the rain-drenched foliage was dark and soothing. It lasted only a moment, though, because Neil wasn't done talking yet.

"Is she still as pretty as I remember?" the other man asked.

"Thought you were happily married," Remo replied evenly.

"Oh, I am. Doesn't mean I can't dream." Neil's tone was just shy of lascivious. "And I've done that plenty over the last half decade. Trust me. Celia was always so—"

A sudden jerk of the car saved Remo from hearing whatever other vulgar thing the other man was about to say, but it also earned him a solid bump of his forehead on the dashboard. There was a clatter from the back seat, too, followed by a curse from Teller, then the click of a seat belt right after that. Vaguely—through sharp pain and watering eyes—Remo realized the detective must've dropped his gun and was trying to recover it. But the mental notation was no sooner made than it slipped to the back of his consciousness. Because as he righted himself, his gaze slid to the windshield, which offered him an unexpected view. Three women were making their way up the road in the pouring rain, and he knew each one. His mother. Celia. And Neil Price's very pregnant wife.

Remo blinked, half expecting them to disappear like the mirage they had to be. They stayed exactly where they were. As he accepted that they weren't a manifestation brought on by the bump to his head, the car jerked again. Only this time, it was with forward momentum. Not only that, but the three women suddenly seemed to be getting closer.

It's not them getting closer! growled an urgent voice in his head. *It's you!*

Belatedly, he figured out what was happening. Neil was accelerating. But not *just* accelerating. Pressing the gas down harder and harder with the vehicle trained right at the three women.

Remo could see that no matter how quickly they moved, they wouldn't stand a chance of getting out of the way. Not all of them, anyway.

Acting on desperate instinct, he shot out his hand and grabbed the wheel, then yanked as hard as he could. The car careened wildly to the side, and Neil yanked back. For a second, the other man regained control, but Remo didn't relent. He tugged harder. The vehicle jerked and swayed, then bounced over the gravel shoulder, not slowing in the slightest. It sailed past Remo's mother, Mrs. Price, and Celia. Remo was thankful, but only for a heartbeat. The relief no sooner hit than he saw that their new path had them headed for a disaster. A towering cedar loomed ahead. He started to raise his arms in defense just as the front end of the car slammed hard into the tree.

For an indecipherable amount of seconds after the air bag deployed in what sounded like an explosion, the world around Remo echoed unnaturally. Every noise and every feeling were amplified. His forearms burned. His mouth stung. Metal creaked, and glass cracked. Something, somewhere hissed like an angry snake. As he dragged his eyes open, he swore he even heard the flutter of his lashes. But his first glimpse of the interior of the car sent all other concerns away.

The impact had thrown Detective Teller from his recently unbuckled position in the back seat to the front, and things had taken the worst turn possible for him. His legs hung on the console, his torso was slumped over the dash, and his eyes were wide, splotched with burst blood vessels, and completely sightless. Remo didn't have to check for a pulse. His professional experience told him the other man had died instantly. It wasn't that, though, that was drawing his concern. It was the fact that on the other side of Teller's body, the driver's door hung open, and Neil Price wasn't anywhere to be seen.

A half a dozen curses popped to mind, but Remo didn't take the time to say them aloud. He had to concentrate on doing something about the missing man. And it *did* take some concentration, because his ears were ringing like nobody's business, and lifting his arms and legs was a groan-inducing chore. He made himself do it anyway.

Forcing his hand up, he pressed his fingers to his seat belt and clicked it free. Next, he fumbled for the door handle. Thankfully, he found it with ease. He gave it a quick tug at the same time as he jammed his elbow forward, and a moment later, a rush of acrid air filled the car. Stifling a gag, he flopped his way out of the vehicle, pushed to his feet, then wiped at his eyes and attempted to see through the black smoke and sheets of rain.

What he spied made his heart drop. Neil had already managed to reach the three women, and in spite of the fact that he was outnumbered, there was no denying that he had an advantage. He held a gun in his hand, and he was waving it a little wildly at Celia. The fact that he hadn't simply fired was a minor miracle.

Why hasn't *he fired?* Remo wondered.

Half-afraid to move forward for fear of triggering a reaction, he squinted through the smoke, and quickly figured out the answer. While Celia and Remo's mother were both on their feet, Neil's wife was on the ground, her hands behind her, her head tucked to her chest, and her eyes squeezed shut. She was in labor. Over the course of his career, Remo had seen it enough times to know. In spite of the gun, and in spite of the fact that he'd been ready to mow down the whole group just minutes earlier, the older man looked more than a little lost.

So take advantage of that fact before it's too late.

Remo started to step toward the small group, then stopped and turned back to the car instead. Doing his best not to attract any attention, he reached into the space he'd just exited and folded the passenger seat forward. Every muscle in his body screeched a protest as he leaned into the back, but he pushed on anyway, feeling around for Teller's discarded weapon. At last his fingers closed on the cool metal. Flooded with relief, he tightened his grip on the gun and drew back. He was forced to go still, though, when something hard poked between his shoulders, and Neil's voice cut in over the ringing in his ears.

"Put it down and turn around very, very slowly," ordered the other man.

Cursing himself for not being thirty seconds faster, Remo did as he was told, spreading his fingers wide so that Neil would know he was unarmed. And when he finished his spin, he was glad he'd listened. The corrupt councilman not only held the gun in one hand, but he held Celia by the hair in the other.

"What do you want?" Remo asked immediately.

"You're going to deliver my baby. Your lovely mother said something's wrong with my wife, and that you'd know what to do to make sure the baby was born safely."

"And why would I agree to that?"

"Because I'll shoot Celia *and* your mother if you don't."

"You're going to kill us all anyway," Remo pointed out.

Neil shrugged. "Maybe true. But I might do it with some mercy if I get what I want." For emphasis, he gave Celia's hair a rough yank.

"Now or never, DeLuca," the other man snapped.

Celia looked like she was trying to shake her head, but the grip on her hair was too tight, and the pain in her eyes was more than Remo could stand.

"Fine," he snarled. "Just stop hurting her."

The other man gave Celia another quick tug, then shoved her forward so hard that her face met the muddy ground. Every bit of Remo's being wanted to reach for her, almost as badly as he wanted to deliver a solid punch to Neil Price's face. He forcibly restrained himself from doing the latter, but couldn't quite stop himself from doing the former. He took a step in Celia's direction, a hand already stretched out. He didn't make it any farther, though, before a bloodcurdling scream carried through the air.

The noise made Neil jerk his head toward it, and the split-second distraction was all Remo needed to act. He changed direction and made a move to dive at the other man. Neil was a hair quicker. The gun swung forward, its barrel aimed in between Remo's chest and shoulder. He braced for impact, but it was unnecessary. As the shot fired, Celia came flying at Neil's knees, knocking him over and sending the bullet up to the trees instead of into Remo's flesh. But he didn't waste time on relief. He picked himself up and strode to the man on the ground. Neil's eyes were closed, his mouth open, and his breathing shallow.

"I think he hit his head," Celia said, spitting out a mouthful of dirt. "Sorry."

"Sorry?" Remo echoed incredulously. "I think you mean you're welcome for saving your life."

"That, too," she agreed.

He pulled her in for a mud-flavored kiss. For a moment, the world stopped. It was just him and Celia. Their lips and the rain. Perfection inside their own little bubble.

Then a siren roared to life in the distance, reminding him soundly that there was more work to be done. He needed to secure the other man, then attend to Mrs. Price, and check on his mom, too. When he leaned back, though, he was surprised to see the pregnant woman standing in front of them, her labor magically halted. She eyed her unconscious husband with a mix of wariness and disgust, then bent down and retrieved the gun he'd dropped.

"What can I say?" she asked, as she straightened and caught the look on Remo's face. "Before I went into architecture, I wanted to be an actress."

His mom appeared then, too, a set of handcuffs dangling from one finger. "I got this off that evil man in the car. Mind if I do the honors? I've always dreamed of putting the cuffs on a bad guy like him."

Remo didn't have the energy to laugh at the insanity of it all. He just grabbed hold of Celia again, pulled her in close, and sat back to wait for the police.

Epilogue

One year later

As they pushed through the side doors of the courthouse, deliberately avoiding the sea of reporters who'd dominated the front of the building for the last six weeks, Celia took a deep breath. For the first time in seven years, she truly felt like she could breathe. There'd been some reprieve in knowing for certain that Neil was arrested and charged. There was more than a bit of relief in discovering that his known associates had abandoned him to the wolves, and that the police were sure Celia and Xavier were safe from retaliation. With Teller dead, and only Neil's own accounts of who existed on the wrong side of the law, there was little chance that anyone would seek revenge. But now—knowing that the man was behind bars for twenty-five years on eight separate charges—Celia really, truly knew she was free.

She cast a glance over at Remo. His handsome profile

currently showcased a small smile. It made her smile, too. Not a day had gone by that she didn't feel thankful that the universe had made *him* the one to drive by and stop at the scene of her accident. She couldn't wait to actually have time together without the police.

They took a few more steps, and Remo's smile became a grin. And when Celia followed his gaze, she knew it was more than just the guilty verdict that brought it on. His mom stood on the corner beside her car, and Xavier clasped her hand.

Celia waved, then frowned as she spotted her son's formal wear. He was dressed in a miniature tuxedo, complete with blue bow tie. And now that Celia was paying attention to the details, she realized Wendy was also wearing something unusually fancy—a satiny, knee-length dress just the same shade as Xavier's tie.

She started to turn and ask Remo if he knew what was going on, but before she could speak, she spotted Felicity— who'd changed her name back from Price to Wallace— stepping out of the car, too. The pretty brunette wore a dress that matched Wendy's, and when she pulled her daughter from the car seat, Celia saw that the baby was clad in a sparkly little dress. Blue, as well.

Celia blinked, and realized that two suit-wearing men also stood beside the car. The first was Riley Hank, the young cop whom Remo had befriended after Neil's initial arrest. The other was his friend, Freddy Yan.

"Remo, what's—" Her words cut off in a gasp as she turned to face her favorite, six-foot-something paramedic.

He'd dropped to his knees, and his grin was now so big that it looked like it might hurt. He still wore the suit he'd had on all week, but he'd plucked a small, blue flower from some hidden place, and had it pinned to his breast pocket. In his hand, he held a tiny, unmistakable box.

"Celia Poller," he said, sliding the box open to reveal a diamond-encrusted sapphire set in white gold. "Since your dad is no longer with us, I asked your son for your hand in marriage. He agreed. With some conditions that involve a new bunk bed. So if you'll do me the honor... I'd love to make you my wife."

"Yes!" She exclaimed it so loudly that a blush crept up her cheeks, but she had no intention of dialing it back.

Remo chuckled, clearly amused by her enthusiasm, then slipped the ring onto her finger. "Good."

He held out his hand, and Celia gladly took it. "Remo?"

"Yes?"

"In case I forgot to mention it today... I love you."

"I love you, too," he said. "Which is why I brought the groomsmen and bridesmaids and ring bearer and that teeny tiny flower girl. And there's a different kind of judge waiting in that courthouse to sign some paperwork. Oh. And some people waiting for some dinner and cake at a fancy hall a few blocks away."

Celia glanced down at her attire, an earlier comment from Xavier coming to mind and making sense.

Put on the blue dress with the flowers, Mom, he'd said.

At the time, she'd just thought it was a quirky suggestion. Now, though, she could see that the request had a purpose. It wasn't a gown, but the colors exactly matched the rest of the bridal party's ensembles.

Smiling so much that her cheeks hurt, Celia squeezed Remo's hands. With fingers clasped, they spun back toward the door they'd just exited. And Celia thought it was quite fitting to start their new chapter at the same place they'd just closed the last.

* * * * *

*For more great thrilling reads, be sure to check out
Melinda Di Lorenzo's Undercover Justice series:*

Captivating Witness
Undercover Protector
Undercover Passion
Undercover Refuge

*Available now wherever Harlequin Romantic Suspense
books and ebooks are sold!*

#2055 COLTON ON THE RUN
The Coltons of Roaring Springs • by Anna J. Stewart
With no memory of who she is while trying to evade the man who kidnapped her, Skye Colton has no choice but to trust Leo Slattery, the handsome rancher who found her in his barn.

#2056 COLTON 911: TARGET IN JEOPARDY
Colton 911 • by Carla Cassidy
After a one-night stand, Avery Logan is pregnant with Dallas Colton's twins. He's thrilled to be a dad, even if relationships aren't his thing. All he has to do is keep her safe when deadly threats are made against her—and somehow *not* fall for Avery while living in tight quarters.

#2057 COLD CASE MANHUNT
Cold Case Detectives • by Jennifer Morey
Jaslene Chabot is determined to find her best friend, who's gone missing in a small West Virginia town. But when she enlists the help of Dark Alley Investigations, Calum Chelsey is so much more than she bargained for, and the search offers them more opportunities for intimacy than either can resist.

#2058 HER DETECTIVE'S SECRET INTENT
Where Secrets are Safe • by Tara Taylor Quinn
After fleeing her abusive father, pediatric PA Miranda Blake never dates in order to keep her real identity a secret. But as she works closely with Tad Newbury to save a young boy, will she finally be able to let someone in? Or will Tad's secrets endanger her once again?

Get 4 FREE REWARDS!

We'll send you 2 FREE Books plus 2 FREE Mystery Gifts.

Harlequin® Romantic Suspense books feature heart-racing sensuality and the promise of a sweeping romance set against the backdrop of suspense.

FREE Value Over $20

SPECIAL EXCERPT FROM

H HARLEQUIN®

ROMANTIC suspense

*After fleeing her abusive father, pediatric
PA Miranda Blake never dates in order to keep her
real identity a secret. But as she works closely with
Tad Newbury to save a young boy, will she finally
be able to let someone in? Or will Tad's secrets
endanger her once again?*

*Read on for a sneak preview of
USA TODAY bestselling author Tara Taylor Quinn's
next book in the Where Secrets are Safe miniseries,*
Her Detective's Secret Intent.

"You're scaring me."

"I'm sorry. I don't mean to. I just have something to tell you that I think you'd want to know."

"Are you leaving Santa Raquel?"

"Make the call, Miranda. Please?"

Less than a minute later, she had him back on the phone. "All set. You want to go to my place?"

"No. And not mine, either. You know that car dealership out by the freeway?" He named a cash-for-your-car type of lot. One that didn't ask many questions if you had enough money, which made her even more uneasy.

"Yeah."

What was he doing? What could he possibly have to say?

Unless he'd found out who was watching her…

"Head over there," he told her. "I'll be right behind you."

"You're sure I'm safe?"

"Yes."

"You're really scaring me now, Tad."

"Call Chantel," he said. "She'll assure you that my request is valid."

"You've talked to her today?"

"I had to tell her I wouldn't be at the High Risk meeting."

Oh. So he was leaving. Which didn't explain why she was on her way to a car lot.

And suddenly she didn't want to know. Life without Tad was inevitable. But did it have to happen right now? When the rest of her world could be caving in?

Don't miss
Her Detective's Secret Intent *by Tara Taylor Quinn,*
available September 2019 wherever
Harlequin® Romantic Suspense books
and ebooks are sold.

www.Harlequin.com

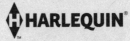

Love Harlequin romance?

DISCOVER.

Be the first to find out about promotions, news and exclusive content!

Facebook.com/HarlequinBooks

Twitter.com/HarlequinBooks

Instagram.com/HarlequinBooks

Pinterest.com/HarlequinBooks

ReaderService.com

EXPLORE.

Sign up for the Harlequin e-newsletter and download a free book from any series at **TryHarlequin.com.**

CONNECT.

Join our Harlequin community to share your thoughts and connect with other romance readers!
Facebook.com/groups/HarlequinConnection

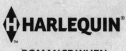

HARLEQUIN®

ROMANCE WHEN YOU NEED IT

HSOCIAL2018

Reward the book lover in you!

Earn points on your purchase of new Harlequin books from participating retailers.

Turn your points into **FREE BOOKS** of your choice!

Join for FREE today at
www.HarlequinMyRewards.com.

Harlequin My Rewards is a free program (no fees) without any commitments or obligations.